The Victorian Pendant

The Victorian Pendant

BOOK ONE

THE HEARTBOUND CHRONICLES

AMARYLLIS MADSEN

Piece Of Pie Publishing

11923 NE Sumner ST Ste 826515

Portland, OR 97220-9601"

To my Grandmother

Thank you for being the most amazing woman and the best grandma a girl could ask for. I can only hope I have made you proud.

"Love alters not with his brief hours and weeks,

But bears it out even to the edge of doom."

— *William Shakespeare, Sonnet 116*

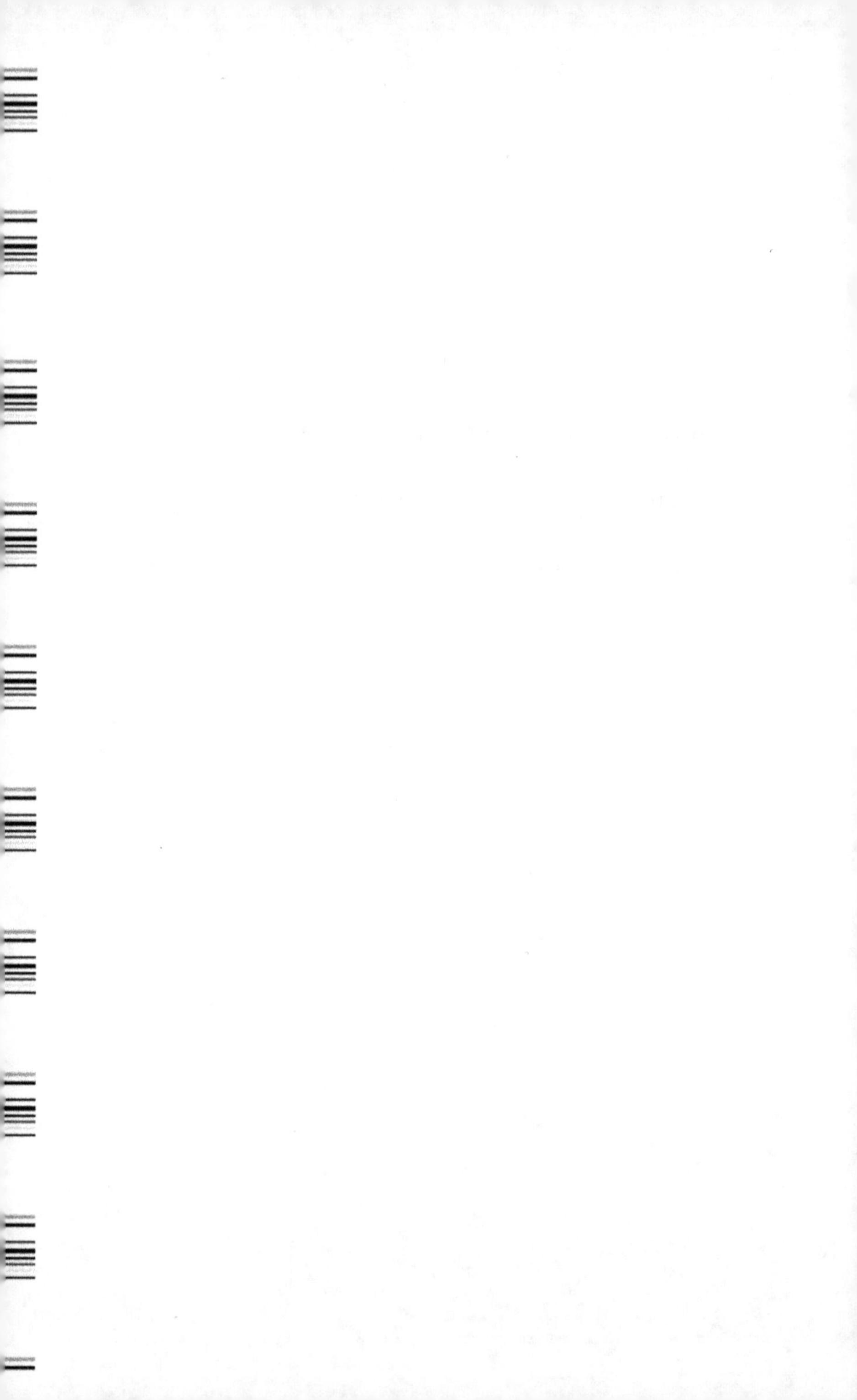

Some loves are not born in their own time.

They are remembered.

CHAPTER 1

Welcome Home

Creak, creak, creak...

Penelope took the three steps up to the front door of her new home. She'd spent over twenty years without a home of her own. Twenty years of borrowed rooms, temporary beds, other people's rules. Twenty years of being the girl no one could fix. The girl whose parents died in the accident that she survived. The girl who carried that guilt like a stone in her chest, so heavy sometimes she couldn't breathe around it. The girl no one wanted. Because no one wanted a broken child.

But this house? This house was hers. No one could take it away. No one could decide she didn't fit. And now, this place, and all its history, was hers.

The house she was moving into was almost 130 years old, and it was showing every one of those years. Yellow paint had faded to the color of old bones, chipping away in curls. The wood of the porch overhang sagged and darkened with rot, and the porch itself wasn't much better. Black ceramic pots with dead plants sat like sentries near the railing, their dry stems clawing at the air, giving the place a haunted-house feeling.

"Alright, Pen. This is either a brilliant idea or the stupidest thing you've ever done," she muttered.

She slid the long skeleton key into the lock and tried to turn it. Nothing. She tried again. It would not move. The pet carrier in her left hand rattled with a grumble of feline outrage.

"I know, I know," she sighed, setting the carrier down. "Hang on, baby."

She tried the key again. "Please let this work," she whispered to no one.

It turned easily this time, as if someone inside had recently oiled it and opened the door for her.

The heavy wooden door, complete with an oval glass panel, creaked with age and protest as she used both hands to push it open. If sadness had a scent, it would be the one wafting from the entryway: old wood, earthy and sweet, wrapped with a faint, sour hint of neglect.

Still, she stepped over the threshold, picked up the carrier, and forced a smile.

"Well, Mina," she breathed. "Welcome home."

The word echoed in her chest. Home. Her life was about to change. Hopefully, for the good. Possibly disastrous. She was going into it blind. She hadn't had a real home in... well, ever.

Orphaned at seven when her parents died of carbon monoxide poisoning in their brand-new house, Penelope's life had split cleanly into *before* and *after*. Before: laughter, bedtime stories, the smell of her mother's shampoo. After: sirens, questions, and a police officer's kind but pitying eyes. And guilt. She would forever carry that.

A sharp, familiar "Mrrrrooooo" snapped her back to the present.

"Oh my God, I'm so sorry," she crooned, crouching to unzip the carrier door.

Mina burst out in a fluff of white, black, and orange. Her nose and toe beans were a bright, improbable pink. Before Pen could set her down, Mina twisted in her arms and scrambled up to her shoulders, settling there like a living stole, face burrowing into Pen's blonde ponytail.

"There you go," Pen murmured, fingers finding the cat's soft fur. "We did it. This is ours now."

Mina's tail flicked against her cheek, a tiny, vibrating metronome of anxiety and curiosity.

Pen stepped farther into the foyer.

To her right, a beautiful curved staircase climbed toward the second level, colored light spilling over the steps from a pane of stained glass on the landing. Dust motes drifted through the beams like tiny suspended constellations.

To the left, a wide wooden archway framed the entrance to the parlor. Hidden pocket doors waited there, half-buried in the walls. Pen tugged gently at one; it resisted, the small wheels clearly in need of oil.

"Add that to the list," she muttered.

Beyond the foyer, straight ahead, was the dining room. Inside, a slightly curved wall held five tall windows. Each one wore stained glass along the top panels like a crown. The rest was simple glass, cloudy with age. On the ceiling, a chandelier hung crooked, missing half its crystals. The fireplace on the right wore soot stains like bruises across green tile. It was clear it hadn't been cleaned in years.

"Or decades," she whispered to the empty room.

Mina gave a complaining "mrowl" as Pen moved from room to room.

The wallpaper in some rooms hung in shredded strips, as if an angry predator cat had taken its claws to it as a scratching post. In other rooms, dust lay thick as a shroud. Every step she took made the warped floorboards groan like old bones waking up.

Here and there, pieces of abandoned life remained: a brass headboard, a broken chair, an old wardrobe crouched in one corner like a wooden sentinel. Most of it needed repairs. Some of it was beyond saving. But Pen wanted to keep as much as she could.

The house needed more than a little TLC.

But as she walked through it, with Mina's claws kneading gently at her shoulder, dust swirled in the fractured sunbeams. Pen couldn't escape the feeling that the house was... listening.

Watching.

Waiting.

It should have been unsettling.

Instead, it felt almost like a shy welcome.

Her chest tightened, and she swallowed against the unexpected wave of emotion.

"This is it," she whispered to herself. "We're really doing this."

For the first time in her life, Penelope was standing in a place that was hers. Not borrowed. Not temporary. Not conditional on someone else's whim.

Whatever this house had been before, whatever stories its walls remembered, it was hers now.

And she did not know yet how literally that was about to become true.

FOR THE FIRST three days in the house, Penelope spent them cleaning out the debris. On more than one occasion, when her body ached with the constant movement and her heart felt heavy with loneliness, she'd second-guess herself.

"Am I really cut out for taking on such an intense project?"

While cleaning out the upstairs bathroom so she'd be able to use the facilities, she paused in front of the fractured mirror that hung over the porcelain sink. Her reflection shattered into uneven shards, each one catching the light differently, taking Pen's breath away. It looked like a collage of her old life... broken, useless, and quietly asking whether she had really come here to put the house back together... or herself.

"Damn it, Pen!" she chastised her misplaced reflection. "This *is* right. We are where we were meant to be!"

Mina chirped at Penelope from her spot on the tile floor, warmed by the sunshine pouring in through the frosted glass window. Pen leaned down to give her best friend a little love. A flash of memory filled her eyes as she cat made a sound.

The first time she'd heard the cat make a noise, it was thin, desperate, and impossible to ignore.

A kitten's cry.

She found the cardboard box by the dumpster behind a grocery store, lined with an old towel. There were three tiny bodies and one still moving, a mottled calico with a too-loud voice for such a small body.

Pen's throat had closed up around a familiar, awful ache.

She scooped the surviving kitten into her coat, cradling it against her chest. "I've got you," she whispered. "I swear you won't end up like them."

She smuggled the kitten into the women's shelter she'd been staying in, bottle-feeding her in the bathroom and hiding her in her coat at night. By day five, she was found out and given a choice: the cat or the bed.

Pen chose the cat.

She named her Mina.

They moved together after that. Tiny Mina rode in coat pockets and duffel bags until she grew too big and graduated to a carrier. The one non-negotiable in Penelope's life became this: wherever she went, Mina went too.

They were each other's family. The only one either of them had. And that was alright.

By MID-AFTERNOON, Penelope had filled two black trash bags and dragged them outside. She lined them neatly along the sidewalk, though "neatly" may have been generous. The piles towered together like the silhouette of some slumbering forest creature guarding the end of her tangled yard.

It was ridiculous how proud she felt every time she added another bag. Each was a victory. Each one dragged her a little closer to restoring the house's past glory.

Mina supervised from a windowsill, tail thumping rhythmically against the glass as if tapping out her opinion of Pen's technique.

"Don't judge me," Pen huffed, wiping sweat from her forehead. "You're not the one wrestling expired mousetraps."

Mina flicked an ear in snobbish defiance.

Pen laughed despite herself. "Alright, fine. Demanding boss."

Her focus in the first days had been the main bedroom. She needed it clean enough to sleep in. Her meager possessions had fit in a backpack and a duffel bag. She'd taken the brass headboard she'd found in the faded yellow painted bedroom that was at the top of the grand staircase, and polished it until it shone, and ordered a mattress and box spring to fit it. It was her very first bed. One that only *she* would sleep on. Well, Mina, too. This was becoming home.

As she moved from room to room, cleaning the years of dust and debris, Pen quickly understood why a certain piece of furniture had been left behind. It was upstairs, in what she could say was the smallest bedroom in the house. Possibly a child's room? But most importantly, it was *heavy*. Not to mention tall and imposing. A thick layer of dust dulled its carved floral designs. How old was it? Late 1800s? Early 1900s? Part of her wanted to keep it because it *belonged* to the house in a way modern furniture never could. It took her over an hour to move the old wardrobe from the room it was abandoned in, down the hall to the main bedroom. Slowly, she pushed one end, then the other, with a towel underneath to keep it from scratching the wooden floor. Once she got it into place, she began cleaning it with wood oil. Stroke by gentle stroke, Penelope imagined what it might have looked like when it was new.

"Alright, old girl," Pen whispered to the wood. "What things did you hold?"

The hinges groaned when she swung the doors open to dust and oil inside. The smell that drifted out was something between attic musk and forgotten perfume. She pulled the bottom drawer out to oil it as well. Setting it down on the towel beside her, Pen began giving it the care it needed. When she was about to slide it back into place, she noticed something pressed against the back panel. She reached for it carefully, aware that her breath felt too heavy for the fragile paper. The envelope nearly disintegrated between her fingers. Only the wax seal, broken long ago, held it together. Hands trembling, she nudged the brittle paper open. Inside was a single folded page, thinner now than onion skin.

She held her breath—and unfolded it.

The handwriting was slanted, elegant, old-fashioned.

And the first line nearly broke her.

Pen sat hard on the nearest dusty crate.

Sept 18th, 1892

My Dearest Clara.

It has been forty-three days since I lost you and our sweet boy, yet I wake each morning expecting to hear your voice. I still turn toward the stairs, listening for footsteps that will never come.

The doctor tells me no man could have saved you, but I cannot make myself believe it. I was your husband. I should have protected you, kept you safe, given my life for yours if that was what fate required. Instead, I stood helplessly as both of you slipped beyond my reach.

I cannot enter the nursery. I stand outside the door until my strength leaves me, but I cannot turn the knob. I fear what waits inside—your absence, his absence, the future we will never have.

The house is unbearably quiet. I have taken to working the land until the sun sets, for exhaustion is the only thing that dulls the grief.

But when night comes, when the lamps burn low, the silence presses so hard upon my chest I can scarcely draw breath.

I write only because there is no one left to speak to. People avoid my sorrow. They look at me as if grief were a sickness they might catch.

Forgive me, Clara—

For every moment I failed you,

For every breath I still take without you.

I will try to live as you would have wanted. I will plant the trees you dreamed of. And I pray that one day, in whatever lies beyond this world, I may see you holding our son.

Until then,

Your devoted husband,

Connor James Halden

PENELOPE'S HANDS trembled by the time she reached the last line. The paper crackled softly between her fingers, the fragile sound jarring in the otherwise still room. She blinked hard, but the ink blurred anyway, swimming behind a sheen of tears she didn't realize she'd been holding back.

Connor's grief poured out in raw, unguarded lines. His guilt, heartbreak, and admission that he didn't know how to keep living in the house they'd built together.

She swallowed, eyes stinging.

His pain wasn't distant history. It felt poured fresh onto the page.

The wardrobe around her smelled of cedar and wood oil, but beneath it lingered something gentler, something floral, faint as a ghost. Clara's perfume? Or maybe Penelope wanted it to be.

A soft weight brushed her knee. Mina hopped silently into Pen's lap, as if sensing the cracking of her heart. Penelope pressed a hand into the warm fur, grounding herself, before leaning down and burying her face in the cat's sunshine-warm fur.

Her throat ached.

Not from crying, but from *feeling* too much.

Connor's words clung to her, heavy as iron. Every sentence felt like a bruise pressed directly into her chest. She could almost see him sitting at a desk lit with a single lamp, his hands shaking as he wrote Clara's name. Could almost imagine how the ink smudged. Not by accident, but because he'd touched it after wiping his eyes.

Pen's heart squeezed painfully. "This poor man..." she whispered, her voice barely more than a breath. The letter felt heavy in her hands. The grief in it was heavier still. She understood that more than most. The grief of not being able to save their loved ones. She carried it as well. Heavy, never-ending weight that nothing had helped heal.

Behind the last page was a photograph. The picture was cracked across one corner, but the image was still clear. A tall, striking man with dark hair and solemn eyes, standing beside a woman in a simple but elegant wedding gown. Clara. Her expression was bright, open, and radiant. Connor looked like a man trying to smile through nerves and devotion all at once.

She couldn't help imagining them—this young couple building a life together, only for fate to hollow it out. Pen pressed the letter against her chest, closing her eyes.

She knew the feeling of losing everything at once. Of staring down the ruins of a life that used to feel safe. Of wishing someone, anyone, could tell her what to do next.

Pen's stomach fluttered with something like recognition, though she knew that made no sense. She traced the edges of the image with a hesitant fingertip, shivering when the old paper crackled beneath her touch.

A soft creak above her made Pen glance upward. The old house always made noise, but this sounded almost... *aware*. As if it remembered the man who had written these words. She shook her head, releasing her silly thoughts. Pen had watched too many scary movies in the foster homes. She knew houses weren't actually haunted.

Pen swallowed hard. "Oh, Connor," she breathed, her voice cracking. "You poor, broken man..." She looked again at the wedding photograph. Clara's smile was warm enough to soften a winter morning. Connor's gaze rested on his bride with a tenderness that made the grief in the letter even sharper. Pen felt something twist deep in her belly, sympathy, sorrow, and a strange, quiet connection she couldn't explain.

This house...

This letter...

This man...

There was a story here.

And she had stumbled into the beginning of it.

Pen rubbed the cat's back, suddenly unsettled but unable to walk away. She tucked the photograph against her chest, the paper warm from her hands.

She didn't know why, but she felt certain of one thing: whatever happened in this house, whatever grief lingered here, she was going to help heal it, and do the same for herself in the process.

Pen's chest squeezed too tight. The letter trembled in her hands—not from the fragile paper, but from her own shaking fingers. She knew this grief. She lived in this grief. Connor's guilt, his desperate wish that he could have saved them, the way he kept replaying every moment wondering what he could have done differently—

She couldn't breathe.

She stood too fast; the wardrobe door swinging shut behind her with a soft thud. Mina chirped, startled. Pen grabbed her keys, her jacket, anything that would get her out of this house and away from the weight pressing down on her ribs.

She needed air. She needed distance. She needed to not feel this much.

. . .

THE AFTERNOON SUN hit her face as she stepped outside, warming her chilled skin. She locked the door behind her and walked toward town, letting the breeze in the trees unwind the knots in her chest.

The town had little: one stoplight, a library, a feed store, a hardware shop, a beauty salon that looked like it specialized in perms from 1985, and a cafe called *The Tipping Bean* wedged between a thrift store and a barber. It was the kind of place with chalkboard menus and overstuffed chairs.

A bell chimed as Pen stepped inside, letting in a rush of warm air that smelled like hazelnut, cinnamon, and roasted espresso. A chalkboard sign above the counter read:

WELCOME! TODAY'S SPECIAL: Lavender Vanilla Latte— Tastes like spring, even when the weather can't commit.

Pen smiled despite her fatigue. She took two deep, grounding breaths before stepping toward the counter. She had to let go of the tight hold grief had on her.

The barista, a woman in her sixties with lavender-gray hair and glittery cat-eye glasses, perked up when she saw her.

"Well, hey there! You must be new in town."

Pen blinked. "That obvious?"

The woman gave a knowing laugh. "Small town, honey. We notice everything."

Great, exactly what I need.

The barista continued, her voice kind and welcoming. "I'm Gale. I own this place."

Pen took the older woman's outstretched hand. "Penelope."

"Nice to meet you, Penelope. I hope I see you in here more often."

Pen ordered a hazelnut latte, needing something sweet, comforting, and grounding. The barista handed her a warm cup and a printed receipt. She folded the receipt without thinking - February 12th, 2026 printed neatly at the top - and slipped it into her pocket. Pen sat at a corner table, sipping slowly. The sweetness coated her tongue, calming her heartbeat. But her thoughts were not calm. She kept seeing the letter.

Seeing the ink. Seeing his name. *Connor James Halden.*

She'd left the house to get him off her mind, not to make it worse. Penelope thanked the barista and pushed her way outside to wander down Main Street, letting herself absorb the quiet charm.

Penelope didn't see the two older women sitting on the bench outside *The Tipping Bean* until she was nearly past them. Their coffee cups steamed in the cool morning air as they watched her over the rims, the kind of watchfulness that lived somewhere between curiosity and ritual.

"Excuse me, sweetheart," one of them called out.

Pen stopped, startled. "Yes?"

The speaker wore a knitted shawl and a hat decorated with so many artificial flowers it looked like it might pollinate something. The other woman, all sharp eyes and sharper cheekbones, leaned forward.

"You're the one who bought the Halden house."

It wasn't a question.

Pen forced a polite smile. "Yes. I... just moved in."

The women exchanged a look heavy with meaning and a dash of theatrical concern.

"Well," the flowered-hat woman said, patting the bench beside her, "someone had to. That place's been empty too long."

"Yes," the sharp-cheeked one agreed, lowering her voice. "Houses get... lonely."

Pen blinked. "Lonely?"

"Oh, yes," Flower Hat replied dramatically. "Buildings remember things. Especially old ones. They get used to footsteps, to voices, to life, and when all that disappears, they start aching for it to return."

Pen wasn't sure how to respond to that. "Aching?"

"Mmm-hmm." The sharp-cheeked woman nodded with unsettling certainty.

Pen tightened her grip on her latte cup.

"What do people usually say about the house?" she asked carefully.

The two women leaned together in an unspoken conference.

Finally, Flower Hat spoke. "Some say the Halden house is a blessing. Others say it's cursed. Depends who you ask."

"Depends what you believe," Doris added.

Pen felt a chill brush the back of her neck. "What do *you* believe?"

Flower Hat gave her a long, appraising look, head tilting slightly, as though she were measuring Pen for something more than conversation.

"I believe," she said gently, "that houses know when the right person walks through their door."

Pen's heart thudded once, too hard. She could feel the pain of it throughout her ribcage.

The women smiled as if they had delivered useful advice, not the opening monologue to a gothic horror film.

"Well, thank you," Pen managed.

"Welcome to town, dear," Flower Hat said with a little wave. "You and your pretty eyes. We're all very excited to see how things turn out."

"Very excited," Doris echoed ominously.

Pen stepped away, their eyes following her down the sidewalk like benignly concerned vultures.

She forced a breath.

Small-town charm, she told herself. Simply quirky old ladies.

But as she walked away from them, the weight of their words settled into her bones.

Houses get lonely. Houses remember. The Halden place has been waiting.

Waiting for her?

The thought was absurd.

And yet... it clung.

CHAPTER 2

The Library

All the talk about the house and the letter she found sent her into investigation mode. What she needed was the factual information, not some hocus pocus. Houses weren't haunted.

The town library was tucked beside City Hall, a squat brick building that looked older than most of the town, with mismatched windows and a ramp that had been painted six times too many. Inside, it smelled like dust, old encyclopedias, and eucalyptus from a diffuser behind the front desk.

The librarian was a thin, sprightly man wearing suspenders, and a bowtie covered in tiny books. He looked up at Pen with immediate curiosity.

"Well, hello there! Haven't seen you before."

Pen lifted a hand in a sheepish wave. "I just moved in."

He lit up. "Whereabouts?"

"The old Victorian on Willow Bend."

A beat of silence.

"Ohhh," he said slowly. "*That* house."

Not again.

She swallowed. "Is that... good?"

He tilted his head. "That house has a story. Not all of it is happy. But if you're living there, you ought to know it, don't you think?"

"Um... sure?"

(She wasn't totally sure.)

"Do you like scandals?"

"...Not particularly."

"Well," he clapped his hands. "You will. Follow me."

He led her to a tall bookshelf labeled *Local History & Genealogy*, pulled down a binder thick enough to stun an ox. "This one has newspaper clippings all the way back to the 1800s. The Haldens were prominent folks. Timber farmers. Donated half the early lumber that built this town."

Pen opened the large binder and was sure the air around her shifted.

It's only your imagination.

Connor J. Halden. A photograph from the 1890s showing a tall man standing beside a wagon stacked with timber saplings. His hair was darker in the photo; his expression stoic but proud.

She traced his face with her eyes.

He looked exactly like the picture she'd found. Exactly like the handwriting in the letter felt.

She read the accompanying article:

"Local Landowner Devotes Efforts to Reforesting Project ... Connor Halden, a respected community member and early settler, has planted over 100 acres of timberland with plans to expand..."

Pen blinked. "A hundred acres?" she whispered.

The librarian nodded. "He was considered one of the most active timber planters in the region. A real visionary. There is so much more. See here," he pointed to another clipping. "Mentions of him establishing timber advocacy groups." He flipped the pages. "Here are notes about community meetings he led." Another few pages turned. This time the older man's voice was somber. "A brief mention of his wife Clara, her charitable work, her 'delicate' disposition."

Pen knew what would come next. An obituary.

Her breath caught as her eyes skimmed the short notice:

Mrs. Clara Halden and infant son passed away after a grueling childbirth... survived by her husband, Connor Halden...

The words blurred. She knew this grief. She'd lived in this grief—the guilt of surviving when someone you loved didn't. Clara and her baby boy. Pen's parents. Different centuries. Same bottomless ache.

She turned away, not wanting the librarian to see her unshed tears. The sound of the binder gently closing brought her palm up to cover her mouth.

The man behind that letter...

The grief...

The heartbreak...

It was real.

He was once real.

His pain, echoing across 130 years, was real.

Pen whispered, barely audible, "When did... when did he pass?"

"If I remember right, he died up there in that old house. The Victorian that has sat empty for so long. Not sure when, but the whole town knew about his broken heart. He never recovered from his loss." He sniffled into a handkerchief. "Well, I hope the ghosts don't bother you much."

"I'm sorry?" Pen blurted out.

"Oh, everyone knows about the ghost of Mr. Halden. Kids used to break into the place through the storm doors on the east side, since the woods block it from view. I'd suggest getting a padlock right away to keep them from coming back. But I digress. The ghost. Yes. It's said he roams the halls, still crying for his lost love. I hope he doesn't haunt you."

Too late. He was in her thoughts, and his grief haunted her heart.

The librarian left her alone with her reading.

Page by brittle page, Penelope read about the house she'd

moved into. It seemed Mr. Halden never recovered from his lost love, losing his respectability with the townfolk, and eventually leaving the property to his housekeeper.

Pen looked for the old deeds, wanting to know all the history of the house, all the people that had lived there. Ghosts or not, this house had a story, had families. Loved ones. She didn't. And if she was to call this home, Pen wanted it all.

In one of the yellowed ledger books, she found the deed from Mr. Halden. The land was purchased in 1857. The house was completed in 1860. In 1897 it was sold to a Mr. Wallace P. The writing had been smudged, so Pen wasn't sure of the surname. In 1955 it fell into the possession of the local bank.

Penelope found nothing after that. And without a surname, her research came to an end.

Pen started scrolling through grainy newspaper scans, looking for anything more about Connor Halden after his wife's death, in which there was very little, when footsteps approached the genealogy section.

She glanced up.

Two teens, maybe seventeen, hovered at the end of the aisle, whispering behind cupped hands. One nudged the other forward. The braver one stepped closer.

"Um... excuse me?" he asked, voice cracking.

Pen blinked. "Yes?"

"You're the girl who bought the Halden place, right?"

Pen's stomach dropped. *How does everyone know already?* She managed a polite, if tight, smile. "Yeah. I just moved in."

The boy's eyes widened with something between awe and alarm. "Seriously? Like... seriously?"

The other teen hissed, "Jacob, don't freak her out!"

Jacob ignored him. "Do you, like... hear anything yet?"

Pen frowned. "Hear what?"

The second teen groaned under his breath. "Dude..."

"No, I mean it!" Jacob insisted, turning back to Penelope with earnest curiosity. "People say the house used to... y'know... *talk.*"

Pen stared. "Talk."

"Not with words," the quieter teen clarified, stepping closer now that the weirdness threshold had been breached. "More like... sounds. Doors closing when no one's home. Floorboards creak when the place is empty. Lights flickering even though it doesn't have wiring—"

"Leo!" Jacob snapped. "Don't scare her!"

Leo shrugged. "She already bought it. Too late for that."

Pen shifted on her feet. "Guys... I'm sure it's simply an old house settling. No big deal."

"Sure," Jacob said. "Totally normal house stuff." He paused. "Except the piano."

Pen's heartbeat stuttered. "The... piano?"

Leo elbowed him hard. "Jacob, STOP."

"What?" Jacob protested. "It's not a ghost story! It's history!"

He turned to Pen again, bright-eyed. "Back when my grandma was a kid, she swore she walked by your house one summer evening and heard a piano playing. Real soft. Like the kind people play when they're sad. She said the windows were dark, no lights on. But the music kept going."

Pen swallowed. "So someone... lived there?"

"No one lived there then," Leo said quietly. "The house was empty for decades after—"

Jacob jabbed him again. "Dude. Boundaries."

Leo rolled his eyes but backed off. "Fine."

Jacob studied Pen for a long moment. "Sorry. We're probably being weird." He hesitated, added softly: "It's that... people say the Halden house remembers its owners. All of them."

Pen's skin prickled.

"Anyway!" Jacob blurted. "Welcome to town! Let us know if you, uh... need anything."

The boys retreated faster than they'd arrived, whispering fiercely at each other as they disappeared behind the nonfiction stacks.

Pen stood frozen, heart thumping in uneven beats.

The house remembers its owners. All of them.

When she finally exhaled, she wasn't sure why her hands were shaking.

It was only small-town superstition.

Only rumors.

Only stories.

Right?

...Right?

Penelope made her way out of the library, feeling heavier of heart and mind than before.

"I wish you'd had a second chance," she whispered to the wind. She felt a warmth spread through her bosom, that flutter you get sometimes.

She didn't know why she whispered to a man long dead.

But for one strange, impossible moment, while standing on the library steps with the cold wind biting at her cheeks, she could have sworn she felt him listening. She didn't know why she felt drawn to him.

But one thing she did know:

She wasn't done learning about him.

Not yet.

The strange tension Pen had felt at the library clung to her long after she returned home, like dust in her throat she couldn't clear.

The house remembers its owners; the teen had said. *All of them.*

Pen shook off the thought and pushed open the heavy front door. Mina trotted up to her with confident entitlement, tail flicked high as if she owned the place.

"You," Pen muttered, dropping her keys into a chipped bowl

that sat on a built in shelf by the door, "are either the bravest crea-ture alive or too chaotic to know fear."

Mina answered with a chirp and darted toward the dining room, her favorite hunting ground for abandoned spider webs and stray pieces of trash.

Pen almost followed, but paused.

Something felt... different.

Not visually. The house looked the same: dim light filtering through dusty stained glass, debris scattered across the floor, drafts winding lazily through the rooms.

But the *temperature* felt different. The *air* felt thicker. The *space* felt watchful.

She couldn't shake the words she'd heard in town:

Houses get lonely. Houses remember. The Halden place has been waiting.

A shiver crawled along her spine, and she forced a breath.

"Okay, Pen. Enough ghost stories. Houses aren't haunted. Back to work."

She grabbed her gloves, intending to tackle the dining room again... when Mina's startled yowl sliced through the silence.

Pen's heart jumped. "Mina?"

She hurried into the dining room and found the cat crouched low, pupils blown wide, tail puffed to maximum Halloween-cat proportions. Mina swatted furiously at something near the far wall.

"Mina! Hey! Don't rip up the —"

Then Pen saw it.

A piece of yellowed paper, wedged under the baseboard. The more Mina tugged, the more the paper tore.

Pen set her gloves down and knelt. Her fingers brushed the edge of the baseboard. It was cold. Not "old wood," cold. Not "drafty room" cold.

It was *unnatural*, the kind of cold that seeped straight into the bones.

She glanced at Mina.

The cat's fur remained puffed, ears flat.

"Sweet girl," Pen whispered, "I've never seen you like this."

Mina's gaze never left the paper. She hissed softly, but it wasn't hostile. It was... afraid.

Pen swallowed before trying gently to remove the paper. It wouldn't budge, but ripped more. She let out a soft breath and wiggled it slightly. With no effort at all, the slip of paper almost flew upward, away from the baseboard, on an imaginary wind.

"Oh," Pen breathed. "Okay. That's... new."

She caught the paper when it made its descent. It almost disintegrated in her hands. Like the wallpaper, it flaked away like dried flower petals, leaving nothing but dust. Pen stared at the faint outline of musical notes left behind in that dust. Sheet music. Hidden beneath the baseboard. She thought of the teen's story—a piano playing when the house was empty—and her throat tightened.

Someone had hidden it. Someone wanted it remembered.

She didn't know why that made her chest ache.

TWO DAYS LATER, Penelope was working on the main floor, where the house needed the most work, outside of the debris. Mina took her new supervisory position very seriously, darting between Pen's ankles, brushing her fluffy calico body across Pen's shins every time her human dared to attempt productivity. "Sweet girl, you are *not* OSHA-approved," Pen muttered, bending to give her a quick stroke before continuing.

The foyer had become a staging zone of chaos. Boxes of supplies crowded the narrow entry like a regiment waiting for orders. Sheets of plastic, new brushes, painter's tape, bottles of cleaner, spackle, a sander, Pen wasn't entirely sure she could operate. Everything a first-time homeowner might need, and several things she probably didn't.

Which meant, of course, Mina found the packing straps.

Right when the sun was setting, and darkness was creeping around the corners of the room, Mina grabbed one with her teeth, dragging it proudly across the dining room like she'd caught a prize snake.

"Mina," Pen announced as the cat darted by with the strap, "you're going feral."

The cat ignored her entirely, dragged them around the front sitting room, chasing after the end, like a dog chasing its tail. Pen watched, finding joy in the cat playing. But she wasn't getting much work done. Her heart and thoughts were still upstairs with the letter she had found, the information she'd learned at the library. The image of Connor burned deep in her mind.

She crossed back into the dining room to see Mina, crouched near the east wall in the front room, pupils huge, tail puffed like a feather duster on high alert.

"Mina? What are you doing?" Pen walked over, and she saw it.

The cat had gotten the jagged edge of one strap stuck, wedged at the corner of a warped floorboard. Pen set her tools down to help the cat. Crouching beside her feline companion, she brushed her blonde hair from her face as she leaned forward to inspect the culprit. The poly strap wasn't simply caught. It was wedged deep beneath the warped edge of the old floorboard, its jagged tip disappearing into a splintered gap that Pen hadn't noticed before.

"Seriously?" Pen sighed, reaching for the strap the cat still had in its mouth. "You couldn't chase dust bunnies like a normal cat?"

Mina tugged at it again, growling in that weird half-kitten, half-mountain-lion sound she made when she was determined. For such a tiny creature, she committed with her whole body. Her black and orange ears flattened, white paws braced, and rump wiggling in preparation for one heroic yank.

Pen laughed. "Okay, okay, let me—"

Before she could finish, Mina pulled with surprising force.

Something underneath the board shifted.

Pen froze. That... *wasn't* normal.

A faint shimmer rippled across the floor, subtle, like heat rising off summer pavement. She blinked, unsure if it was simply dust motes catching the light like she'd seen often over the last few days. But Mina's tail puffed even bigger, her body arching like she'd felt a silent pop beneath her paws.

"Whoa," Penelope whispered. "What was that?" She reached for the strap again, giving it a gentle tug. The board responded, lifting with a dry, tired *creak*, almost as though it had simply been waiting for her touch. Dust curled upward in a lazy spiral, moving unnaturally slow. The air felt like time thickened for a heartbeat.

Penelope's breath hitched.

The shimmer came again.

Mina darted behind her for safety, then sprang gracefully onto Pen's shoulders, cat claws hooking into the fabric of her T-shirt. The feline flattened herself against her owner's neck. Pen steadied her with one hand, the other still gripping the strap.

"Okay, sweetheart," she murmured, heart thudding. "You saw that too, right? Please tell me I'm not going crazy alone. I shouldn't have listened to those people. Houses aren't haunted." She repeated those three words like a mantra.

The cat pressed her face into Pen's hair and growled low in her throat.

Taking a steadying breath, Pen slipped her fingers beneath the lifted floorboard edge. The wood was cool beneath her fingertips. Too cool. And when her skin brushed the seam, she hesitated as a shiver crawled up her spine. The board rose easily, far easier than rotted wood had any right to do.

And the moment her fingertips brushed the underside—everything stopped.

Not sound. Not movement. Something deeper.

Time.

For one impossible heartbeat, the house held its breath. The air thickened. The light dimmed. Pen's pulse stuttered in her chest, and she felt—

Him.

Not a ghost. Not a presence. Just... a feeling. Grief so old it had soaked into the wood. Longing so deep it had nowhere else to go but down, into the bones of the house, waiting to be found.

Her throat tightened.

'Connor,' she whispered.

The name left her lips before she knew why.

Then, just as suddenly—the world returned. Sound. Light. Air. Mina's claws pricked her shoulder.

Pen gasped, blinking hard, her hands trembling.

What the hell was that?

Beneath the board, the cavity sunk deep between the joists, its darkness thick and lightless. Dust clung to the edges in a smooth, unbroken layer, untouched by footprint or finger, undisturbed by time or chance. The air that drifted up was stale and dry, carrying the faint scent of old wood and sealed years.

No one had opened this space in decades.

But something inside was waiting for her.

Nestled within, wrapped in brittle, yellowed cloth, was something that caught the dim evening light—a muted glint, dull but unmistakable. Metal.

Pen's pulse kicked hard against her ribs. "What the hell..." she breathed, shifting Mina's weight on her shoulders as she reached inside.

Pen eased the fragile cloth bundle from the hollow, half-expecting it to disintegrate the way the sheet music had. The cloth felt lighter than air, the threads giving way with a papery sigh as she lifted it into her lap. Mina dug her claws into Pen's shoulder for stability, her warm body trembling with silent intensity.

"Claws, Mina!" she blew out a short breath. "It's okay," she murmured, though her voice came out thin. She wasn't sure who she was trying to comfort: herself, or the cat currently latched onto her like a furry backpack. Mina's claws dug through cotton and into skin, a steady sting that kept Pen grounded.

The bundle split as she unwrapped it. Strips of fabric slipped through her fingers and floated to the floor like wilted petals.

What remained in her palm stole her breath.

A pendant.

It wasn't a simple charm or locket. It was a delicate lattice of interwoven metal loops, each ring twisting into the next like a chain-mail flower frozen mid-bloom. At the heart of the looping pattern nestled a small stone, smooth and cool-looking. Its surface caught the dim light and shifted, not like glitter or glass, but like something deeper—sapphire one moment, smoky gray the next. The loops around it cradled the stone like protective hands, forming an intricate cage that seemed crafted with reverence rather than decoration. As Pen tilted it, hints of green and silver flickered beneath the surface, like a storm trapped behind glass.

Her fingers tingled where they touched the metal. A warmth spread from her palm up her wrist in a slow, deliberate crawl.

Pen swallowed. "Okay," she whispered. "That's... weird."

The cat let out a low, uneasy trill near Pen's ear, her tail puffed and wrapped around the back of Pen's neck like she was trying to anchor them both in place.

Pen's gaze stayed locked on the pendant. It was beautiful. Old, but not rusted. Strange, but not gaudy. It felt out of place and yet perfectly right for this house, like it belonged here more than anything else they'd found.

And completely irrationally, it felt... familiar.

A soft breath of cool air brushed the back of her neck.

Pen froze.

Her eyes flicked to the nearest window. It was closed. So were the doors. No vents near her. No obvious source.

"Right," she muttered. "Totally normal. Random indoor breeze. Houses do that."

Her voice didn't sound convinced.

Her heart thudded hard against her ribs, each beat echoed by a faint, answering thrum in her palm where the pendant sat.

She lifted it higher to examine the chain. The metal links were surprisingly fine, each one matching the looped design of the pendant itself. No clasp—simply one continuous strand, like it had never been meant to be taken off.

She couldn't rationally explain it, but she felt the *need* to put it on. "I'm letting the town gossip get to me. It's only a necklace, right? Mina," she said softly, turning her head just enough to bump her cheek against fur. "If this kills us, I hope you know I love you."

The cat responded by pushing her face firmly into Pen's hair, ears pinned flat against her skull.

A normal person, Pen thought distantly, would probably put the weird antique back in the hole, shove the floorboard in place, and never think about it again. But normal people didn't buy haunted-looking Victorian houses sight unseen and talk back to old ladies who claimed buildings got lonely.

"Curiosity is going to be the death of me," she muttered.

Pen guided the chain over her head, careful not to jostle Mina. The metal slid across her fingers with an uncanny smoothness, like water rather than solid links. When it settled against her collarbone, the pendant slipped under the collar of her t-shirt and seemed to find its own place, drawn to the center of her chest as if magnetized to her skin.

And the world exhaled.

For one suspended heartbeat, everything went utterly still.

Mina went rigid, claws frozen in place. Dust motes hung in the air, no longer drifting.

The hum of the refrigerator in the kitchen cut off abruptly, like someone had severed a wire.

Pen felt the hairs on her arms and the back of her neck lift.

The warmth from the pendant flared.

Heat bloomed across her chest, not burning, but intense. The air thickened, pressing against her skin like invisible hands. Her ears rang with a high, clear tone that made the world feel far away.

She tried to suck in a breath and found her lungs working through syrup.

"Wh—" she started, but the word stretched, distorted, like it came from underwater.

Light bled in at the edges of her vision, silver and pale gold, rippling in slow waves. The room wavered. The walls pulsed. The chandelier's crooked shape seemed to straighten, then blur, then straighten again.

The floor gave a strange, subtle lurch under her knees.

Not physically.

Reality itself seemed to tilt.

Mina stopped trembling; she went statue-still; her claws still embedded in Penelope's shoulder.

"Mina," she gasped, grabbing at the cat with one hand, clutching the pendant through her shirt with the other. "Mina—"

Her fingers brushed the back of a nearby broken chair as she tried to steady herself.

Her hand went straight through it.

Her stomach dropped.

The chair was still there, solid to her eyes, but intangible under her skin. The wood wavered around her hand like smoke.

Panic clawed up her throat.

"Nope," she choked. "Nope, nope—this is not happening—"

The pendant went from warm to hot to *searing*. The heat shot through her like an invisible tether being yanked. Her vision tunneled, collapsing into a narrow corridor of sparkling light.

For a moment, she felt weightless.

Like the world had stepped away from her, leaving her suspended in a place that wasn't a place at all.

With a soft, decisive *snap*, like a camera shutter closing, everything shifted.

Not just the light. Not just the air.

Her.

For one impossible second, Pen felt herself split—half in the ruined dining room, half somewhere else—before the world made its choice and yanked her forward.

Pen's knees slammed into a surface.

Not raw, warped wood.

Something softer.

A rug.

She toppled forward onto her hands, air rushing out of her lungs. Mina dug her claws in deeper with a furious hiss, clinging to Pen's shoulders like she, too, was trying not to fall out of the world.

Pen coughed, inhaled—

And froze.

The musty, stale scent of dust and disuse was gone.

The air smelled like lemon oil, beeswax, and a hint of wood smoke.

Slowly, heart pounding against the pendant, she lifted her head.

The dining room was... wrong.

Or maybe it was finally right.

The crooked chandelier above her now hung perfectly centered, every crystal in place, catching light from flames flickering in the polished glass shades of oil lamps. The wallpaper, once torn and sagging in sad strips, now lay smooth against the walls... tiny flowers on a pale background, the pattern delicate and new.

The five tall windows along the curved wall gleamed. Their stained-glass crowns glowed with late-evening sunlight, casting ribbons of color over a polished floor.

The fireplace had been scrubbed clean; green tile glossy. A modest fire crackled inside, sending out gentle waves of warmth that kissed Pen's cheeks.

The debris, the boxes, the trash bags...

Gone.

Everything looked exactly the way it must have when the house was young.

Pen's heart hammered so hard it hurt.

"What the..." she whispered, voice dazed. "No. No way."

Mina made a strangled sound—half-growl, half-yowl—and launched off Pen's shoulder. She hit the floor in a crouch, fur standing on end, pupils blown so wide her eyes looked black. Her tail lashed once, twice, then she froze, staring at the fire with a low, continuous growl rumbling in her chest.

She didn't run.

She didn't hide.

She just... stared. Like she could see something Pen couldn't.

Pen forced herself up onto her knees, fingers digging into the thick braided rug beneath her. It was real. Coarse texture under her hands. Finally, getting to her wobbly feet, she turned slowly in a circle.

The archway to the foyer was no longer chipped and shadowed. The wood gleamed with fresh varnish. In the distance, beyond the stairwell, she could make out the faint sound of something clattering, like metal on wood. The kitchen?

Her mind rejected every possible explanation it threw at her.

Hallucination. Fever dream. Carbon monoxide leak—too on the nose and definitely not it. Stress.

None of it accounted for Mina's claws, which had been painfully embedded in her shoulder. For the smell of smoke and polish. For the warmth of the fire.

The pendant lay heavy and pulsing against her chest, as if it had its own heartbeat.

A voice drifted from somewhere deeper in the house—low, male, humming a melody she didn't recognize.

Pen's blood turned to ice.

Someone was here.

Someone alive.

Her stomach dropped.

She wasn't alone.

"Who are you?" a voice demanded, deep and edged with steel, "and what are you doing in my house?"

Pen's spine locked.

CHAPTER 3

The House Remembers

Penelope's breath stopped.

Every muscle locked. The pendant pulsed hot against her sternum, but she couldn't move. Couldn't think past the voice behind her—low, sharp, *real*.

The cat let out a low, guttural growl. The kind she only made when a dog got too close.

Pen swallowed. Her throat felt like sandpaper.

Turn around, her brain screamed. *Turn around and—*

She turned.

A man stood in the arched doorway to the dining room.

He was tall—the kind of tall that made the doorframe look slightly too small. His hair was pitch-black, swept neatly back from his forehead. Lamplight caught the angles of his face: a strong jaw, a straight nose, cheekbones that would've made modern casting directors weep.

He wore a dark waistcoat over a white shirt, his shoulders straight and unyielding. His boots were dusty. His hands roughened with calluses that spoke of real work, not office hours.

He looked like he had walked straight out of that sepia photograph- from a century where women didn't wear jeans, messy buns, or calico cats like a scarf.

He was staring at her like she was an intruder from the wrong side of hell.

But it was his eyes that rooted her in place.

Blue. Clear. Intense.And currently fixed on her with a mixture of disbelief, outrage, and something darker.

She knew that face. Not from this room. From a photograph —a brittle piece of paper inside an old wardrobe. From a letter that tore at her heart.

Connor James Halden.

Her mouth went dry. "Connor," Pen breathed, his name slipping out like it had been waiting on her tongue.

His expression tightened. "How," he said, voice low and dangerous, "do you know my name?"

Pen stared at him, heartbeat pounding against the pendant, against her ribs, against the thin barrier of reality that had already torn.

How could she tell him that she'd read his grief? Held his heartbreak? Seen the version of him who lost everything. How could she tell him that somehow—impossibly—his house had brought her here?

"Oh," she breathed, heart hammering. "Oh, no."

He strode into the room with the kind of confidence only men in old photographs seemed to have. "I will not ask again. State your name and your purpose here. Immediately." His voice was crisp. Formal. Heavy with authority.

"I—I can explain," she stammered.

She could not explain. Not even to herself.

Connor's gaze traveled from her messy blonde hair to her vintage pink T-shirt with her favorite band, Razor's Edge, faded across the front—down to her dirty jeans, then her beat-up sneakers. His eyes snapped back to the cat plastered to her shoulders.

His brows lowered with every inch he registered.

If judgment were heat, Pen would have burst into flames.

Mina hissed again—loud, vicious, her whole body still arching like a Halloween cat, complete with bottlebrush tail.

Penelope reached down to pick her up. Soothe the cat. Or herself. She wasn't sure.

Pen thought back to what he had said. Her mind was still as disoriented as her body. *State your name and your purpose here.*

She tried to steady her voice, but it wobbled like a loose floorboard. "I'm Penelope."

His expression didn't change. Not even a flicker. "I did not ask for a given name alone. Continue."

Right. Last name. Easy. Normal. People had those.

Except her brain had left the building.

"Ward," she managed.

She was talking to a man who shouldn't exist anymore. If not for the pain of her cat flexing dagger-like claws into her shoulder, she would've sworn she was dreaming.

"Miss Ward." His tone was edged with disbelief. "Why are you in my home, dressed in..." he gestured stiffly at her clothes "...that?"

Pen opened her mouth again. Closed it. Opened it. She was a gasping goldfish of confusion.

"And the animal?" Connor pressed, still glaring at the cat.

"This is Mina." Pen's voice trembled.

"Mina." He repeated it flatly, as if the name itself was suspicious. His voice dipped lower. Colder. "And where is your escort?"

"My...?" Pen blinked. "My escort?"

"Husband. Father. Brother. Someone." His gaze was relentless. "No respectable woman travels unaccompanied."

Respectable. Right.

She'd just time-traveled into someone else's house in pajama-adjacent clothing and an emotional support cat.

Respectability was not high on her priority list right now.

"I don't have an escort," Pen said carefully. "I live alone."

If Connor's expression had been severe before, it turned glacial. "You. Live. Alone."

"Yes."

"And entered my household. Unannounced. Unaccompanied. Dressed in whatever manner of costume you've conjured." His jaw tightened. "Miss Ward, I do not know what theatre you believe you're performing, but I assure you—"

"I think there's been a misunderstanding." Her voice wobbled, "This house is mine."

His arms crossed over his chest.

Wrong thing to say.

Penelope felt her breath catch at the sight of the fabric of his shirt pulling tight over muscled biceps.

Connor's jaw clenched. "I assure you, it is not."

She opened her mouth. Nothing coherent came out. Her mind scrambled through explanations like a prize wheel spinning out of control:

You're Connor. I found your letter. Your wife died. In 1892. I'm not supposed to be here.

No version of those thoughts sounded sane.

Instead, all she managed to blurt out was, "I just... I bought the place a few days ago."

He stared. Hard. Those blue eyes were as cold as a blizzard in winter.

Penelope wanted the floor to swallow her whole.

Mina grumbled, flexing her claws again into Pen's skin.

His voice turned hard. Cold.

"If you cannot give me a straight explanation, I will take you to the sheriff. He can determine what to do with you."

A bolt of panic shot down her spine.

Mina hissed again, low and warbling, pressing deeper into Pen's neck.

He took a step back as if the cat might leap at him.

Pen didn't blame him. Mina looked ready to commit murder.

He stared at her. Not only at her, but *through* her. Like every word she'd said scraped his nerves raw.

"You," he said slowly, "expect me to believe you *purchased* my home... a few days ago."

Pen winced. When he repeated it like that, yeah, it sounded unhinged.

"It wasn't like this," she whispered.

"What did you say?"

She swallowed. "The walls were... different. The floorboards. The..." Her voice trembled. "It was old. Worn. And now it's... new." She took a deep breath, trying to steady herself. "I know how it sounds," she rushed on, words tumbling over themselves. "But I have a signed contract, and a realtor, and a loan officer, and a whole stack of papers back in—" She stopped herself just in time, swallowing the word *my office*.

"Back in *where*, Miss Ward?" His tone sharpened. "Because it certainly cannot be here."

Her mouth went dry. "Back in... Missouri."

He blinked once. "Missouri?"

"Uh. Yeah. The state. Gateway to the Midwest." She flapped one hand weakly, as if that clarified anything.

One dark brow arched, slow and disbelieving. "I am acquainted with geography, Miss Ward."

Heat flooded her face. "Right. Of course, you are. Sorry. I'm... I'm really not good at... this." At *whatever the hell this is*.

"That is enough," he bit out. "I will not be made a fool in my own home. I asked you a direct question, and in return, you offered me nonsense. If you will not answer plainly, I will take you to the sheriff and let him decide whether you are mad or lying."

Panic surged, hot and suffocating.

No! Please, you can't..." The wobble in her voice made her hate herself. "I don't know what's going on here, but this is my home." Her chest tightened. "I'm not trying to trick you. I swear I'm not." The words rushed out, desperate. "One minute, this house was falling apart around me. The next, I'm here. With you. And the walls are fixed, and the lights are wrong, and nothing makes sense, and I just—"

Her voice broke.

"I don't know what's happening." Her vision blurred. "This doesn't look like 2026!"

Oh, no. Absolutely not.

She was not crying in front of this infuriatingly composed Victorian man she'd accidentally time-traveled to meet. She blinked rapidly. Her throat burned.

Mina let out a low, rumbling growl—directed at Connor, at the house, at the universe; Pen couldn't tell.

Connor opened his mouth, clearly ready to deliver some cutting retort.

But then, finally, he seemed to see her.

It could have been her white-knuckled grip on Mina, or maybe the wobble in her knees she couldn't hide. Her face had gone pale beneath the dirt smudges, eyes wide with something beyond confusion.

Fear.

Real fear.

His jaw flexed, a muscle ticking near his temple. Something flickered behind his stern expression—not softness exactly, but recognition.

A man who knew the shape of grief and panic when he saw it.

"You are near to swooning," he said, voice still firm but no longer sharp. "Sit down before you fall."

Pen stared at him, breath shuddering.

He stepped closer—not enough to frighten, but enough to shield her from collapsing onto the polished floor.

"Miss Ward," he said, low and almost reluctant. "Sit."

Pen swallowed hard.

That tone wasn't a threat now.

It wasn't anger.

It was... concern. Buried deep. Wrapped in iron.

She sank onto the nearest chair before her legs gave out entirely, Mina pressing tight against her neck like a small, vibrating shield.

Connor watched her for one careful moment, unreadable as ever.

Not accusing now.

Simply wary.

And in the shifting firelight, Pen realized:

Whatever this was, whatever had happened to her, she wasn't getting out of this anytime soon.

CONNOR ~

Connor Halden had seen many strange things in his thirty-five years. Things that could not be explained.

Like the harvest season ruined by locusts. A river frozen solid in late April. And a man who survived a logging accident that should have split him in two.

But he had *never* seen anything like the woman standing in his parlor.

She looked like she'd been dropped into his house from a fever dream.

Or a painting he did not remember commissioning.

Or a life he had not meant to want again.

Her hair was unbound, falling in loose waves that no respectable lady would ever allow. Her clothing was tight on her legs like a second skin, her shirt printed with garish ink—the faded faces of five men.

Not to mention the cat perched on her shoulder like a sentinel, tail flicking with offensive confidence.

He didn't know which was more alarming: the woman or the animal.

She stared at him with wide, startled eyes.

Blue.

But not Clara's shade. Different. Brighter. More alive than any expression he'd seen in this house for a very long time.

"I think there is a misunderstanding. Um... this house is mine," she stammered.

Misunderstanding?

In *his* house? In his locked, orderly, grieving house?

It was the most ludicrous thing he'd ever heard. The audacity.

"I assure you, it is not." His pulse roared in his ears. She was lying. She had to be.

She blinked rapidly. "I... I just bought the place a few days ago."

He nearly laughed.

Nearly.

The sound caught in his throat and died. This was his house, his life's work, memories made with wood and nails and widowhood.

"If you cannot give me a straight explanation, I will take you to the sheriff. He can determine what to do with you," he snapped.

Her cheeks colored. Not with guilt, but with something else.

Fear. Confusion. Sincerity?

That last part troubled him.

Because he knew liars. He'd learned to know them intimately after Clara's death, when everyone had lied in some small way to comfort him. *"You did all you could." "She was strong." "It wasn't your fault."*

It was always his fault.

But this strange woman... she didn't lie the way others did. She lied like someone who believed her own falsehoods.

Or like someone telling the truth that no sane man would accept.

He examined her again: methodical, cautious.

Her shoes were ragged, and her hands were ungloved. Her golden hair was loose. Her accent was odd, and her mannerisms were all wrong. Everything about her challenged the order he'd carved into this house with his bare hands.

And yet...

When she glanced behind her, as if looking for escape, something in his chest twisted sharply.

It was a feeling he didn't want, didn't need, didn't permit.

She was afraid.

And he, damn him, didn't want her afraid of him.

He pushed that thought away ruthlessly.

But he needed answers. "You," he said slowly, "expect me to believe you *purchased* my home... a few days ago."

Her lips parted. She looked down at her hands, at the room, then, strangely, at the chandelier overhead.

"It wasn't like this," she whispered.

Something cold shivered through him. "What did you say?"

She swallowed. "The walls were... different. The floorboards. The..." Her voice trembled. "It was old. Worn. And now it's— new."

He gathered a bit more information out of her, but when her voice cracked, and she said, "I don't know what's happening. This doesn't look like 2026!" Connor felt a pull inside that he could not explain. He stared. No one could know what this house had looked like years ago except... except Clara and him. He felt the old grief lurch inside him, clawing at the walls he'd built to contain it. *No.* He would not let this stranger chip away at the order he had rebuilt. He would not let softness enter his home again. Not from her, not from anyone. But another truth gnawed at him.

She looked lost. Not deceitful or cunning. Simply... Lost. And her words made no sense.

This doesn't look like 2026.

And despite everything, his battered heart screamed at him to do, to order her out, to remove temptation, to defend what remained, but he found himself saying, "You are near to swooning. Sit down before you fall."

Her eyes snapped up to his.

He hated the way the relief there struck him like a blow.

Because it felt... familiar.Like the way Clara once looked at him on her wedding day, trusting him to keep her safe. He stepped back quickly, spine rigid once more. This woman was not Clara, nor family. Not welcome.

And yet... he could not stop wondering who she was. And why she felt less like a trespasser...

...and more like the beginning of something that terrified him.

PENELOPE WIPED at her cheeks with the heel of her hand, embarrassed at her own tears. She'd imagined many ways her first days in her new house might unfold. Unpacking boxes. Hanging curtains. Maybe battling a stubborn window latch.

Finding the previous owner still inside hadn't made the list.

And yet here she was, standing in what should have been her parlor, staring at a man who very much looked like he owned the place.

Mina finally released her claws and slipped onto Pen's lap, sitting firmly, her fluffy tail wrapped around her front paws, staring at the man with sharp cat eyes.

Connor remained standing, as if sitting near her might somehow legitimize her presence.

Mina shifted, rumbling a shaky, sympathetic purr—as if trying to knead her human back into one functional emotional piece.

Pen bent her head, pressing a soft kiss between the cat's ears. "It's okay, baby," she whispered. "We're... we're figuring it out."

A lie. Or maybe a hope.

Up close, Connor was overwhelming. The faint scent of smoke

and pine clung to him, threaded with something clean. Soap, maybe.

He stood near the fireplace with the stillness of someone who'd spent years commanding rooms without raising his voice. Tall—taller than she'd expected from the photo—with broad shoulders that filled his dark vest and coat like they'd been tailored to intimidate. His sleeves were rolled to his elbows, revealing forearms corded with the kind of muscle that came from real work, not a gym membership.

A logger's arms.

A builder's hands.

Of course, he did real work.

"Water," he muttered, almost to himself, and crossed to a side table.

Pen followed his movement with wide eyes as he poured from a ceramic pitcher into a glass. Not a faucet, not a filtered dispenser. Just water. In a pitcher. Because, of course.

He handed her the glass with a curt nod. Their fingers didn't quite touch, but the nearness of his hand made her pulse jump, anyway.

"Drink," he ordered.

She did. The water was cool and clean, and for a second, the simple act of swallowing grounded her more than anything else had since she'd clasped the pendant.

"Thank you," she managed.

He grunted, as if courtesy physically pained him, and resumed his position across from her, arms folding over his chest again. It made his shoulders look broader.

Which she absolutely did not need to notice right now.

"Let us begin again," he said. "Your name is Penelope Ward. You claim to have... purchased,"—he said the word as if it offended him—"this house. Recently."

Pen nodded weakly.

"You have no papers on you to prove it."

Another nod.

"I'm assuming you have no family here."

Her throat tightened. "No family anywhere."

Something flickered inside his expression. That one hit too close to home; she could feel it without knowing why. He masked it quickly.

"Then you are either orphaned and alone," he said, "or a very poor liar."

"Can't I be both?" The words slipped out before she could stop them.

For a fleeting second, the corner of his mouth twitched. Not quite a smile, but close enough.

Her chest squeezed.

Damn it. Do not be charmed by the grief-stricken man who thinks you broke into his house.

"I am not ignorant of hardship, Miss Ward," he replied, the brief softness gone. "And I am not unsympathetic to it. But I will not have vagrants or charlatans using it as an excuse to trespass on my property."

Vagrants. Charlatans.

If she weren't so terrified, she'd have laughed. She'd been called awkward, quiet, too much, and not enough. No one had ever accused her of being interesting enough to be a charlatan.

"I'm not a thief or a liar," she said quietly. "I'm not here to hurt you. I just... I don't know how to leave. God, I don't even know how I got here."

He studied her, head tilted slightly, like he was trying to pin her to some category in his mind and failing.

He turned and looked toward the front door.

"I wish it were that simple," Pen said, stroking the cat. Sleek white fur, mottled with black and orange in no pattern.

"But it is. Stand up, walk that way, push the handle, and step out."

"That won't get me home," she whispered, fighting the sting in her eyes, the inevitable tears that were pricking at the corners. Her stomach churned.

"I thought you said *this* was home," he said, like he was trying to catch her in a lie.

"It was going to be. My first home. The first place I could ever call mine. Mina and I." She leaned down and kissed the top of her cat's head. "She's the only family I have. This was our new start."

Silence stretched between them. The fire in the hearth crackled. Somewhere deeper in the house, wood settled with a soft groan—familiar and strange all at once.

Connor finally exhaled, the sound long and low.

"Very well," he said. "For the moment, we will set aside whether I find your story credible. The fact remains, I cannot, in good conscience, turn a woman out into the night with nowhere to go."

He spoke the words like each one scraped his throat on the way out.

"Nor will I have you paraded through town like some spectacle without cause. The sheriff is not a toy to be summoned on a whim."

Relief hit so hard her eyes stung. "So... you're not taking me to him?"

"Not tonight." His gaze sharpened. "Do not mistake that for trust.

A pause.

"You need rest," he said quietly.

Pen startled. She hadn't expected gentleness, not even this tiny, gruff version of it.

Connor shifted his weight, as though fighting himself. "You may use the lounge in the parlor tonight. Until your mind is clearer. You will stay where I can see you. This room, or the dining room. No wandering around the house. No slipping out in the dark. Am I understood?"

She nodded quickly. "Yes. Completely. No wandering. I can be very... un-wandery."

A flicker of something—exasperation, maybe—passed through his eyes. "We will speak again in the morning," he said. "When, I hope, you will have discovered how to explain yourself in a manner that does not sound like the ravings of a lunatic."

Pen winced. "I'll... do my best."

His eyes met hers. "I do not yet believe your tale. But I... can see your distress is not feigned."

Pen swallowed. "I'm not lying."

"We will find the truth in the morning." He cleared his throat and stepped back. "Try to sleep."

He gave another curt nod—a temporary truce he wasn't thrilled about but would honor, anyway.

As he turned toward the doorway, Pen's fingers found the pendant at her chest. Cool now, as if it hadn't ripped her out of her life and dropped her into someone else's.

The metal loops pressed into her skin like a question.

If it brought me here, it can take me back!

She started to pull the chain off, then stopped.

Mina!

She snatched her cat into her arms. If the pendant brought them there together, it could take them home. She steadied to cat back on her shoulders and slowly removed the necklace.

Nothing happened.

The pendant was cool.

On, off. On, off.

On.

Nothing.

Tears blurred her vision. She was stuck.

Pen dropped onto the chaise lounge, Mina still draped across her shoulders. She smoothed a hand down the cat's back, gaze drifting over the gleaming room once more.

Connor Halden—flesh and blood—walked into the hall of the

house she'd bought over a phone call and legal forms and blind hope.

A house that clearly belonged to him, in a year that shouldn't be hers.

Penelope swallowed.

She was almost a hundred and thirty years from home, trapped in a stranger's life, wearing what she could only call *magic* around her neck and with a furious Victorian on the other side of the wall.

And somehow, inexplicably, she had the sinking feeling that this impossible, terrifying, wildly wrong moment was exactly where she was meant to be.

Pen stood there a moment, holding Mina like a lifeline as the silence settled around them. Only the faint crackle of the fire carried around her.

Finally, she sank into the chaise lounge; surprisingly soft—softer than anything she'd slept on in the years of moving from couch to spare room to temporary housing.

Mina circled once and collapsed against her hip with a soft *whump*.

Pen drew her knees up.

She had no way home. No phone. No contacts. No familiar world outside that window.

Only Mina. And the pendant. And Connor.

Her hand found the pendant again. Cool and lifeless. She traced the pattern with her fingertip.

"What am I supposed to do?" she whispered. "Why did you bring me here?"

Mina butted her forehead against Pen's arm.

Cuddle and survive.

Pen pulled the blanket over herself and lay down. Tears prickled her eyes, but exhaustion was stronger.

Slowly, with Mina's weight curled warm beside her, she drifted into sleep.

CHAPTER 4

Truth Be Told

Penelope awoke to voices in a house that should have been empty. Footsteps where there should be none. Pots clattering in the distance.

Her mind surfaced with sleepy normalcy: new house, sore muscles, tomorrow's to-do list. The faint buzz of the refrigerator. The far-off sound of a car. The vague glow of her phone some-where nearby.

None of that came.

Instead, the soft pop of the dying fire. Murmurs beyond the wall. The clatter of metal on ceramic.

And the air smelled like wood smoke and... bacon?

Pen's eyes snapped open.

She wasn't on the mattress she'd set up in the main bedroom. She was on a narrow, green chaise with carved wooden legs and a crocheted blanket half-slipped off her chest.

Mina lay on her legs, purring, as if nothing at all was wrong.

"Oh God," Pen whispered. Memory rushed back: the letter, the photograph, the pendant, the light, the voice behind her.

Connor.

She sat up too fast. The room tilted. She caught herself with one hand on the armrest. "Okay," she told herself under her breath. "Let's make sure you didn't dream the entire Victorian widower situation."

Mina yawned, pink tongue curling.

Morning light spilled across the floral wallpaper.

Two matching chairs sat in opposite corners, flanking the front window. Small tables beside each held unlit oil lamps. Against the far wall: the chaise where she'd slept, two pillows still indented from the night. In the center of the room, a round walnut table held a white doily and a red bowl.

Connor had brought her a blanket and stoked the fire in the adjacent dining room.

Pen pushed herself upright. Everything felt too quiet, too soft. Too... 1896.

"Okay, Penelope," she whispered. "You've survived twelve hours. Gold star."

Mina chirped in agreement.

Pen stroked her absently, then stood, sending the cat to the ground with a harrumph. The wooden floor was smooth and cool beneath her socks. She still wore her jeans and T-shirt from... before. Her muscles ached from hours of cleaning the house that wasn't ruined anymore.

She reached into her jeans pocket—lint, a folded paper, hair tie. She pulled out the hair tie and secured her hair back.

She crossed to the entryway and peered out.

The dining room was empty. Morning light slanted through clean windows, splashing golden rectangles across the polished floor. The chandelier above her head glowed faintly—not too bright. Not electric. Lamps on side tables flickered.

No light switches.No outlets.No power cords trailing anywhere.

Her throat went dry.

Clue number one.

"Miss Ward."

Her arms flailed as she spun around in shock.

Connor's voice came from behind her. Again. What was it with this man and emerging from nowhere like some sort of judgmental specter?

She turned to find him standing at the base of the main stairs, sleeves rolled to his forearms, dark hair smoothed back. He'd changed his shirt, this one a pale tan, open at the throat, the fabric worn soft from use. He looked slightly less furious and no less intimidating.

"I see you survived the night." His tone suggested he'd half-expected her to vanish.

"Barely," she muttered.

One of his brows twitched. "Come. The morning meal is on the table. You may eat before we talk."

The way Connor said *"talk"* made her stomach tighten, but the smell of food overrode everything else. When had she last eaten? Lunch? Yesterday felt at least a hundred and thirty years ago.

She followed him into what had been—in her timeline—a depressing, half-gutted dining room buried in boxes and trash bags.

Now it was beautiful.

Sunlight poured through lace curtains. The long table gleamed, flanked by high-backed chairs. A sideboard held covered dishes. In the center: eggs and bacon, a basket of biscuits, and a ceramic pot that smelled like coffee.

Her knees nearly buckled.

"Please. Sit." He motioned to the chair at the end of the table.

Penelope hovered. "Are you sure? I don't want to—"

"Yes," he said. "I am capable of offering basic hospitality without collapsing in on myself, Miss Ward."

She bit back a retort. He sounded like he might actually collapse at any second, but it felt rude to say so.

She slid into the chair. Mina hopped into her lap, folding herself into a neat furry loaf.

Connor took the seat at the other end. He bowed his head, murmured a quick grace she couldn't hear, and picked up his fork.

Pen waited a beat, then helped herself cautiously to a strip of bacon. The first bite almost made her moan. Crispy, salty, hot—real, solid proof that this wasn't some bizarre dreamscape. Her dreams never had this much texture.

They ate in strained silence for a few minutes. Pen shoveled in eggs and a biscuit like she was afraid he might change his mind midway through and snatch the plate away.

Finally, Connor set his fork down.

"Now," he said. "We talk."

Pen's appetite shrank.

"Let us begin with where you came from. You say Missouri."

She nodded, swallowing. "Yes."

"And why, precisely, do you believe this house to be yours?"

She picked up her coffee, mostly, so she'd have something to hold. It was stronger than she was used to, a little bitter, grounding.

"I told you," she said. "I bought it. The listing said, 'Needs love, lots of potential, TLC required.' Which was a nice way of saying, 'This place has been through hell and probably has mold.'"

His brows drew together. "Listing?"

"An advertisement. On... paper. And on... other things." Her brain screamed don't say internet. "I signed papers with a real estate agent. Put down a deposit. Everything was legal. On my end, anyway."

"And when was this?"

"Last month." Her mouth went dry. "For me."

"For you," he echoed.

Pen's gaze dropped to her plate. No point in lying about it. He already thought she was crazy. "In the year 2026. I know this sounds insane."

"That word does come to mind."

She flinched. He hadn't yelled or screamed when she mentioned the year. Had he not heard her?

He exhaled, the sound heavy. "You offer explanations that speak of futures, of purchase and sale, of agents I have never heard of, yet you possess nothing to substantiate your claims. No documents. No one in town who might vouch for you. No husband, father, or brother in whose care you reside." His voice cooled further. "Do you see why I might be inclined toward skepticism?"

She bristled. "I don't need a man to be in charge of me."

Something like surprise flickered across his features. "That is not a view I have often heard expressed."

"I'm full of unpopular opinions."

He studied her. "And yet you stand here in my dining room, reliant on my goodwill."

"Technically, I'm sitting."

He wasn't wrong.

Then, the realization of what he said and what she had hit her. *No documents.*

That was correct. She had no proof of owning the house, or of who she was. But laying in her pocket was proof.

She set down her cup.

"Wait! I have this!" She pulled the folded receipt from her pocket and offered it to him.

He looked it at briefly, dismissing it immediately.

"It's a receipt of the coffee I bought, in my time. Just look at it, please," she cried.

"Nothing that small could prove what you are telling," he said.

She put it back in her pocket. Now was not the time for pushing it.

"I know you have no reason to believe me. But I'm not lying. I woke up one day in the women's shelter, and a few weeks later I had keys to this place, and black trash bags piled higher than my shoulders on the curb, and a cat with bad manners, and more dust in my lungs than oxygen, and then—"

She broke off, chest tight.

His voice was quiet. "And then?"

She looked up. Met his gaze. "I found this pendant." She pulled it out from underneath her shirt.

Something flickered across his face. It was gone before she could read it.

She reached for the metal at her throat, fingers brushing the intricate loops. "It was hidden under a floorboard in the front parlor. Wrapped in cloth. As soon as I put it on, everything... changed."

"Changed."

"The house. The light. The air." She swallowed. "This thing —" she held it up—"started heating up. My vision got blurry, and the room started changing. From one hundred and thirty years old and falling apart, to brand new."

His jaw tightened. He looked like he wanted to call her mad and be done with it. Instead, he pushed his plate away and leaned back.

"And you truly expect me to believe," he said slowly, "that some trinket transported you here from one hundred and thirty years in the future? Like H.G. Wells would write?"

Silence.

Penelope's face burned. "I know how that sounds. I don't even know what year it is."

"1896. And yes, it does sound like the ravings of a woman who has spent too much time alone."

She winced. "You're not wrong."

Mina chose that moment to leap onto the table, landing between the basket of biscuits and the plate of eggs.

"Mina! No!"

The cat strutted forward like a queen surveying her domain.

She sniffed Connor's abandoned fork, his plate, and batted a crumb toward the edge.

Connor's eyes widened. "Absolutely not."

He stood so fast his chair scraped against the floor. Mina fluffed to twice her size, hissed like he'd insulted her ancestors, and darted away, knocking over Penelope's glass.

Water spilled across the table, soaking into the cloth and dripping onto the floor.

"Oh, crap, I'm so sorry—" Pen scrambled for the hand towel near the pitcher, blotting frantically. Mina raced across the sideboard, sending a silver spoon clattering, before launching herself onto the back of a chair and from there to the doorway.

"Get that creature off the table," Connor barked, as if she hadn't already tried.

"She moves faster than I do!" Pen protested, mopping up water. "And she has knives for feet."

Connor muttered something that sounded like a curse under his breath. He crossed the room in three long strides, scooped the towel from Pen's hands, and finished drying the mess with quick, efficient motions.

Penelope watched him, cheeks burning. Mina had disappeared into the hallway, tail flicking like a banner of defiance.

"Is she always like that?"

Pen's lips twitched. "That was her being polite."

He shot her a look that should have withered her on the spot. Instead, it made her want to laugh for the first time since this began. She bit the feeling down. Hysterical laughter probably wouldn't help her case.

When the table was mostly dry, Connor straightened.

"Your... pet," he said, as if the word offended him, "is disrupting my home."

"She's also the only one who listened when I cried on the bus for three hours the night I moved states."

His expression shuttered. She hadn't meant to say that out loud.

"Miss Ward," he said after a beat, "I am not blind. I can see that you are frightened. And alone." His mouth thinned. "I know something of those conditions."

The admission startled her. It felt like an opening—small and grudging, but there.

He went on before she could respond. "But I cannot simply assume your story is true because it is imaginative. I must think of the safety of my household."

"Your household?" She glanced around. "It's just you."

He paused. The silence was so heavy she wanted to snatch the words back. Her mind flicked to the letter. To Clara's name. To the son who never took a breath. She swallowed. "I didn't mean—"

"Regardless." His voice clipped the word short. "You are a stranger here. No acquaintances here. No employment. No means of support. You tell tales of the future and magical jewelry. You see my difficulty."

"I do," she whispered.

He watched her. "You said yesterday you had nowhere to go. Is that still the case this morning?"

Penelope thought about it. She pictured herself stepping out of his front door into 1896—into a world without phones or IDs or any way to prove she existed. She didn't even have cash. The contents of her pockets: a hair tie and a piece of paper.

"Yes," she said eventually. "It is."

"Do you have any living family you might appeal to?"

"No." The word came out hoarse. "They're dead."

He nodded once, as if that answered something. Connor looked toward the window, where sunlight glowed against the glass.

Pen's chest squeezed as she watched his profile. For a heartbeat, his face was unguarded—tired, lonely, haunted.

"May I..." She forced herself to ask, though every prideful bone protested. "May I stay? For a little while. Until I can figure out what to do. How to get home."

The request hung between them, fragile as the cloth that had wrapped the pendant.

Connor's jaw worked. She could see the war behind his eyes—like instinct telling him to close the door, habit telling him to lock the world out, something else whispering that turning away a woman with nowhere to go might be one cruelty too many.

He inclined his head.

"One more night," he said. "You may stay under my roof for one more night."

Relief washed through her. "Thank you," she murmured.

He held up a hand. "Do not thank me yet. There will be rules. You will not leave this house without my knowledge. You will not go near the outbuildings or the timber. You will not rifle through my personal affairs." His gaze sharpened. "And you will not lie to me. If I find your story has changed, or you have concealed something, this arrangement ends at once. Do we understand each other?"

"Yes. I understand."

He gave her one last searching look and nodded. "Very well. I will see to some matters on the property. You may remain in the parlor and this room." Without another word, he left.

Pen sat there listening to his footsteps fade down the hall and out the back door. When she was sure he was gone, she slumped in her chair.

Mina reappeared as if summoned, leaping onto her lap.

"Well," Pen said, scratching behind her ears. "We're officially strangers in 1896, crashing at a grieving man's house with nothing but sarcasm and a haunted necklace. Super-duper."

Mina purred.

Pen looked down at the pendant resting against her T-shirt, the metal loops warm under her fingers.

She still had no idea how she'd gotten here.

Her hand drifted toward her pocket—the receipt. The one from the coffee shop with the date stamped clear as day: February 12, 2026.

But Connor was already gone. And even if he wasn't, what would a piece of paper prove to a man who'd already decided she was a liar?

She left it where it was.

But for the first time, she had something that looked almost like a choice:

Trust him. Or try this alone.

Her fingers tightened around the pendant.

"One more night," she whispered. "Just one more night."

But somewhere in the back of her mind, she knew one night was only the beginning.

PENELOPE SPENT the next hour pacing the front parlor, trying not to unravel like cheap yarn.

She searched the floor for the warped board that had held the pendant—the one she now wore. But nothing was loose. No signs of tampering. Everything had happened in a rush and a whirl of... what? Magic? She didn't know what to call it. Couldn't remember where it had been.

Maybe by the edge of the carpet, where I fell to my knees?
Nothing.

Finally, she slumped down on the chaise lounge, where Connor had instructed her to stay, mostly because wandering looked like a guaranteed way to end up in the stocks or whatever they did to suspicious women in 1896. Mina made herself at home on the parlor sofa, grooming furiously as if she'd personally chosen violence with every hair.

Pen tried to reconcile the impossible:

The house was whole. Connor was alive. She was a stray in another century, dependent on a man who looked at her like she was dangerous.

Too soon, she heard the heavy tread of boots in the hall.

Connor appeared in the doorway, sleeves rolled, vest buttoned, hair wind-tousled. "I will send Mrs. Porter to assist you in dressing. She manages the house."

"Wait— a housekeeper??" Pen sputtered.

"You did not imagine the house ran itself, did you?"

"You don't live alone?"

Connor sounded insulted. "Of course not. A house of this size requires proper staff."

Pen's stomach dropped. She hadn't *considered* there would be people here. A housekeeper. A cook. Groundsmen?

Oh God. She was about to meet real 1896 humans in her Razor's Edge T-shirt.

Connor cleared his throat. "Mrs. Porter will come momentarily. Please allow her to assist you."

Pen swallowed. "Okay. Yes. Thank you."

"And Miss Ward?"

"Yes?"

"Do not allow the cat to terrorize her."

Pen stared at Mina.

Mina licked her paw with the air of a creature who terrorized on purpose.

"I'll... try," Pen said weakly.

Then his words really hit her. "Wait—assist me in dressing?"

"You need something suitable to wear beyond this room."

Pen looked down at herself: pink band tee, jeans, scuffed sneakers. "What's wrong with this?"

He blinked. Once. Slowly. "Everything."

She winced.

"Right. I forgot that women's fashion back now is... more... fabric."

Mrs. Porter arrived with a fitful knock. She was a round-cheeked woman in her late forties, her graying hair tucked neatly under a cap, her eyes bright and curious. Too curious.

"So this is the young lady?" She looked Penelope up and down like she'd discovered an exotic bird in the pantry. "Lord above, Mr. Halden, she's nearly naked."

Pen choked. "No. I—okay, maybe a little—"

Mrs. Porter tutted sympathetically. "Don't worry, dear. We'll have you in something proper." She thrust a folded stack of clothing at Pen. "You can change in the washroom."

Connor cleared his throat. "See that you hurry. We must go into town."

Pen's stomach plummeted. "Town? Why? I can't possibly—"

"There is a matter that requires attention," he cut in. "And the sheriff will expect to meet you."

"The sheriff?" Her voice shot up an octave. "But—I thought —last night you said—"

"I said I would not parade you before the sheriff *last night.*" His eyes narrowed. "Today is another matter."

Oh, fantastic.

She was going to be marched into town dressed like a Victorian Barbie, accompanied by a man who barely tolerated her.

"Go change." He jerked his chin toward the hall. "Mrs. Porter will assist you."

Pen swallowed hard. "Do I... have a choice?"

"No." Then, as if remembering she might cry again, he added, "It is better you appear respectable."

Mrs. Porter hooked an arm through Pen's before she could argue. "Come along, dear. Before your cat gets any more ideas."

Walking down the hall, Mrs. Porter chatted away. "Oh my. You are a peculiar one."

Pen opened her mouth to defend herself, but Mina hissed first.

Mrs. Porter raised a brow. "Is that beast quite tame?"

"No."

The housekeeper nodded, as if she respected the honesty. "Well. We shall manage. Come, dear. Let's make you presentable before Mr. Halden sees you again."

Pen blushed. "He already saw me."

"Yes," Mrs. Porter said dryly. "And I imagine he is still recovering."

Pen groaned.

The washroom was small, bright, and full of unfamiliar hygiene tools. A porcelain basin, a pitcher, neatly folded towels— and on a chair, a stack of clothing that looked more like an architectural project than an outfit.

Mina hopped onto the basin stand and sauntered toward Mrs. Porter, tail flicking in judgment.

"Oh, good heavens," the housekeeper's voice dropped. "It's looking at me."

Pen stifled a laugh. "She's friendly. Sometimes."

"I see."

Mrs. Porter reached into her apron pocket and pulled out a bit of dried fish.

Mina perked.

"Ah," Mrs. Porter smiled. "We shall be friends."

"Well... that's two of us," Pen murmured.

The older woman softened. "Don't fret, dear. Mr. Halden may appear stern, but he is a good man. He has weathered much grief."

Pen's chest tightened. "I know."

Mrs. Porter's eyes flicked up, sharp. "Do you?"

Pen looked away.

No explanation she could give would make sense.

Not yet.

Penelope reached for a folded square of linen from the stack on the chair. It was softer than she expected, worn smooth by years of washing. She held it up. "There's... a lot going on here."

Mrs. Porter sorted garments with military precision.

"Chemise, drawers, petticoat, stays, stockings, dress," she recited briskly. "Not so much once you're used to it."

Pen glanced at the chair again. Followed by the second chair. Every surface was occupied by fabric. "Uh-huh," she said faintly. "I'm still emotionally attached to T-shirts."

Mrs. Porter gave her a considering look. Not disapproving, but puzzled, as though Pen had confessed a fondness for wearing potato sacks.

"We'll cure you of that," she said mildly.

Pen swallowed. "Is all of this really necessary?"

"Of course." The answer came without hesitation. Like gravity.

Pen's shoulders slumped. "Do I have to breathe?"

Mrs. Porter smiled as she reached for the chemise. "Optional. But discouraged."

Pen wasn't entirely sure that she was joking.

The chemise went on first—cool and loose, settling against her skin. Pen relaxed a fraction. *Okay*, she thought. *This I can handle.* It felt almost like a nightgown. Harmless.

Then came the drawers, which Pen accepted with a raised brow and no comment. Then the petticoat.

"Oh," she said as it settled around her legs in a soft, rustling cloud. "I feel like a baked good."

"A respectable one," Mrs. Porter replied, smoothing the fabric with practiced hands. "Stand still."

Pen stood. She always stood when adults told her to. Old habits.

The stays were another story.

"Not a corset, dear," Mrs. Porter said, holding them up. "These are more sensible."

Pen eyed the boning, the laces, the unmistakable implication. "Those look... structural."

"They are," Mrs. Porter said cheerfully. "Arms up."

Pen obeyed. The stays wrapped around her middle, firm hands guiding them into place. The fabric hugged closer than anything she was used to, pressure blooming slowly, deliberately.

Mrs. Porter pulled the laces with steady, unhurried efficiency.

Pen inhaled—and paused.

Her breath didn't go as far down as it usually did.

"Breathe out," Mrs. Porter instructed, pulling the laces.

"I am breathing out," Pen wheezed.

"Then breathe out more."

"Oh," she said, startled. "That's... different."

"You'll adjust."

Mrs. Porter tied the knot and stepped back. Pen looked down at herself. Her posture had changed without her permission. Shoulders back. Spine straight. Everything held where it apparently belonged.

But Pen felt like she was being politely squeezed by an overenthusiastic sofa.

She shifted experimentally.

The stays didn't shift with her.

"This is hostile clothing," Pen muttered.

Mrs. Porter snorted. "You look proper."

Proper felt suspiciously like *contained*.

Stockings followed, the soft slide of fabric up her calves, followed by the dress itself—heavier, warmer, the final layer that transformed her from a woman borrowing clothes into something that belonged in this house, in this century. It was a soft lavender fabric, long sleeves, a high neck, and rows of buttons down the front.

It was pretty, in a way that made her feel like she was about to be presented to someone's grandmother for approval.

Mrs. Porter finished fastening the last button. She stepped back and nodded once.

"There," she said. "You clean up nicely, Miss Ward. You look like someone who won't cause comment."

"Thanks," Pen said faintly. "I feel like an overdressed sausage."

Pen stared at the woman in the mirror.

Unfamiliar. This wasn't Pen from 2025.

This was Miss Ward, 1896.

Same eyes. Same hair, pinned up in a loose, rebellious bun. But everything else softer. Framed. Like she'd been placed into a painting she'd never meant to be part of.

"I feel like I can't slouch," Pen said.

Mrs. Porter smiled. "That's the idea."

Pen exhaled—shorter than she was used to—and tried to convince herself this was fine.

Totally fine.

She was not mourning her T-shirts.

Not at all.

She touched the pendant through the fabric. Still warm. Still the only piece of her own life she carried.

"There now," Mrs. Porter said warmly. "You look like a proper young lady." She patted her arm. "Mr. Halden is waiting."

Of course he was.

CONNOR STOOD in the parlor with his back to the door, staring out the window. Morning light edged his hair with silver and turned his shoulders into sharp, solid lines beneath his dark vest.

When he turned, the air stopped in her lungs—and it had nothing to do with the stays.

His gaze swept over her, from her pinned-up hair to the lavender dress to the gloves Mrs. Porter had tugged onto her hands before sending her out. For a heartbeat, his expression went completely blank.

His gaze swept over her—pinned-up hair, lavender dress, gloves Mrs. Porter had tugged onto her hands.

He froze.

Actually froze.

His expression went blank. Then something flickered. Surprise. Something warmer. Appreciation, maybe—quickly strangled into something that looked like guilt.

His jaw tightened. He looked away too quickly, as if the sight of her in his world was something he hadn't been prepared for.

"That will do," he said, voice a little rougher than usual.

Mrs. Porter beamed. "Doesn't she look lovely, Mr. Halden?"

Connor cleared his throat. "It is... acceptable attire." He turned to Pen. "You look... respectable."

Pen raised an eyebrow. "Respectable. Wow. Be still, my beating heart."

The corner of his mouth twitched, then flattened. "It's important," he said stiffly, "that the town understand you are a lady under my protection, not a vagrant I found climbing through a window."

"Great," she said. "So I'm... what? Your guest? Your... what did people even call this? 'Suspicious female loose in the wild'?"

"You are my cousin, Miss Ward."

She blinked. "I'm your what?"

"Distant cousin," he amended. "Visiting from back East. It will not satisfy everyone, but it is better than having no explanation at all."

A cover story. She supposed that was the most reasonable option—if any of this could be called reasonable.

"Okay," she said slowly. "What's my tragic fake backstory? And why do we care what they think?"

"You are recently bereaved," he said without missing a beat. "Having lost your parents and inherited enough to travel, you wished to see more of the country before... settling." The faintest shadow crossed his features. "It will excuse your unfamiliarity with our community."

Penelope swallowed.

Recently bereaved wasn't exactly a stretch. It simply wasn't the kind of bereaved they'd think.

"And it will give people pause before they pry too deeply," Connor said. "Most have the decency not to pick at fresh wounds. But if they don't know about you before you're seen in my home, it could be catastrophic for us both."

Pen thought of the letter she'd found. The wound that hadn't closed.

"Do they offer you that same decency?" she asked quietly.

He hesitated. "It is not important."

It was. She could see it in the tightness around his mouth. But he'd closed that door with the same finality he probably used on actual doors.

So you're taking me into town to stop gossip before anyone sees me here?" Pen said. "Just in case I actually need time to figure out how to get home?"

Assuming your wild tale is actually true." He paused. "But yes. This town loves gossip. They'll tear down anyone respectable if it brings them entertainment. I'm not willing to risk that."

He reached for his hat near the door, then looked pointedly at her gloves. "Those aren't fastened properly."

Pen glanced down. "They're just gloves."

"You may as well wear no gloves at all if you are going to expose half your wrist," he said, exasperation edging his voice. He stepped closer, hand outstretched. "May I?"

The question startled her almost as much as his nearness.

"Yeah," she said softly. "Sure."

He took her left hand in his, his fingers warm and calloused. The contact sent an unexpected little jolt up her arm. She watched, oddly transfixed, as he straightened the glove, tugging it gently until the fabric smoothed over her skin. His thumb brushed the inside of her wrist for the briefest heartbeat, feeling her pulse hammering there.

His eyes flicked up as if he'd heard it too.

Color rose along his cheekbones. He dropped her hand as though it had burned him.

"That will do," he said, voice abruptly brisk. "We should go."

Penelope flexed her fingers, skin still tingling where he'd touched her. For a moment, she'd seen something in his face, not only duty, but something almost tender.

And then it was gone.

CHAPTER 5

Lessons In Town

C onnor ~

Connor closed the parlor door and leaned against it, waiting for his pulse to settle.

Miss Penelope Ward.

He turned the name over in his mind like a puzzle, but it refused to make sense. She'd sat only feet from him moments ago—pale, trembling, dressed in clothes he couldn't explain—and he still had no idea where she'd come from.

Her story was impossible. And yet...

Connor rubbed the back of his neck, pacing the length of the hallway with long, restless strides. The house creaked overhead, ordinary sounds he knew as well as his own breath, but today they felt different. Sharper. Attentive.

As though the house itself knew something had changed.

He thought the pushed aside. *Nonsense.*

He stopped at the base of the staircase, fingers brushing the banister. Clara's hand had rested there once, gliding down the railing as she descended for supper.

The memory hit like stepping into a room he'd locked years ago.

He pressed his eyes shut. *Not now.*

He had enough turmoil without summoning ghosts.

He turned from the stairs and shut himself in the study. The fire was burning low. He crossed the room to stoke it, needing something to do with his hands.

Because they *had* shaken.

When he'd handed her the water. When she'd looked at him with those wide, frightened eyes. When she whispered, *I don't know how to leave.*

His jaw tightened.

She was trouble. Confused. Possibly unwell.

But not malicious.

He dropped a fresh log onto the embers. Sparks flared. His thoughts scattered with them.

He should take her to the sheriff. That was the sensible route. A stranger in his house, offering riddles instead of answers, appearing out of nowhere. He should turn her over and let the law decide.

But...

He ran a hand across his face.

She'd looked at him as though she expected him to save her.

He hadn't felt that in years. Not since Clara.

Clara's pale hand slipping from his grip. The doctor shouting orders he could not obey. The room spinning with blood and lavender water.

The silence afterward.

The way the house had swallowed his grief whole.

Connor forced the memory away and paced.

Penelope Ward was not Clara. He owed her nothing. She was a stranger who spoke in nonsense and wore men's trousers like a reckless actress from a traveling show.

But the moment she'd said she had no family, something inside him had stirred. Long torment. A soft ache under the breastbone he'd thought buried.

He sat heavily in his desk chair.

Hell.

He didn't want this.

Didn't want to care whether the strange, trembling woman in his parlor had anywhere to go. Or why she claimed his home looked "new". Or why her eyes had gone glossy with more sorrow than any charlatan would bother to fake.

He didn't want to care why her cat glared at him like a tiny, furry sentinel.

And he certainly didn't want to notice the way she softened when she touched the animal. Or the way she had spoken to it as if it were the only steady thing in her world.

Connor exhaled sharply.

This was dangerous ground.

He leaned forward, elbows on his desk, fingers laced.

"She needs guidance," he muttered. "Structure. Someone to keep her from wandering town and causing a scandal."

He'd already made the decision, hadn't he?

The moment he told her she could stay the night. The moment she'd whispered, *this was my home...*

Connor swallowed hard.

He rose and crossed to the window overlooking the land. Rows of young timber swayed in the winter wind—a promise he'd made to Clara. One he'd kept after she was gone.

Second chances, the pastor called them. Connor had never believed in such things.

He wasn't sure what to make of the woman who'd appeared on his parlor rug, but she was a disruption. His careful routines. His ordered silence. His grief carved so deep it had become a home of its own.

She unsettled all of it.

He watched the trees bend under a gust of wind.

"She may stay," he murmured, as though the land were listening. "For now."

His mind was made. He'd take her into town. Present her as a distant cousin—a story he hated, but better than parading her before the sheriff like a criminal.

Penelope Ward was frightened.Lost.Broken in ways familiar to him.

And damn him, he understood broken things.

Connor pressed a hand to the windowsill and bowed his head.

"God help me," he whispered. "This is a mistake."

But even as he said it, a truth rose in him.

It felt good—dangerously good—not to be alone in the house anymore.

PENELOPE WALKED STIFFLY BESIDE CONNOR, every step dictated by stays and petticoats. The borrowed dress swished around her legs, and every breath felt like it had to be negotiated with the corset.

This was her personal hell.

Connor walked just close enough that no one could mistake her as unaccompanied, but never close enough to brush her arm. Too intimate. Too improper.

Too dangerous.

The fields and young trees gave way to packed dirt streets. The streets gave way to orderly buildings. And the moment they crossed into the main street, she felt.

The stare.

Not one stare.

Many.

Whispers slid through the winter air.

Connor didn't react. Of course, he didn't. He wore his stoicism like armor.

But Pen felt her cheeks burn.

"Do they always look this long at... cousins?" she whispered.

Connor's jaw tightened. "They always look this long at anything new." Then, softer: "Don't take it personally."

Easier said than done.

"Mr. Halden!" An older woman called, leaning against the bakery doorframe. "And who's this pretty thing?"

Pretty thing. Pen nearly inhaled her own tongue.

Connor blushed. Subtly. But enough to notice. "Mrs. Abernathy. This is my cousin, Miss Ward," he said firmly.

Mrs. Abernathy's smile said: *I do not believe you.* But aloud she said: "Welcome, dear. You'll find the town quiet, but we do like entertainment."

Fantastic. She was entertainment now.

Whether 2026 or 1896, small towns had little to do but gossip. For the briefest moment, Pen was grateful of the attention she had received in her time. It semi-prepared her for what was to come.

The comments kept coming as they walked.

"Cousin?"

"Did anyone know he had a cousin?"

"She's rather... striking."

"Poor man, after all he's endured..."

"Or perhaps this will finally do him good—"

Pen wished the dirt road would split open and swallow her.

Connor angled his body slightly in front of her. A subtle shield.

It helped more than she expected.

More people greeted Connor, some formally, some with hesitant warmth. Every introduction followed the same pattern:

"This is my cousin, Miss Ward."

"From back East."

"Visiting for a short time."

Each repetition nailed the lie more firmly into place. Every time he said *cousin,* an ache pressed behind her ribs. It was protection, she knew that. But it still felt like being kept at arm's length.

Connor steered them toward the general store. As they stepped inside, a bell above the door chimed. The air smelled of coffee, sawdust, and something sweet. Shelves lined the walls, stacked with canned goods, bolts of fabric, jars of candy, tools, and everything in between. On one wall hung a cluster of framed photographs—families, couples, stern men in their best suits.

Penelope's gaze drifted at first.

Then snagged.

There, centered among the others, was a portrait she recognized.

Clara and Connor.

Clara's hair was pulled back in soft waves, her dress simple but elegant, her eyes full of quiet joy. Connor stood beside her—younger, stiffer, less worn, but unmistakably him. His arm rested near hers, close but not quite touching.

Pen drifted toward the photo. She didn't touch it—that felt like crossing a line. The photograph looked newer than the one she had in the house, in her time. Cleaner. No cracks through the corner. The store's lamplight reflected faintly on the glass, but it didn't dull the warmth in Clara's smile.

"Ah," Mr. Talbot, the store owner, said from behind the counter, following her gaze. "Fine portrait, that one. Taken right after they married, if I recall. Sad business, what happened." His voice dropped. "Such a shame. Young as she was. And the babe…"

"I know," Pen said softly.

She sensed, more than heard, Connor draw up beside her.

They stood shoulder to shoulder, staring at the image of his other life.

Penelope glanced at his profile.

His face was stone. No expression. But his hand, at his side, had curled into a fist so tight his knuckles had gone white.

Pen's chest tightened. "She's beautiful," she said quietly.

A muscle in his cheek twitched. "Yes. She was."

Past tense. The word hung between them.

He stepped away.

Pen lingered a heartbeat longer beneath Clara's smiling gaze.

Connor pulled in a breath, forced his hand to relax. "I wanted to take you to meet the sheriff," he began.

His words hit her hard in the gut. Fear brought bile tickling the back of her throat.

"But he is over in Dodge County right now. Come," he said. "I have what I need."

Pen exhaled. She followed Connor, but her eyes lingered on Clara's smile one last time. His tragedy wasn't abstract anymore.

It wasn't just words in an old letter.

It was right there on the wall, level with her heart.

They left the store with a parcel in Connor's hand holding flour, coffee, a few other necessities. The whispers followed them out like a breeze.

"Cousin, is she?"

"Poor man. Maybe it'll do him good."

"Or trouble him worse."

Once they'd left town, the road was quiet around them. Penelope blew out a breath she hadn't realized she'd been holding. "Well," she said, trying for lightness. "I think your cousin story is officially under review by the town committee of Suspicious Old Ladies."

He huffed out something that might almost have been a laugh. "They would be suspicious if the sky declared itself blue."

"And they think I'm pretty," she added, and immediately wanted to smack herself.

He shot her a quick, sideways glance, then looked ahead again. "They are not blind," he said shortly.

Heat shot straight to her face. "I... I didn't mean... I..."

"You need not respond," he said, more sharply than necessary. "It was an observation. Nothing more."

But she'd seen the guilt in his eyes when he'd looked at her in the parlor that morning. Saw it now, in the rigid set of his shoulders. He didn't want to see her that way. Didn't want to feel anything at all.

They walked in silence for a while. The house came into view, sunlight pooling across its fresh paint and gleaming windows.

"Thank you," Penelope said suddenly.

Connor glanced at her. "For what?"

"For... all of it. For the ridiculous cousin lie. For not letting them tear me apart with gossip. For adjusting my gloves so I didn't accidentally flash a scandalous wrist in public." She smiled. "You didn't have to do any of it."

He looked away, jaw working. "You are under my roof," he said. "It would reflect poorly on me if you were..." He hesitated. "...mistreated."

"That's not the same thing as caring," she said gently.

Something flickered in his gaze—a softening, then a closing.

"It is," he said quietly, "what I can offer. For now."

Her heart squeezed.

It wasn't much. But it was more than nothing.

Penelope nodded. "For now."

As they walked the last stretch toward the house, Mina appeared in the front window, paws on the sill, tail flicking. Pen couldn't help it—she smiled.

But somewhere beneath Connor's rigid control, she'd seen it. A crack. A glimpse of the man who adjusted her gloves instead of letting her flounder. A man who still cared, even when he didn't want to.

And that was the thing that scared her most.

Because if she wasn't careful, she was going to start caring back.

DINNER WAS a quieter affair than Penelope expected.

Mrs. Porter moved around the dining room with her usual

calm efficiency while Connor washed his hands at the pump near the back door. Pen lingered at the threshold, uncertain whether she should help or stay out of the way. Every instinct she had seemed to be wrong in this century.

"Sit, dear," Mrs. Porter said, nodding toward the table. "You've had enough excitement for one day."

Pen obeyed, easing herself into the chair with care, skirts arranged as best she could manage. Mina jumped into an empty chair beside her as if invited, curling her tail neatly around her paws.

Connor paused mid-motion.

"She eats with us?" he asked.

Mrs. Porter didn't even look up. "She lives here now, sir."

Mina flicked her tail smugly.

Connor sighed and took his seat across from Pen, posture precise, hands folded loosely before him. For a few moments, the only sounds were the soft clink of cutlery and the crackle of the fire.

The house felt... different in the evening. Less like a museum of grief. More like a place where people lived.

Pen took a bite, and another. Her nerves eased.

It was Connor who broke the silence.

"You mentioned earlier that the pendant belonged to the house."

Pen looked up. "I... yes. I think so."

His gaze didn't leave her face. "What do you know about it?"

She set her fork down. "Not much. Only that I found it under a floorboard in the parlor. It felt... important. Like it had been waiting."

Connor's brow furrowed. "Waiting."

"Yes." She hesitated. "The cloth it was wrapped in disintegrated when I touched it. The dust... at least a century's worth."

Mrs. Porter paused, though she said nothing.

Connor leaned back a fraction in his chair. "Do you know where it came from?"

"No. But I want to. I think... I think understanding it might explain why I'm here."

Connor considered her for a long moment, then nodded. "Then we will look into it."

"We will?"

"This house has records," he said. "Old ledgers. Deeds. Correspondence. My father kept meticulous notes. If the pendant belonged here, it will be mentioned somewhere. And I have access to county archives."

Pen blinked. "You'd help me?"

"You are under my roof," he said more quietly, "and it would be... prudent to understand such an object."

She smiled despite herself. "Prudent. Right."

Mrs. Porter cleared her throat pointedly and resumed clearing plates.

After dinner, Pen rose. "Connor?"

"Yes?"

"I can show you where it was," she said. "If you'd like."

His nod was immediate. "Yes."

They moved into the parlor. The room felt different at night —shadows longer, corners deeper. Pen crossed to the section of floor near the rug and knelt carefully, hoping the stays didn't pierce her.

"Here," she said, pressing her fingers against the edge of the board. "This one."

Connor crouched beside her, close enough that she could feel the heat from his body. He watched as she tried to find an edge of the wood to lift.

"The board was loose when I found this," she said. "No. It wasn't." Penelope scrunched her brow. "Mina had gotten a polystrap stuck. She fought like hell to get it out. It wouldn't budge. Then I tried, and it came right up. I can't explain it."

Connor stared at the floor. "That floor has not been disturbed since before my father's death. Perhaps longer."

Pen touched the board. "Whatever it is... it wanted to be found. Should we get something to pry it up? See if it's already there?"

Connor straightened. "No, Miss Ward. We will not be tearing up my parlor. But tomorrow, we begin looking for answers."

Tomorrow.

Connor led her upstairs and down the hall, the house's polished floorboards gleaming beneath her feet. She'd stepped into the restored version of her renovation daydreams. The thought twisted her stomach.

He stopped at a room on the left and opened the door.

Pen gasped.

Elegant wallpaper in pale gold, stenciled with curling vines. A white coverlet tucked neatly over a perfectly made bed. A vase of white lilies on the small dresser, their petals bright and fresh.

She had seen this room before. Curled wallpaper peeling. The brass headboard looking old and dingy. The floor sagging.

But here... Here, it looked like the house was in its prime.

"You may take use of this room while you are in residence here," Connor said.

"Thank you," she whispered.

Connor hesitated, his hand still on the doorframe. "Miss Ward."

She looked up.

"Sleep well." He turned and left her standing there, still in disbelief over the events of the day.

PENELOPE WOKE the next morning with a stiff back, a dry mouth, awareness that she was still in 1896.

The lavender dress was folded on a chair near her borrowed bed. No longer sleeping on the chaise lounge in the front sitting room, but in a guest room at the top of the main stairs. The brass headboard from her modern-day main bedroom stood against the far wall. Off-white lace curtains with embroidered flowers covered the windows, morning light filtering through.

Next to the chair, on the chest-of-drawers, was a fresh blouse and skirt, each piece aligned with the edge of the wood.

Mina was curled against Pen's hip like nothing about the last thirty-six hours had been unusual.

Downstairs, she could hear movement: boots on floorboards, the clank of a stove, voices that sounded like Connor and Mrs. Porter discussing something in clipped tones. It had the rhythm of a household already in motion, smooth and structured.

Timetables. Expectations. Morning routines. This world had rules. Written and unwritten.

She was going to break all of them if someone didn't intervene. Penelope dressed, stumbling through the unfamiliar layers. She was halfway through buttoning the blouse when she heard Mina sprint out of the room like a tiny, furry missile.

"Oh no. No, no, no," Pen muttered.

She tore after the cat.

Penelope found Mina skidding across the polished dining room floor, fur puffed, chasing what looked like...

"Is that a mouse?" Pen squeaked.

Mrs. Porter shrieked and dropped a spoon. Connor turned from where he stood pouring coffee, his expression somewhere between horror and resignation.

The mouse darted underneath a cabinet. Mina attempted to follow and nearly wedged herself into the baseboard.

Pen scrambled to scoop her up. "No! Not today! You cannot cause a scandal before breakfast!"

Connor stared at her. "You are shouting. In the dining room."

Penelope blinked. "You're criticizing my volume during a mouse incident?"

He set down the coffeepot. "Ladies do not raise their voices—"

"Oh, buddy. I am not a lady *yet.* You have seen me fall out of a wagon."

"Precisely why you require lessons."

Mrs. Porter cleared her throat. "Miss Ward, perhaps after breakfast, Mr. Halden might teach you a bit of local custom?"

Pen gasped. "He's going to teach me etiquette?"

Connor nodded. "For the sake of us all."

"We haven't even *started* the meal."

"Which makes your outburst all the more unsettling."

"You're gonna have to give me more specific instructions if you expect me to blend into 1896."

Penelope crossed her arms. "I am perfectly capable of basic etiquette."

Connor inhaled deeply. "We will begin with proper introductions. Followed by posture, conversation, and general decorum."

Pen narrowed her eyes. "Are you saying I'm indecorous?"

"I am saying that the people of this town will find you... unconventional. And unconventional women attract attention."

Penelope stared. "So this is a 'don't embarrass me' lesson."

He didn't deny it.

Mrs. Porter busied herself with the plates, humming a tune that sounded suspiciously cheerful.

Breakfast was eggs, biscuits, strong coffee, and carefully measured silence. Pen did her best to emulate the way Mrs. Porter sat—straight spine, feet flat, ankles demurely crossed—and still managed to clatter her fork more than once. Every time she forgot herself and reached for something without asking first, Connor's gaze flicked to her.

By the end of the meal, her shoulders ached from sitting so straight, and they hadn't even started the day.

After the last dishes were cleared, Connor stood and straightened his vest. "We will begin your lessons in the parlor. Then outside. Dress warmly."

"Outside?" she echoed.

"There is more to life here than afternoon calls and napkins. If you expect to remain, even temporarily, you must understand the work that supports this household."

Pen's brain snagged on the word. Remain.

She swallowed. "Okay. Yes. Outside. Sure. Great."

Mina, perhaps sensing she was about to be left out of something interesting, trotted after them down the hall.

CHAPTER 6

The Timber Lesson

C ONNOR ~

Connor Halden had always believed a well-run household required structure.Predictable movements.Predictable people.

Penelope Ward was neither.

He stood at the edge of the dining room, arms folded, as she *attempted* to fold her hands correctly in her lap.

How one woman could look both determined and exasperated at the same time baffled him.

Mrs. Porter hovered nearby, offering gentle corrections.

"No, dear, your wrists together, yes, just so. Chin slightly up. Shoulders back."

Penelope shifted, wincing. "Is there a rule about breathing? Am I allowed?"

"Breathing is advisable"

Penelope muttered something under her breath that Connor suspected was profanity.

He should not have noticed the way her hair caught the morning light, or that the lavender dress suited her... too well. He should not have noticed that her frustration was oddly endearing. But he noticed everything. More than he wanted to.

"Back straight," Connor added from the doorway. "You cannot present yourself to the town as a lady of good breeding if you sit as though you are about to fall asleep."

"I'm not about to fall asleep," Penelope mumbled. "I'm about to pass out."

"Same thing."

She glared at him.

She took a deep breath, straightened in her chair, lifted her chin precisely one inch... and immediately sneezed from the scent of the lemon oil Mrs. Porter had used on the furniture.

"Bless you."

Penelope groaned. "This is impossible."

Connor stepped forward before he could stop himself. "It is not impossible. It simply requires discipline."

Penelope narrowed her eyes. "Oh yes, because nothing says discipline like trying to hold perfectly still while wearing fifteen pounds of upholstery."

His lips twitched. "You must adapt," he said. "This society will not adapt to you."

"You really think I can do this?"

Connor's chest tightened.

He should have said no. He should have told her to return to Missouri. He should have reminded her that her stay was temporary.

Instead: "Yes. With effort."

He turned away, warmth creeping up his neck.

"Very well. Stand. We will practice walking."

"Oh good. My favorite."

She learned how to cross a room without tripping over her skirts, without letting her arms swing wildly, and without fidgeting with the pendant. Connor corrected her.

"Shorter steps. Do not stare at the floor. You are not hunting for loose coins. Your hands, Miss Ward. They are not flags."

She stopped and threw her hands up. "I would like to register a complaint with the universe about clothing."

"Complaint noted. Continue walking."

Mrs. Porter laughed. "Mr. Halden, if you work her to the bone before mid-day, she'll be too tired to learn a thing outside."

"Thank you. I knew I liked you," Penelope said with a smile.

"We will take a short respite. Then we go to the fields."

"The fields?"

He tipped his head toward the back of the house. "You read about them, did you not? In your... listing. This land is not decorative, Miss Ward. It feeds the town. Feeds the future."

Penelope touched the pendant through her blouse.

"Okay," she said softly. "Show me."

THE FIELDS STRETCHED WIDE and golden under the late morning sun. Penelope had seen these acres in grainy photos and bullet-pointed real estate copy—"twenty-seven acres of wooded land, former timber farm."

They walked past the kitchen garden and the outbuildings, past a weathered barn and a smaller shed that would, in her time, be half-collapsed. The air smelled like earth and sap, the faint tang of sawdust on the breeze.

Rows of young trees stood in straight lines, their leaves flickering in the light. Farther off, near the tree line, she saw men in work shirts and flat caps hauling cut logs, the thud of wood on wood punctuated by the ring of metal against a wedge. Shouts carried across the field.

"This is..." She stopped and tried again. "This is yours."

Connor's gaze stayed on the rows of saplings. "It is labor. Necessary labor. Nothing more."

"You planted all these. You... did this."

Penelope touched the pendant through her blouse. It felt strangely heavy.

He shrugged one shoulder. "Not alone. The men you see back there, and some before them. It is a long task. Longer than one life-time, perhaps."

Pen swallowed. In her own time, she'd read: "historically important timber stands." Nothing about the man who planted them.

"You're growing a forest."

His jaw flexed. "Come. We will begin with something simple."

They walked toward a shaded area near the edge of the yard where several smooth-cut logs had been arranged around a sturdy sawhorse. Tools lay arranged on a small bench—hatchet, handsaw, wedges, a mallet.

Pen's steps slowed. "Uh. Is this... spectator sport? Or are you about to hand me something sharp?"

Connor picked up the smaller hatchet and held it out to her.

She stared at it, then at him. "I'm sorry. What?"

"You are going to learn something. Etiquette can wait. You should know the work that keeps you warm and fed."

"I can boil water. Mostly."

His expression didn't change. "Take it."

She took it.

The hatchet was heavier than it looked, the wooden handle worn smooth by long use. It sat awkwardly in her hand.

"I am not completely without self-awareness. Giving me an axe might be a poor life choice."

"Hatch—" He caught himself, exhaled, and stepped closer. "Your grip is wrong."

His hands closed around hers, one adjusting her fingers on the wood, the other steadying the top of the handle. The contrast between his roughened palms and her borrowed gloves—her breath hitched.

"You must stand square." His voice close enough that the back of her neck prickled. "Feet firm. Shoulders aligned. If you lose your balance, you risk more than embarrassment."

She swallowed and nodded. "Right. No decapitation. Got it."

He guided her stance, nudging her right foot back, shifting her left shoulder with the edge of his hand.

"Do not swing wildly. Aim. Let the weight of the blade do part of the work. You are not beating the wood into submission; you are cutting it."

"Okay. Aim. Not murder."

He stepped back.

A small, square chunk of wood sat on a low chopping block in front of her. It looked harmless.

She lifted the hatchet.

Everything in her body screamed that this was a bad idea.

The first strike landed with a thud, glancing off to the side and denting the wood.

"Well. That was anticlimactic."

"Again. Focus. Choose a point. Strike that point."

She inhaled, exhaled, and tried again.

The second swing was better. Not perfect, but better. The blade bit in, splitting a shallow notch. Her arms vibrated with the impact all the way up to her shoulders.

By the fourth, she'd found a rhythm. Lift, aim, drop, thud. Sweat prickled along her hairline. Strands of hair slipped loose from their pins and tickled her cheeks.

"Good."

She looked up at him, panting. "Yeah?"

"You are stronger than you appear. Most would complain by now."

"Oh, I'm absolutely complaining." Breathless. "Only... internally."

"Keep the complaints there. At least while Mrs. Abernathy is within earshot."

She snorted. "You mean the town's head gossip? Pretty sure she can hear thoughts."

"All the more reason to practice discretion."

He handed her a different piece of wood, this one larger, then circled around the chopping block to watch her from the side. His gaze followed her movements.

Her swings started losing their aim. The hatchet slipped off a corner and jarred her wrists.

"Ow," she hissed, shaking out her hands.

"That is enough." He stepping forward. "You will bruise."

"Too late," she muttered. "Everything is already a bruise."

He reached for her hand before she could pull it back, turning her wrist palm-up to examine the inside of the glove. "Do you feel that?"

"Feel what?"

He pressed against a spot right below the base of her thumb. A sharp ache radiated through the muscle.

"Ah. Yeah. That. I definitely feel that."

"You are holding too tightly. You must allow the handle to move a little, or you will damage your hand."

"Excellent. Can't wait to explain to my non-existent doctor that I have a time-travel-related axe injury."

He frowned at her phrasing. "Sit," he ordered, nodding toward one of the logs.

She sat.

He crouched in front of her and tugged at the fingertip of her glove. "May I?"

"Yes."

He slid the glove off. Her skin looked pale daylight, faint calluses at the base of her fingers.

He turned her palm upward and pressed gently along the base of her fingers. "You will blister here. And here. Mrs. Porter has salve that will help."

Pen swallowed. "Okay."

He let go quickly.

"Enough for today." he rose to his feet. "You will do more harm than good if you push past what your muscles know."

"But I was just starting to feel competent."

"One hour of chopping does not make you a lumberman."

"Lumberwoman."

He gave her a look. "Absolutely not."

THEY WALKED BACK toward the house at a slower pace, her hand tingling where he'd pressed the sore muscle, her shoulders already aching.

"You did well."

She glanced at him. "That almost sounded like a compliment."

"It was an observation. You did not complain as much as I expected."

"I complain constantly. You're simply tuned to the 'silent suffering' station."

He huffed something that might have been a suppressed laugh. Might.

For a few steps, they walked side by side. The house rose up ahead of them, all fresh paint and shining glass, looking like it was exactly where it belonged in time.

"Thank you."

He looked at her. "For what?"

"For... all of it." She picked at a loose thread on her borrowed skirt. "For not letting me make a complete fool of myself at breakfast. For trying to teach me not to trip over my own feet. For trusting me with sharp objects."

"I did not say I trusted you."

She smiled. "You didn't have to."

He looked ahead, jaw tight. "You are under my roof, Miss Ward. It would reflect poorly on me if you were... mistreated."

"But you're looking out for me. And you don't have to. You could have turned me over to the sheriff yesterday."

His shoulders stiffened. "I have no intention of parading you through town as a spectacle."

"That's not what I meant."

He didn't answer. The crunch of gravel under their boots filled the space between them.

"There is already enough suffering in this town. I will not add to it by turning a woman out into the road with nowhere to go." He paused. "Whether or not I believe everything you say."

Something loosened in her chest.

"So..." Heart thumping against the pendant at her breast. "Does that mean I can stay? For... a while?"

He exhaled. "It means that for now, you have a roof. And food. And work to do."

Work. Lessons. Rules.

But it was safety.

For now.

She nodded. "For now," she echoed.

As they reached the back steps, the kitchen door banged open and Mrs. Porter stepped out with a drying cloth in hand. Mina slipped between her ankles, darted onto the back stoop, bounded toward Pen with an excited chirp.

"You"—Mina attempted to climb her skirt—"are not allowed near hatchets."

Mina ignored her and scrambled up, anyway.

Connor pinched the bridge of his nose. "Your creature is determined to be underfoot at all times."

"She's very passionate."

"About chaos," he muttered.

Pen followed him back inside, her shoulders aching, her palms throbbing, her body tired in a way she hadn't felt in years.

But under all of that, something else:

Almost.

Almost belonging.

Almost wanted.

Almost home.

She wasn't there yet.

She didn't know if she ever could be.

But as she stepped over the threshold, the scent of soap and wood polish around her:

Maybe Conor was learning too.

CHAPTER 7

Powdered Ghosts

Penelope had finally managed to sit properly, as Connor had instructed, perched on the edge of the parlor chair with her ankles delicately crossed and her hands folded.

Back straight. Chin up. No slouching. No fidgeting.

If posture were a full-time job, she deserved a raise.

Mina chose this moment to attempt murder.

The cat slunk into the room with the silent determination of a jungle predator, whiskers forward, shoulders low, pupils blown.

Pen saw the line of her cat's gaze and went cold.

"Oh, no," she whispered. "Mina... don't you dare."

Mina's eyes narrowed on her newest enemy: A highly polished, deeply innocent, extremely antique rocking chair.

The calico's tail puffed to full bottlebrush capacity.

"Oh God," Pen muttered, scrambling to her feet. "No, ma'am. Absolutely not. We respect antiques in this house—"

Too late.

The cat launched.

She struck the rocking chairs curved runners like a furry torpedo—sliding underneath it, hitting the carpet, spinning in a half circle, then BAT-BAT-BAT-ing both legs as if punishing it for standing upright in her presence.

The chair rocked violently, nearly tipping backward.

"Mina!" Pen yelped, lunging. "Stop fighting the furniture!"

The rocking chair banged into the wall with a thud and rocked wildly, creaking.

Pen dove—or tried to, trussed up like she was.

Mina juked sideways at the last second like a tiny, tri-colored NFL running back and shot out from under the chair. Pen's hand met empty air, and momentum did the rest.

She slid across the rug, skirt tangling around her ankles, and landed on her side with an *oof.*

Mina bounded up onto the velvet settee and sat there, tail wrapped primly around her paws, looking exactly like she had won this century.

That was when Connor appeared.

He stopped in the doorway, taking in the scene: the rocking chair listing, Penelope sprawled on the floor, hair coming loose from its pins, and Mina on the settee.

Connor stared.

Utterly still.

Pen scrambled upright, hot from cheeks to neckline. "This isn't... she doesn't usually..." She winced. "Okay, she always does this, but still!"

Mina blinked at him slowly, then licked her chest.

Connor exhaled slowly, pinching the bridge of his nose. He did that a lot around her. She was starting to take it personally.

"I see," he murmured. "Your... pet appears to have declared war on my furniture."

Pen scooped up the cat, who hissed, claws kneading into Pen's bodice. "She's very passionate."

"About destruction?" he asked dryly.

"About architecture," Pen corrected, hoisting Mina higher, cradling her like an oversized, baby. "She has strong opinions."

Mina, hearing this, meowed as if agreeing: *Death to all rocking things.*

Connor closed his eyes for three beats, like he was counting to something. Eternity, maybe. "Miss Ward... remind me again why we agreed she may remain indoors?"

Pen brightened. "Because she's adorable?"

Mina chirped.

Connor opened his eyes and gave the cat a long, unimpressed look. "Adorable," he said slowly, "is not the word I would have chosen."

The rocking chair groaned behind them.

Pen smoothed her skirt. "I'll keep her away from the breakable things. I promise."

His glance flicked to the rocking chair, then to the fine porcelain vases on the mantel, the lamps on spindly tables, the framed photographs.

"There is little in this house that is not breakable," he said.

"Great," Penelope muttered. "No pressure."

Mina stretched in her arms and swatted at the dangling tassel of a nearby curtain.

Connor's eye twitched.

"Control her, please," he said abruptly. "Before she decides to test the integrity of the ceiling as well. I will leave you to your... lessons. There is... something I must attend to upstairs."

He turned and strode out.

Mina wriggled free of Pen's grip with the grim determination of a creature born to commit minor crimes and trotted after him like a furry lieutenant.

Pen followed her cat.

That was the official story, at least.

Really, she'd caught a look on Connor's face as he'd turned. His shoulders had dropped, just slightly. Not the squared-off tension she'd come to recognize—something else.

She drifted up the stairs behind them, fingers tracing the polished banister. Smaller photographs lined the wall: men in dark suits, women with tight expressions, children in stiff Sunday clothes. A vase of dried flowers sat on a side table, faded but carefully preserved.

Connor reached the top landing and paused. She was sure he hadn't heard her yet. He stood at one closed door, the one right past the room he'd offered her, and stared at it.

Penelope didn't need to ask what room it was.

The nursery.

She held her breath as he lifted his hand toward the doorknob.

Stopped.

Lowered it.

His shoulders rose and fell once, shallow, controlled.

Pen took one tiny step closer. "Connor?"

He didn't flinch, but his eyes closed briefly before he turned.

"Miss Ward," he said. "I asked you not to wander."

Pen pressed her lips together. "I wasn't wandering. I was... following Mina. Who is clearly a menace to society."

As if on cue, Mina hopped up onto a small hallway table and knocked over a decorative wooden horse with one decisive paw.

The little carving clattered to the floor.

Connor's eye twitched. "I see."

Pen scooped the cat up quickly. "She's very sorry."

Mina cleaning her paw said she was not sorry.

Connor exhaled through his nose. "Come downstairs," he said. "There is something you must learn."

Pen glanced back at the closed nursery door. Something inside her whispered, *Don't leave him alone with that.*

But he'd already turned away, walking toward the stairs with measured steps, leaving whatever task he had upstairs for another time.

She followed.

The kitchen was warm, all steam and movement and the smell of baking bread. Mrs. Porter stood at the worktable with her sleeves rolled up and her hair escaping its cap as she worked dough with efficient hands.

She looked up and smiled when Pen entered, with Mina in her arms and Connor not far behind.

"Ah, good, dear," the housekeeper said. "I was about to fetch you. Mr. Halden says you'll be helping tonight."

Pen blinked. "Helping with what?"

"Domestic necessity," Connor said, stepping around the table. His sleeves were rolled up. Somehow, it made him look less like a carved monument and more... human. Still annoyingly handsome, but human. "The stove needs tending," he went on. "You must learn to use the pump, gather wood, and prepare a simple meal. Should you remain more than—"

"I get it," Pen cut in with a wince. "I need to know basic survival."

"Precisely," he said. "And it may help you avoid burning my house down."

Mrs. Porter coughed into her hand. "It is not an entirely unreasonable concern, dear. You did look at the stove yesterday as if it might bite."

"In my world, things turn on with knobs and buttons," Pen said weakly. "Fire usually stays hidden. It's very civilized."

"Here," Connor said, opening the iron door of the cookstove. "We are less civilized."

The next hour was a blur of near-disasters.

Penelope pumped the water too hard and soaked the table and herself. The pump handle apparently had two modes: unwilling and vengeful. On her third attempt, she got the rhythm right, and Mrs. Porter clapped in delight.

"See? You're getting it," the older woman said.

"I'm getting arthritis," Pen muttered.

She nearly dropped a cast-iron skillet twice. The thing weighed approximately half a Mina. The stove hissed and popped when she added wood, and she startled so violently she banged the back of her head on the open warming shelf.

"Language," Connor said when she cursed under her breath.

"I didn't even say anything that bad," she protested, rubbing her skull.

"In my house, even small blasphemies are unwelcome."

"Then you shouldn't let me near the fire," she muttered. "I'm a walking hazard."

Butter in 1896 did not behave like butter in 2026. It refused to melt at the speed she wanted, then suddenly turned into a bubbling puddle of chaos. Flour didn't come in neat bags; it came in sacks that wanted to coat the world.

And Mina, of course, got into the flour.

One moment, the cat was sitting upright on a chair. The next, she'd leapt onto a low stool, then onto the table, then directly *into* the open sack of flour with the commitment of a soldier going over a trench.

"Mina!" Pen gasped.

The cat disappeared.

"Mina?" Mrs. Porter said faintly.

A tiny, flour-coated head emerged slowly from the sack, ears ghostly white, whiskers thick with dust. Mina shook herself. A mushroom cloud of flour exploded through the air.

Pen coughed, waving her hand. "Oh, my God—"

Mina shot out of the sack like a powdered cannonball, skidding across the tabletop, leaving miniature paw prints in every direction before launching herself to the floor. She raced in circles, trailing white dust like the world's smallest snowstorm.

Mrs. Porter grabbed for a towel.

Pen lunged for the cat.

Connor... sat down.

Actually sat. In a chair.

Pen blinked through the flour haze.

He had one hand covering his mouth, but it didn't entirely hide the sound: a low, huff of laughter.

Penelope froze. "Was that a laugh?"

He dropped his hand, his face settling back into its usual lines. "It was a cough."

Mrs. Porter, sputtering flour from her lips, muttered, "It was *not* a cough."

Mina streaked past again, a puffed-up white ghost with gold eyes.

Pen scooped her up at last, holding a struggling, powdery demon to her chest. "This is why we don't get invited anywhere nice," she told the cat. "You know that, right?"

Mina sneezed flour directly into her face. Pen closed her eyes and accepted her fate.

By the time Mrs. Porter had the worst of the mess cleaned and Pen had wiped down the cat with a damp cloth (earning herself several yowls), the kitchen looked almost normal again.

Pen, on the other hand, looked like she'd lost a fight with a bakery.

Mrs. Porter shooed them both toward the door. "Out, out, the lot of you. Miss Ward, go wash. Mr. Halden, stop hovering like a barn owl. I can manage from here."

Connor straightened, his expression smoothing, but something remained in his eyes—a softness at the corners, a brightness that hadn't been there before.

He met Penelope's gaze.

"You did not set anything on fire," he said. "That is... progress."

Pen blinked. "Wow. High praise."

His mouth almost twitched. "Do not grow conceited."

She wanted to say something light, something deflecting, but her throat tightened, her chest suddenly warm.

As Pen stepped out of the kitchen with Mina in her arms, a slightly less powdered ghost now, she let herself think:

Maybe, just maybe...

She could learn how to live here.

If only for a while.

CHAPTER 8

Ghosts at the Piano

By early evening, the house had settled into a quieter rhythm. The clang and chatter of the morning gave way to the soft thud of steps, the whisper of skirts, the murmur of low voices.

Penelope wandered into the front parlor, still smelling faintly of flour and wood smoke, Mina padding at her heels. The cat was mostly back to her normal calico coloring, though the occasional streak of white across her fur testified to earlier crimes.

"I loved you more when you were only emotionally messy," Pen told her.

Mina flicked her tail in what Penelope could only interpret as: *You're welcome.*

Pen told herself she was not waiting for Connor to reappear.

She absolutely was.

Instead, she found something else.

The piano was dark wood with clean lines, no ornate carvings or flourishes. In her time, it had been cracked and silent in a room that smelled of mildew, occasionally haunting passersby who claimed to hear notes drifting from the empty house. Here, the finish still shone faintly. Pen's fingers brushed the edge, the wood smooth beneath her touch, worn to a soft sheen by years of use.

When she pressed a single key, the sound bloomed into the room —low, resonant, unfinished.

The note lingered.

And beneath it, for a heartbeat, something else stirred in the air —or in her, she couldn't tell.

The pendant warmed against her skin.

Not sharply. Not enough to startle. Just a faint heat spreading beneath the metal, like a pulse answering a call she hadn't known she'd made. Pen stilled, her breath catching as the warmth faded as quickly as it had come. She frowned, fingertips hovering over the keys.

The house remained silent. No sound. No movement. Nothing she could point to and say *this happened.*

But the warmth in her chest lingered. As if the music had reached somewhere deeper than the room.

A book sat on the closed lid. It looked like it had been placed there long ago and then forgotten: edges softened, pages yellowed, a thin layer of dust turning its dark cover gray.

Pen laid her fingertips lightly on the book's cover.

Dust smeared under her touch.

She opened it carefully.

A music book.

Neatly inked notes filled the pages, flowing like tiny black birds across the staves. At the top corner of the first page, written in delicate, looping script, was a name:

Clara Halden.

Pen's chest tightened.

She traced the letters gently, like touching the past through paper. "You played piano," she whispered.

A voice behind her said, "She did."

Pen jumped, the book wobbling in her hands. She spun to find Connor in the doorway, one hand braced on the frame. His face was still, eyes steady on hers.

"I'm sorry," she blurted. "I didn't mean—I wasn't—I was just looking. I shouldn't have touched—"

"You may," he said quietly, cutting off her spiral. "It... belonged to her. I have not touched it since she died."

His voice caught on the last word—barely, a hairline fracture in the syllable.

Her throat ached. "She seemed lovely," she said softly. "In the photograph. At the store."

His gaze flicked to the piano, to the music, then back to her face. "She was."

Pen looked down at the notes again, imagining Clara's fingers on the keys, the room filled with music and light. A life that had once existed here and then... hadn't.

She closed the book and set it back where she'd found it, as if anything more might disturb something sacred. "Thank you for letting me see it," she said.

Connor's jaw worked. "It is only paper."

The words sat hollow between them.

"Please, excuse me. I have pressing business in my study." He turned and strode from the room.

Pen remained in the parlor after he left, a faint hum still hanging in the air, like the house itself hadn't quite decided whether to exhale. She stood there longer than she meant to, fingers curled at her sides, the pendant resting warm and heavy against her sternum.

It had grown warmer since the piano.

Not hot. Just... present. Like something waking.

As though it had stirred at the sound.

She was tracing the curve of the instrument's edge when footsteps approached from the hall. She turned as Connor entered— returned; she realized—a book tucked beneath one arm, his expression drawn tighter than when he'd left.

"I've searched my father's ledgers," he said without preamble.

Pen straightened. "And?"

He crossed the room and set the book on the table, the movement careful, restraint. "There is no record of the floor being repaired. No mention of boards lifted, replaced, or disturbed. Not during his lifetime. Not during mine."

A chill slid down her spine. "So the cavity—"

"Should not exist," he finished quietly.

He opened the book and pushed it toward her. The leather binding creaked in protest. Its pages were yellowed, edges soft with age, the text cramped and formal. A folded scrap of paper marked a place near the center.

"This," Connor said, tapping the margin, "is the only reference I could find that bears any resemblance to what you described."

Pen leaned in, the scent of old paper and dust rising around them.

The heartbound charm: a talisman said to bind its bearer not merely to place, but to purpose—drawing them to the moment or soul required to mend a broken path.

Her breath caught.

"Heartbound?" she whispered.

Connor nodded once. "It appears in multiple collections of regional folklore. Often dismissed as superstition." His mouth tightened. "But it is... persistent. The references repeat."

Penelope's fingers lifted to the pendant beneath her blouse. It warmed at her touch—a gentle pulse of heat against her skin.

"What does it mean?" she asked.

He turned a page, smoothing the edge before releasing it. "The texts are vague. Deliberately so, I suspect. But the implication is consistent." He hesitated, then said the words like they cost him something. "Second chances."

A tightness bloomed behind her ribs. "Second chances at what?"

Connor's gaze lingered on the page, then lifted to her. "Life. Fate. Healing." His voice dropped. "Love."

The air between them went quiet. Even the house's usual creaks and settling seemed to pause.

Pen swallowed. "You think it brought me here for a reason."

"I think"—he paused, weighing each word—"that if such a charm exists, it does not act randomly." His eyes flicked to the pendant, then back to her face. "It binds its bearer to the person or place that must be faced."

Her pulse thundered.

The pendant warmed again. Stronger this time.

Their eyes met and held.

The pull she'd felt since the moment she'd woken on the parlor floor sharpened—not just desire, though that hummed beneath her skin, but something deeper. Recognition. The sense that the air between the held weight, like a word spoken aloud after years of silence.

Connor looked away first.

"We do not know this to be true," he said stiffly. "Folklore is not evidence."

"Maybe not," Pen said softly. "But folklore is how stories survive when people are afraid to write them down."

His jaw tightened. He closed the book, aligning the edges with the table's corner before releasing it. "Miss Ward—"

"Penelope," she corrected, quietly.

He hesitated.

"Miss Ward," he repeated, lower now. "I am not prepared for what this may suggest."

She nodded, because she wasn't either. "Neither am I."

As he drew the book back toward himself, their hands brushed on the tabletop.

A spark leapt where their skin touched, sharp enough to make her inhale.

Connor froze.

For half a breath, neither of them moved.

Then, slowly—deliberately—he withdrew his hand.

The air between them felt thick, charged. Pen's ears rang with the silence.

THAT NIGHT, Penelope watched Connor move through the house.

Connor checked the back door twice before nightfall, fingers testing the latch. When he passed the nursery door upstairs, his hand brushed the wall beside it—never the doorknob, only the wood. The hallway photographs got a quick glance each time he walked by, his eyes darting away just as fast. When she entered a room, he stepped back. When she moved closer, he found a reason to cross to the other side.

His answers stayed short. His eyes rarely met hers longer than a heartbeat.

And yet.

When she flinched at a door slamming somewhere in the house, his eyes snapped to her first, sweeping over her before he turned toward the noise. When she fumbled with the impossible tiny buttons at her wrist, muttering a curse under her breath, his hand half-lifted—then dropped. His jaw tightening.

Penelope pretended she hadn't seen that.

That evening, Mrs. Porter retired early with a warning about the weather—"smells like rain thinking about visiting"—and a fond pat to Pen's shoulder.

"Sleep well, dear," she said. "You look all wrung out."

Pen wasn't sure if that was a comment on the flour incident, the timber lesson, or her entire life.

Mina curled up on the chaise like she owned it. Which, given her attitude, she probably believed.

Pen stood near the front window, fingers resting lightly on the lace curtain. Outside, the sky was a deepening blue; the fields growing indistinct at the edges like the world was dissolving into shadow. A few early stars pricked through the dark.

Everything was quiet.

Too quiet.

"You should sleep," Connor said from behind her.

Pen startled. She hadn't heard him approach.

"I want to," she admitted, her voice small in the big, quiet room. "It's just... hard. When everything feels... wrong."

The word slipped out before she could stop it.

Wrong.

Connor's voice was low, measured. "This house has been wrong for a long time."

She turned.

He stood near the cold fireplace now, one hand braced against the mantel as though the entire structure was responsible for keeping him upright. Lamplight threw warm amber across his features, carving shadows under his eyes and along the line of his jaw. He looked exhausted—not the bone-deep weariness of a day's hard labor, but something older. Something that showed in the set of his mouth, the weight in his shoulders.

Grief-tired.

Too-many-nights-alone tired.

Pen swallowed, fingers drifting to the pendant at her throat. She hated how much she understood that kind of tired.

"Connor?" she said softly.

He didn't move at first. Then he turned just enough that she could see one blue eye, narrowed. "Yes?"

"Can I ask you something?"

"You may ask," he said carefully. "Whether I answer depends on the nature of it."

She hesitated. "Do you believe that the pendant brought me here? For whatever unknown reason?"

His jaw ticked. For a moment, she thought he would shut down completely, the way he sometimes did when the conversation cut too close. Instead, he stepped away from the fireplace and crossed the room, stopping a few feet from her. Not close enough to startle. Close enough that leaving now would be deliberate.

"I believe," he began slowly, "that something is amiss."

Silence. Complete and thick.

"You appear in my home wearing garments I have never seen. Speaking in ways that make no sense. Knowing information you ought not know. This pendant makes no logical sense. I can't tell truth from fiction right now."

Pen's stomach twisted. "I found your letter," she whispered before she could stop herself.

His eyes went hard, pupils contracting. "What letter?" His voice dropped half an octave, soft and cold at the same time.

Penelope's heart hammered. She hadn't meant to bring it up at all, not like this. Not without proof she wasn't... insane. "I... I found something," she admitted, throat tight. "In the house. Before..."

"Before you claim to have arrived from a different time," he finished flatly. "Something else? Something more than a magical talisman?"

She flinched. "Yes."

His gaze pinned her, moving from her eyes to her mouth and back again. His jaw worked. "Why did you not tell me?" he asked quietly.

"Because it felt private," she said, the words tumbling out in a rush. "And cruel. And I didn't know if showing it to you would make anything better. I thought it might..." She swallowed. "Rip you open."

His mouth tightened. "You presume to protect me?"

"No," she whispered. "I presume you deserve to be protected. Even from your own memories."

His breath hitched.

Pen's chest tightened. She'd done that. Made this worse.

Connor turned away sharply, moving to the opposite side of the room. He braced his hands on the back of the settee, knuckles whitening, shoulders rigid. When he finally spoke, his voice was rough gravel. "My letter," he said. "The one saying goodbye?"

"Yes," she whispered.

His grip on the wood creaked.

Penelope took a cautious step closer. Mina, sensing the shift from the chaise, lifted her head and stared between them, tail thumping once.

"Connor," Pen said quietly, "I'm not lying to hurt you. I'm not lying at all. Something strange happened. Something impossible. And I don't know how to convince you without making both of us feel worse."

His shoulders rose and fell, the movement tight. "Every instinct I possess," he said, "tells me you are not who you claim. That this can not be real."

Her throat closed. "Then why haven't you thrown me out?" she asked. It came out more raw than she intended.

Silence.

He let go of the settee and turned back to her. His eyes were darker now, the skin around them tight. "Because," he said slowly, "you do not feel like a danger." His gaze flicked to the pendant at her throat, then back to her face. "You feel like..." He stopped.

Her pulse stuttered. "Like what?" she asked, barely breathing.

His eyes lingered on her. They dipped to her mouth, then jerked back up. "Like something I should not want near me," he finished quietly.

Heat pulsed under her skin, painful and electric.

"Connor..."

He stepped back. His spine straightened, shoulders squared. "I cannot believe your story, Miss Ward. Not yet. But I cannot dismiss it either."

Her eyes burned. "Then let me show you," she whispered. "Not tonight. Not when you're exhausted. But soon."

His jaw tightened. "Show me what?"

"The letter. That I know where it is," she said. "Untouched since you put it there. Until I found it in 2026."

His breath shuddered.

She rushed on. "It's in a wardrobe. I don't know where it is in the house right now, but when I moved in, in my time, I found an old wardrobe abandoned in one of the upstairs rooms. The smallest room. I dragged it down the hall and into the main bedroom. The letter was hidden in the bottom drawer. It had your name. Clara's name. The date."

He went very still.

"I see," he said at last, though the words sounded strangled. "The nursery," he added under his breath, more to himself than to her.

Penelope stepped back. Her chest tightened. "I won't force you to look," she said. "I won't push. But when you're ready... I can prove I'm not lying. It's the only way I know how. I haven't seen most of the rooms in this house. You know that. I couldn't have invented details I've never had the chance to observe."

Mina hopped down from the chaise and brushed against Pen's skirts, then Connor's boot.

Connor's eyes shone, only for a second. Just enough for her to see the shine before he blinked it away.

"Goodnight, Miss Ward," he said quietly. "We will... revisit this matter." He turned toward the doorway.

"Goodnight, Connor," she said softly.

He hesitated. Only a heartbeat. Then he stepped into the shadows of the hall and was gone.

Penelope stood there for a moment, trembling, blinking against the sting in her eyes. Then she sank onto the nearest chair, and Mina promptly climbed into her lap, kneading at her skirts until she settled.

Pen buried her fingers in the soft fur and let out a long, shivering breath.

She had not shown him the letter yet.

But she'd cracked something open between them. Something that made her chest ache just thinking about it..

Connor Halden carried his grief like a locked room he wouldn't let anyone enter.

One day, she hoped, she could open at least one of them without breaking him.

Her hand drifted to the pendant.

A ghost lived in this house.

Another ghost lived inside the man who owned it.

And somehow, impossibly...

She was learning to live with both.

CHAPTER 9

The Man in Town

Penelope was still half-asleep when someone knocked on her bedroom door.

Not a frantic knock.

Not a polite tap-tap of Mrs. Porter.

A firm, measured knock.

"Miss Ward?"

Connor.

She sat up too fast. The unfamiliar bed, the pale yellow wallpaper, the stays digging into her ribs from yesterday because she'd been too tired to fully undress, it all hit at once. "I'm awake," she called, which was only half a lie.

There was a pause. "Mrs. Porter will bring you breakfast shortly. Afterward, we will go into town."

Pen blinked. "Town? Again?"

Another small pause. "Yes."

"Okay," she said cautiously. "Sure."

"Dress warmly," he added. "It will be cool along the road. We leave within the hour."

His footsteps retreated down the hall, steady and unhurried.

Pen frowned at the door.

His voice had been different. Not louder. Not warmer. But... steadier. No edge underneath the words. No weight pressing down on them either.

She pushed herself up, Mina rolling off her hip with a sharp chirp.

"Yeah, yeah," Pen muttered, scooping the cat up and pressing a kiss to the top of her head. "We're going to town. Try to act normal."

Mina blinked slowly, the universal cat sign for *I will do what I want and you will thank me.*

Penelope dressed with less fumbling than the previous day. Her hands remembered which buttons went first, how to adjust the stays so she could at least breathe in shallow, dignified gasps. Mrs. Porter had set out a soft gray dress with a dark blue ribbon at the waist.

It was... pretty.

The part of Pen that still thought in thrift-store racks and clearance tags wanted to check the price. The part of her that had signed legal papers on this house thought, *This is your life now. For as long as you're stuck here, anyway.*

Mina hopped up onto the little dresser and batted at the blue ribbon.

Penelope swatted her away. "Touch the ribbon, lose the whiskers."

Mina did not take the threat seriously.

By the time Pen came downstairs, Connor was waiting in the front hall.

He'd shed his work jacket in favor of a dark coat, his waistcoat buttoned neatly, hat in hand. He looked composed. His shoulders weren't hunched. His jaw wasn't tight. Whatever he'd decided during the night, he'd settled into it.

His gaze swept over her once: hair pinned, gloves on, dress

smoothed, and something flickered briefly in his expression. Not anger. Not disapproval.

Something softer.

Quick.

Gone.

"That will do," he said, voice a little rougher than usual. "You are presentable."

"High praise," Pen murmured.

The corner of his mouth did that almost-smile thing again, the one that made her chest squeeze. "The town will expect as much," he said. "And I would rather they focus on your comportment than your... cat."

Mina chose that moment to trot downstairs like she owned the staircase, tail high, whiskers forward.

Connor stared.

Pen cleared her throat. "She, um... has separation anxiety."

Mina ran straight to Pen, coiled up her skirts like a ladder, and scrambled up to her shoulder, where she draped herself like a calico stole.

Penelope winced. "And no respect for modern fashion."

"Miss Ward," Connor said slowly, "you cannot bring that animal into town on your shoulder."

"Sure, I can," she said. "Watch me."

His jaw tightened. "Cats remain in barns. Or on porches. Or in laps. They do not sit on a lady's shoulder in public like a—"

"Like a parrot?" Pen offered. "We tried that; she didn't like the accent."

He closed his eyes briefly. "Please," he said, opening them again. The word startled her. He so rarely used it. "The gossip is bad enough."

Pen stroked Mina's side. "She'll behave," she said. "Won't you?"

Mina promptly flicked her tail into Connor's shoulder.

His eye twitched.

Penelope bit back a smile. "She's adjusting," she said. "But it's that or leave her screaming at the window the whole time."

He exhaled. His gaze flicked between Mina and the door, then back.

"Fine," he said at last, in the tone of a man signing a terrible peace treaty. "She may come. But if she leaps at anyone, I reserve the right to deny all association."

"Deal," Pen said.

They stepped out together onto the front porch. The air was crisp; the sky a washed-out blue. The fields rolled away toward town, dotted with young trees and the far outline of workers already moving among them.

Connor offered his arm.

First.

Without being prompted.

Pen blinked.

He raised a brow. "It is customary."

"Right," she said quickly, sliding her hand into the crook of his elbow. The fabric of his coat was warm over solid muscle. "Customs. Love those."

They walked.

She expected their usual silence, that careful, brittle thing between wary strangers, but after a few minutes, he spoke.

"You slept," he said abruptly.

Pen glanced up at him. "Is that a question?"

"A statement." His eyes stayed on the path ahead. "You look less... strained. I take it the room suited you?"

She thought of the clean linens, the quiet, the way Mina had curled against her without needing to hide under furniture. "It did," she said softly. "Thank you. For letting me stay there. For letting me stay, period."

His jaw worked. "I meant what I said," he answered. "I will not turn a woman out into the road with nowhere to go."

It sounded different this morning, less like a reluctant obligation and more like a choice.

Pen swallowed. "Is... everything all right?" She asked, then winced. "I mean, aside from the obvious 'my house is haunted and there's a stray time traveler in it' situation."

One corner of his mouth twitched. "My home is not haunted. And... I have had... cause to think," he said, which told her absolutely nothing and somehow everything at once.

She wanted to push.

She didn't.

They walked the rest of the way in something that was not quite silence, not quite conversation. Mina occasionally chirped at birds she'd never catch. Connor's arm stayed steady under her hand.

For the first time since she'd arrived in 1896, the road into town didn't feel like a march toward judgment.

It felt, God help her, almost like being escorted.

Like she mattered to someone.

Penelope had never been stared at so much in her life.

Not at the DMV.

Not during her high-school choir solo.

Not even that one time she'd tried hot yoga and passed out in front of an entire room of overachievers.

But walking into town on the arm of Connor Halden?

Every eyeball in a five-mile radius found her like she was a bright, blinking beacon of *Not From Around Here*. Conversations dipped the moment they hit the main street. Men paused by wagons. Women paused on porches. Two boys on a barrel outright gaped at her before Mina hissed and sent them scrambling. It was like a live-action search bar autocomplete:

Connor Halden... cousin?

Connor Halden... woman?

Connor Halden... scandal?

"Do they always stare this much?" Pen muttered.

"At anything new," Connor said. "And at anyone associated with me."

"That sounded ominous."

He didn't answer.

Mina flicked her tail, brushing against his coat again.

"Can you not control her?" he asked through his teeth.

"She's a free spirit," Pen whispered. "You can't control her; you can only negotiate."

"She is not negotiating," he muttered.

"She's setting boundaries," Penelope corrected. "With your shoulder."

His eye did the twitching thing again.

Mrs. Abernathy was already on the general store porch.

Of course she was.

The woman scanned the street like some sort of social lighthouse whose beams were pure gossip. "Mr. Halden!" she called, bright as church bells. "And Miss Ward. You're looking well today."

Well, was an exaggeration. Pen felt like she'd been pressed, buttoned, and sculpted into a Victorian impersonator. But she managed a polite nod. "Good morning, Mrs. Abernathy," she said, trying to keep her voice steady and ladylike and not like someone who said things like *DMV* in her head.

Mrs. Abernathy's shrewd eyes flicked from Connor's offered arm to Mina on Pen's shoulder to the precise distance between their bodies.

"Tell me, dear," she said, all sugar and arsenic, "how long do you plan to stay with your cousin?"

Penelope opened her mouth.

"We have not decided," Connor cut in, his tone firm but courteous. "My cousin's circumstances are... unusual."

Mrs. Abernathy leaned forward. "Oh? In what way?"

"Private," Connor said. One word, clipped and cold enough to frost the porch railing.

Pen bit the inside of her cheek to stop a smile. Protective Connor was... something.

Mrs. Abernathy hummed. "Well, the town will be very interested in such a mystery. Especially the women."

Connor's jaw tightened. "There is nothing for them to interest themselves in."

Mrs. Abernathy's eyebrows climbed to dangerous heights. "No? A young, handsome widower with a lady in his home?"

Pen's stomach twisted.

There it was.

Widower.

Lady in his home.

Connor's voice dropped to a temperature that could freeze boiling water. "Miss Ward is..." he stumbled a moment. "my cousin. And my responsibility," he said. "Nothing more."

Nothing more.

Pen felt the sting even though she told herself she shouldn't. *Responsibility* was still better than *burden*, she supposed.

Mrs. Abernathy smiled like a woman who had found an entire winter's worth of fuel for her gossip fire. "Of course. Just family."

She said the word *family* like she was holding it with tongs.

"Mrs. Abernathy? What stories do you have to share with *me* about your family?" Penelope asked, not willing to let this old bitty talk to Conner in such a manner.

"Oh, there is nothing to share," the older woman stammered. "No gossip here."

"And I will say the same," Pen retorted. "Unless you want *your* family talked about at the dinner table, keep your words about ours, alone."

A sound rumbled beside her—low, brief, caught in Connor's chest.

Pen escaped as soon as she could into the warmer, quieter aisles of the general store, letting Mina hop down to explore under the shelves. The bell above the door chimed once more behind her as someone else entered.

She breathed out slowly.

Shelves lined the walls, stocked with everything from flour to fabric, nails to ribbons, lantern oil to jars of candy. A large barrel near the back held apples, and the air smelled faintly of coffee and sawdust.

Her fingers drifted over a bolt of fabric, pale blue and soft beneath her touch. It reminded her faintly of the dress Clara wore in the photograph. Simple. Lovely. Real.

Imagine, she thought, *having to choose fabric this way. Piece by piece. Yard by yard. Not just clicking "add to cart."*

"What do you think?" a warm voice asked.

Pen turned.

The man standing a few feet away was tall and blond, with a smile that could probably get him out of parking tickets if those existed yet. His shirt sleeves were rolled, showing strong forearms dusted with gold hair. His eyes were bright and very much fixed on her.

He nodded toward the fabric under her hand. "Would suit you beautifully."

Pen blinked. "Oh. I... um... thanks."

Smooth, Pen. Very smooth.

"You're Halden's cousin, aren't you?" he asked, stepping closer but not too close. "I'm Daniel Brookes."

He offered his hand. She hesitated, then took it, wary but curious. His grip was gentle, warm. But the kiss to her knuckles lingered a fraction of a second longer than strictly necessary.

"Penelope," she said. "And yes. I'm his... cousin."

"Distant cousin," Daniel said with a grin. "That's what everyone's saying."

Her cheeks warmed. Of course that made it around town already.

"Well," he went on, lowering his voice enough to feel conspiratorial, "for what it's worth, I don't believe half the things people say in this town."

Pen huffed out a surprised laugh. "That seems wise."

He tilted his head, studying her. "You don't sound like the rest of them," he observed. "Talk a little... sharper. Like you're trimming words as you go."

Because I'm trying not to say "like" and "totally" and "Wi-Fi," she thought.

"I'm from... farther east," she said. "Way east."

"Hmm," Daniel said, his eyes staying on her face. "Well, wherever you're from, it's good to have some new blood around here." His smile softened. "Must be a change, though. For you."

It was the first time anyone had asked that. Really asked.

Pen swallowed. "It is," she admitted. "A big one."

"Let me guess," he said lightly. "You're used to places where no one knows anyone's name, no one cares where you buy your flour, and if you walked down the street with a cat on your shoulder, no one would blink?"

Mina chose that moment to slink around the corner, whiskers dusted with some mysterious powder from under a shelf. Daniel crouched and held out a hand. "Well, hello there."

To Pen's shock, Mina didn't hiss. She sniffed his finger, then head-butted his knuckles like he'd been pre-approved.

"Traitor," Pen whispered.

Daniel chuckled. "Smart girl," he said to Mina. "You know quality when you see it."

Penelope rolled her eyes. "Wow. Modesty. Love that in a man."

He laughed. "Miss Ward, if I were modest, I'd never survive this place. So. Do you and your rather impressive guardian intend to stay long?"

She hesitated. "We... don't know yet."

"Well," he said easily, "if you do, you should know where to find decent coffee and terrible company. My workshop's behind the livery." He jerked his thumb toward the back window.

"Wheels, leather, a few odds and ends. I'm usually there. You ever need help with anything, repairs, directions, someone to glare at Mrs. Abernathy from across the street, I'm your man."

"That's very..." She searched for the right word. "...forward."

"I prefer 'efficient,'" he said, smile widening. "Life's short. No sense pretending people aren't interesting when they are."

Before Pen could respond, a shadow fell across the aisle.

A very tall, very rigid, very familiar shadow.

"Brookes," Connor said flatly.

Daniel stood, unhurried, and smiled wider. "Halden. Didn't see you there."

"You did," Connor replied, voice smooth as river stone. "You always do."

Daniel's eyes sparkled. "Simply being friendly to your cousin."

"That won't be necessary," Connor said.

Pen turned fully to stare at him. His posture looked relaxed— arms loose, weight shifted back. But the muscle in his jaw was ticking, and his eyes were a shade sharper than usual.

"Um," she said. "Excuse me, I can decide who talks to me."

Daniel choked on a laugh.

Connor did not laugh.

His gaze flicked to her, then back to Daniel. "Mr. Brookes is known to be... liberal with his attentions," he said. "I would not see you misled."

"'Liberal with my attentions,'" Daniel repeated. "You make me sound like a badly written novel."

"If the description fits," Connor said coolly.

Pen cleared her throat. "I'm perfectly capable of recognizing a flirt, thank you."

Daniel put a hand to his heart. "Flattered and wounded, all at once."

"You're not wounded," she said.

"True," he admitted cheerfully. "But I am flattered."

Connor's expression did not change, but the air around him

felt ten degrees colder. "Miss Ward," he said, tone polite but edged. "If you have chosen your fabric, we should conclude our business."

"We're not in a rush," Pen pointed out.

"We are," he said.

Daniel's gaze bounced between them, amused. "Well. I'll leave you two to your... cousinly errands." He gave Penelope a small bow. "Pleasure to meet you, Miss Ward. I hope we see each other again. For repairs, gossip, coffee, or all three."

"Thank you," she said, surprising herself by meaning it.

He tipped an invisible hat at Connor. "Halden."

"Brookes," Connor replied.

Daniel sauntered away, whistling under his breath.

Penelope watched him go. Connor stood beside her, silent, jaw still tight, that muscle still ticking.

She turned slowly. "What was that?"

"What was what?" he asked, entirely too innocent.

"That territorial thing you did," she said. "You went full 'back away from the female, sir.'"

"I merely informed him that his presence was not required," Connor said. "He has a history."

Pen crossed her arms. "Of what? Being charming?"

"Of pursuing whatever catches his eye," Connor said shortly. "And leaving just as swiftly."

She raised a brow. "And what do you think you're doing to mine?"

He went very still.

Daniel's laughter floated faintly from the front of the store.

Connor's throat worked. "It is my responsibility," he said finally, "to ensure no one takes advantage of your situation."

Pen's temper cooled at that. "You think that's what he was doing?"

"I think men like Brookes are drawn to novelty," Connor said. "And you are... novel."

Pen huffed. "Great. I'm a circus act."

"That is not what I meant," he snapped, then drew in a breath, his shoulders dropping slightly. "You are... different. You do not know our ways. You are without family or protection beyond this house. Men like him see that."

"And men like you?" she asked quietly.

His gaze met hers then, heated and unguarded in a way that made her breath catch.

"Men like me," he said, voice low, "should know better."

Her heart stuttered.

He looked away first. "We should go," he said. "Mrs. Porter will be waiting."

When they left the store, Penelope was stunned to realize she'd been smiling.

Not at Mrs. Abernathy's gossip, or the ridiculousness of Daniel Brookes. Not even at Connor's utterly unconvincing *I am not jealous* routine.

But underneath that was something stranger. Warmer.

People had said her name.

They'd greeted her. Studied her. Measured her with their eyes, yes, but also... acknowledged her. After a lifetime of being the extra chair in the room, the easily replaced foster kid, the temporary tenant whose name no one learned, the attention, good and bad, felt like someone had turned a light toward her.

She'd spent years being invisible. Now, for the first time, invisible wasn't an option. And part of her... liked that.

On the walk back, Connor was uncharacteristically quiet. No lectures about posture. No commentary on proper glove length. Only silence and the sound of their footsteps on the packed earth. Mina rode on Pen's shoulder again, tail occasionally brushing Connor's sleeve like she was testing his patience on purpose.

Pen watched him out of the corner of her eye. His jaw was tight, his gaze fixed straight ahead, but his shoulders were not as rigid as they had been on their first walk to town. His stride was different to—less parade-ground perfect, more... actual human.

"You're awfully quiet," she said finally.

"I am often quiet," he replied.

"Quieter than usual," she clarified. "Are you all right?"

"I am fine," he said.

"You're lying," she said automatically.

His head snapped toward her, eyes flashing. "You think you can read me so easily?" he asked.

"No," she said. "But I know what 'fine' sounds like on someone who is very much not fine."

His throat worked. He looked away again. "You should not encourage Brookes," he said abruptly.

Penelope blinked. "I wasn't encouraging him."

"You smiled," he said.

Pen threw her free hand up, nearly upsetting Mina. "Am I not allowed to smile in 1896?"

"You are allowed," he said sharply. Then, softer: "You simply do not... understand."

"Then explain it to me," she challenged. "Because right now, it feels like you're mad at me for not being miserable enough."

He stopped walking.

The sudden halt dragged her to a stop too, her hand tightening on his arm to keep her balance. Mina dug her claws into her shoulder, offended.

Connor turned to face her fully. The wind tugged at his coat, at the edges of Pen's bonnet. The fields around them were quiet; the house still a small shape in the distance.

"You think I wish you to be miserable?" he asked, voice low.

She swallowed. "I think you don't know what to do with me if I'm not."

He flinched.

It was small. Quick. But she saw it.

He drew in a long breath, as if the next words cost him. "I have lost much, Miss Ward," he said finally. "And I do not trust easily. When people circle my household, when they... circle you... it..." He trailed off, jaw flexing. For the first time since she'd arrived, he looked less like a stone wall and more like a man standing in front of one, uncertain which way to go.

"It what?" she prompted gently.

"It feels," he said slowly, "as though the ground beneath my feet is shifting again. And I have had enough of falling."

Pen's throat tightened. She took one small step closer, careful not to crowd him. "Connor," she said softly.

He shook his head. "Do not be gentle with me," he said abruptly. "I can't..." His voice roughened. "I cannot bear that."

She blinked. "You think I'm lying about who I am to hurt you."

"I think," he said, staring at some point beyond her shoulder, "that if you are lying, I will be hurt. And if you are not lying..." His gaze snapped back to hers. Something fierce and desperate burned there. "...then I do not know what to do," he finished.

The wind tugged at her skirts.

Pen's heart hammered against the pendant under her dress. She could tell him about the fractured mirror of her soul, or the way his grief had bled across paper into her hands. Instead, she reached for the one thing she could offer him here, now, in this moment between the past and whatever future awaited them. "Let me show you," she whispered. "Not right now. Not when you're... this raw. But soon. Let me show you the letter. The wardrobe. The proof that I know things I shouldn't know, because I've seen what becomes of this house."

His hands curled into fists at his sides. "No," he said, the word sharp but quiet. "Not yet."

"Why not?" she asked.

"Because," he said, and this time when he looked at her, there was no anger in his face. Only fear. And something that might almost be hope. "Because I am not ready to see myself through your eyes."

Her breath caught. "Connor..."

He stepped back, putting the distance between them again, brick by careful brick. "We should return," he said, voice slipping back into the steadier register she was used to. "Mrs. Porter will be expecting us."

Pen let him have the retreat.

For now.

They walked the rest of the way in silence, but it was not the same silence as before. This one hummed with unsaid things. With questions. With the knowledge that somewhere inside the house ahead of them, a letter waited to be found. And somewhere inside the man beside her something had shifted—she could feel it in the way he no longer held himself quite so rigidly, in the careful space he kept between them that felt less like a wall and more like an invitation to patience.

Beneath the quiet, her heart was loud.

And for the first time, Penelope dared to believe that whatever impossible road had brought her here...

She wasn't walking it alone.

CONNOR ~

Connor Halden had always believed himself a sensible man.

The kind of man who rose before dawn without needing a bell, who measured flour and feed and ledger lines with the same exacting hand, who kept fences upright and roofs patched and emotions locked behind iron.

Emotion, in his experience, was a weakness.

It had undone him once already.

Grief was not meant to be survived, only endured. Day after day. Breath after breath. Until it dulled enough that a man could move through his own house without flinching at every ghost-shaped space.

He had learned how to endure.

He had not learned how to live.

And then Penelope Ward arrived in his home like a storm that had taken the shape of a woman in unusual clothing, sharper words than any respectable lady ought to possess, eyes that missed nothing, and a cat that looked at him as though she were judging the quality of his soul.

He had expected deceit. Manipulation. Trouble.

He had not expected... this.

The way she unsettled him without trying. The way she smiled with her whole face, as if joy were not something a person had to earn. The way her eyes softened when she looked at him; softened in sympathy, not pity. As if she could see the bones of him underneath the coat and the manners and the discipline, and did not recoil.

She was intolerable.

And yet he could not stop noticing her.

Not the tremor in her voice when she spoke truths she did not want to carry alone. Not the way her fingers found the pendant at her throat whenever she thought herself unseen, as though she were tethering herself to something that might otherwise drift away.

Not the way she looked at Clara's photograph.

Not with jealousy.

Not with hunger.

With sorrow.

With a careful kind of respect, as if she understood that Clara was not merely a wife he had lost, but the only warm thing that had ever truly belonged to him, and that losing her had torn the world open.

That, more than anything, made Penelope dangerous.

Because she did not treat his grief like an inconvenience.

She treated it like a sacred thing.

And sacred things did not belong in his life anymore.

But Penelope...Penelope puzzled him.

Every time he decided she was a danger, she did something unbearably kind. When he thought she was lying, she told him something no reasonable liar would dare confess. And every time he tried to pull away, she stepped back just enough to let him breathe.

And damn him, but he noticed that too.

He noticed her courage. Her stubbornness. Her grief, quiet and unspoken, much like his own.

He noticed her softness most of all.

Not a weakness. A resilience.

The kind that worried him, because if softness could survive in her... it might survive in him too.

That was the most dangerous thing of all.

He leaned against the doorframe of his room, staring at the dim hallway lit only by a single oil lamp. He could hear voices from the kitchen—Penelope's laugh, Mrs. Porter's murmur—the sounds of dinner preparation. The cat too, no doubt, switch backing around her ankles.

He should send her away. He knew he should. The longer she stayed, the more the house changed. The more *he* changed. And Connor Halden had no room in his ribcage for change. He had built walls, carefully and deliberately, around a heart that had been left bleeding once. But the truth settled inside him with the weight of something inevitable.

A part of him no longer cared about those walls.

When Penelope walked into town beside him, chin high though tension had tightened her shoulders, something inside him had eased. When she defended herself against gossip with humor rather than shame, something warmed. When Daniel Brookes had smiled at her too long, too boldly, Connor had felt something sharp and unwelcome coil low in his stomach.

Jealousy. Good God. He had no right to be jealous. And yet he'd stepped between them without thinking, instinct tugging at his spine with a single word. *Mine.* Not true. Not appropriate. Not remotely acceptable. But honest. He closed his eyes and exhaled through his teeth.

Penelope was trouble. Not because she lied. Not because she had appeared in his home like a stray pulled from the fog.

But because every day she remained... he remembered what it was like to feel. Not happiness. Not desire. But possibility. And possibility was its own kind of grief for a man who wasn't ready to hope again. He thought of the letter she claimed to have found, the one he had written in a moment of despair unlikely to show any man at his best.

If she truly possessed it...If she knew what he had written...If she understood how deeply he had once been broken...

Connor's breath caught.

He wasn't ready for that truth.

Not from her lips, nor reflected in her eyes. Not brought into the light where he could no longer hide it from himself. He pushed off the doorframe and straightened, jaw tightening. He needed to keep his distance. Tomorrow, he would reinforce the boundaries between them, and he would stop noticing her.

He repeated the intention like a prayer.

Tomorrow. Tomorrow. Tomorrow.

He turned to extinguish the lamp.

And then Penelope laughed again downstairs, soft, surprised, bright.

A sound that did not belong in his house.

A sound that made his chest ache.

Connor closed his eyes.

For one stolen moment, he let himself imagine Clara's voice, gentle as breath.

Be kind to her.

He exhaled, slow and unsteady.

Then he opened his eyes, and the armor slid back into place.

Tonight, he would go down to dinner.

He would keep his distance.

He would be sensible.

He would be Connor Halden.

But as he started toward the stairs, one thought followed him like a shadow he could not outrun:

If loving Penelope was dishonor...

Why did Clara's memory feel less like a chain when Penelope was near?

CHAPTER 10

The Letter

Penelope realized something was wrong, *different,* the moment Connor sat down to supper.

Not wrong the way he had been wrong before.

Not the clipped, controlled quiet he usually wore like a coat buttoned to the throat. This was quieter than that. Brittler. As if he'd spent the day holding something in his chest and now it was pressing against his ribs from the inside.

Mrs. Porter set the plates down with her usual firm efficiency; stew, bread, something green that tasted like perseverance.

Connor barely touched his food.

Mina sat on the windowsill like a queen presiding over a trial, her tail flicking in slow, smug beats.

Penelope tried to eat. Her fork scraped her plate too loudly, and she winced, certain Connor would flinch, certain he'd snap into correction the way he always did.

He didn't.

He stared at the candle for a long moment, like the flame was trying to tell him a secret.

Pen watched him from the corner of her eye, her stomach twisting itself into a knot.

Something had happened.

Overnight, maybe. She couldn't name it, couldn't prove it, but she could *feel* the shift the way you could feel the air change before a storm. Connor seemed... unsettled.

But not by her—or at least, it didn't feel like it was about her. This was something inside him, something he was wrestling with alone.

Mrs. Porter cleared her throat. "Mr. Halden," she said, voice gentle in a way Pen hadn't heard often from her. "Are you unwell?"

Connor's gaze lifted, slow as if it took effort. "No."

Mrs. Porter wasn't fooled. "You've taken more bites of air than stew."

Mina chirped, as if agreeing.

Connor blinked once, then looked down at his bowl. "I am simply... not hungry."

Mrs. Porter's eyes flicked, very briefly, to Penelope, then back to Connor. "Mm," she hummed. "That happens sometimes. When a man carries too much and pretends it weighs nothing."

Penelope's throat tightened.

Connor's jaw flexed. He set his spoon down and, quietly, took another bite, as if to prove a point.

It was the closest thing to peace they'd had all evening.

Pen wanted to ask him. *What happened? Why do you feel different?* But the questions crowded her mouth and stayed there, trapped behind nerves and stays and fear. Because if she asked, he might shut the door again.

And tonight, for the first time, it felt like the door might actually open.

Dinner ended with the scrape of chairs and the soft clink of dishes.

"I'll see to the kitchen," Mrs. Porter said, gathering plates. Her gaze lingered on Connor a second too long. "Try to sleep, Mr. Halden."

Connor didn't respond, but his shoulders shifted slightly, like the words hit some place tender.

Pen waited until the sound of water and plates moved farther away.

Mina yawned dramatically, hopped down from the windowsill, and wove between Pen's ankles like she was tying her to the floor.

Pen wiped her palms against her skirt.

This was it.

This was the moment. Things were shifting between them.

He'd done nothing to help her find out how to get home. What little information he had found was superstition at best, with no real answers. Connor had begun helping her mold to the situation, shaping her to fit in. Did he even believe she was from 2026? Did he want her to leave? Did *she* want to leave?

Connor remained seated at the table, hands folded loosely, eyes on the candle as if he were still listening to something no one else could hear. The silence between them felt alive, charged and waiting.

Pen swallowed. Her voice came out smaller than she meant it to. "Connor."

His gaze lifted immediately.

Surprise.

Wariness.

And something else... something raw, like a bruise pressed too hard.

Penelope's pulse stumbled. "Can you..." she forced the words out. "Can you walk with me? Upstairs."

His head tipped slightly, as if he didn't quite believe he'd heard her. Then he nodded once. Just once. Slowly, like something in him had to be convinced first.

They climbed the staircase in silence.

Moonlight poured through the stained glass window halfway up, blues and reds and soft golds spilling across the wood in fractured patterns. Dust motes drifted through it like tiny, floating sparks. The house creaked beneath their feet, not loudly, not threateningly, more like a warning whispered by old bones.

Pen couldn't stop thinking: *The house knows where we're going.*

Connor followed close behind—close enough that she heard his breath when it caught, shallow and controlled. Close enough that every step sounded like a decision. She led him down the upstairs hallway, past her guest room, past the sitting room, past the places that were merely rooms and not wounds.

And then she stopped at the door he never touched.

The nursery.

Connor halted behind her so abruptly she almost turned and apologized out of habit.

His breath hitched—not loud, but deep, catching somewhere in his chest.

Pen faced him slowly.

His eyes were on the door the way a man might look at a gravestone carved with his own name.

"I want to show you something," she whispered. "But I can't do it alone."

"I do not enter that room," he said quietly. Not sharp. Not cold. Simply... absolute. A boundary etched into his bones.

"I know," Penelope breathed. "But you need to."

His jaw tightened. "Why?"

Pen's heart thudded painfully. "Because the truth you've been avoiding is in there."

A flicker, fear, anger, grief, crossed his face so quickly it might have been imagination.

Pen reached for the knob.

The door opened with a soft, weary sigh, as if the room itself had been waiting a long time to exhale.

The room was small compared to the guest bedroom. But perfect for an infant or growing child. Moonlight slanted across the faded wallpaper. A hand-crafted wooden cradle sat near the window, covered with a yellowed blanket untouched by human hands in years. A wooden toy horse lay tipped on its side, as though dropped mid-play. The room looked ethereal. Like something out of a fairytale. Connor's stillborn son had been truly loved; she could see that in every careful detail, every tender choice.

Penelope felt Connor stop in the doorway behind her. Not only physically—the very air around him seemed to stop. He didn't move. Didn't breathe. Like he'd been turned to stone. It took Pen reaching out for him, her hand finding his arm, to break whatever spell held him. Under her touch, he flinched back into motion.

Pen turned back, her chest aching. "Connor... come in."

His eyes didn't leave the cradle. "I cannot."

"Yes," Pen whispered. "You can."

His throat worked. His voice came out broken around the edges. "It hurts."

"I know," she said softly, and she meant it. "But it's time."

Time.

The word tasted like cruelty. Time had taken him apart. Time had brought her here. Time was the only reason any of this was happening.

Connor closed his eyes. A muscle jumped in his cheek. The silence stretched until Pen thought he might turn away.

Then, like a man surrendering to something inevitable, he took one trembling step inside. Then another.

The air changed. Thickened. Quieted.

Pen felt it like pressure in her bones.

Connor Halden was walking into the past he'd spent years avoiding. He stopped beside the cradle, his body taut as a drawn wire. His hand hovered above the rim but didn't touch. Not yet.

Penelope swallowed the lump in her throat and crossed to the old wardrobe in the corner. The same wardrobe she'd opened in *her* time. The same one she'd touched the day everything shifted.

Her fingers found the drawer knob. Cold. Heavy. Familiar. She pulled it open.

The faint scent of cedar escaped. Inside the drawer was a pile of folded blankets. She gently pulled the drawer all the way out and set it on the ground beside her. Leaning down to peer inside, Penelope found the old letter. The one he had written in 1892. The one she was sure Connor hoped no one would ever read. Pen reached in. Her fingers brushed the ivory paper. The envelope that held the most heart-breaking story. She pulled it out; the edges brittle but intact. She turned to him, holding it gently. "This is yours."

Connor's gaze snapped to it like it was flame.

His voice broke. "How did you know it was there?"

"In this wardrobe," Pen whispered. "Six days ago. Before I came here. Before I found the pendant. Before I knew anything about you."

Connor went very still.

"That is not possible," he whispered.

"I know." Pen took a small step toward him, heart hammering. Her voice trembled as she continued. "I read your most intimate and grieving thoughts; I felt your pain. I felt your guilt, as I carry the same in my own heart. How would I know this if I wasn't from another time?"

Connor didn't reach for the letter. Couldn't seem to make himself move.

The pain on his face said it for him, written in the tightness around his mouth, in the damp shine in his eyes.

So Pen lowered the envelope and pressed it to her chest like a shield. Like a vow. Giving him space to breathe.

Then she crossed to the chest-of-drawers and set it down gently, as if roughness might shatter him along with the paper.

Connor stared at the letter. Then at the cradle. Then at Penelope. His voice came out ragged. "I wrote that."

Pen nodded once. "I know."

"I closed that wardrobe a month after Clara died," he whispered. "I never opened it again."

Pen's throat tightened until it hurt to breathe. "I know."

His gaze snapped to her, sharp with something that sounded like accusation—though his expression showed confusion more than blame. "You should not know."

"I shouldn't be here at all," Pen whispered. "But I am."

Connor took a half step back, as if her existence pressed against something he'd barricaded. His hand lifted, hovered near his mouth, then dropped again. "How?" he breathed. "How is this possible?"

Pen's fingers trembled. She reached into her skirt pocket, into the hidden seam where she'd kept the last piece of proof like a secret prayer, waiting for the right time to try again to present it to him. "Then there is this," she whispered. She unfolded the wrinkled coffee shop receipt that had been in the pocket of her jeans, the ones she wore the day all this happened.

The ink was faded, but still legible.

The Tipping BeanHazelnut Latte – $6.25DATE: 2-12-2026

Connor stared at it, his face cycling through doubt, wonder, and something close to fear.

At the strange lettering.The impossible date.The foreign numbers.The words that meant nothing in his century.

"What is this?" he breathed.

"My receipt," Pen said gently. "From two days before I arrived here. My time. My world."

She held it out.

For a moment, he didn't move.

Then he reached slowly. Reverently. Like touching it might burn him, or prove him wrong, or prove him right.

His fingers grazed the corner. He inhaled sharply, like the paper itself shocked him. Connor took it fully and turned it in his hands, studying the strange printing, the unfamiliar texture, the impossible date. "This... isn't indented," he murmured, voice rough, threaded with wonder and something darker—maybe dread. "Not like a typewriter. This paper is..." He swallowed. "Different."

Pen stepped closer. "This is the truth," she whispered. "I didn't lie to you, Connor. Not once."

He staggered back half a step, like reality struck him in the chest. His hand pressed to his mouth. His eyes stayed locked on the receipt as if it might vanish if he blinked.

Penelope's heart cracked for him. This was too much, too fast; a man with one century's worth of pain suddenly handed proof that the world was wider, stranger, and far less merciful than he'd ever believed.

"Connor..." she breathed, reaching toward him.

He didn't recoil.

But he didn't reach back either.

He stood there, caught between the cradle and the letter and the paper from the future, breathing unevenly, like a man pinned under the weight of impossible truth.

Finally, after a long moment, he spoke.

"You are not possible."

Pen gave a small, broken laugh that wasn't laughter at all. "I know."

"And yet..." His gaze lifted to her, red-rimmed and stunned. "... you are here."

"I am."

His throat worked. "Then everything I have believed since Clara died..." His voice cracked. "Is not what I thought."

Pen's eyes burned. "I'm sorry."

He shook his head, squeezing his eyes shut as if he couldn't bear the pressure behind them. "Do not apologize," he rasped. "You have done nothing wrong. It is I who..." He swallowed hard. "Who does not know how to exist in a world that allows this."

Pen stepped closer, closing the last inches between them. Her hand lifted, not to touch him, not yet, but to hover near his sleeve like a question. "Connor," she whispered, voice shaking.

He opened his eyes. And for the first time since she'd arrived, he didn't look angry. He didn't look suspicious. He didn't look like armor. Connor looked human. Hurting. Hopeful. Terrified.

The house creaked softly, almost like a sigh.

Penelope held her breath.

Their worlds, once parallel, had collided. Quietly. Irrevocably.

Connor looked down at the receipt again, then at the letter. Then, finally, at the cradle. His voice came out like a fracture. "Tell me what happens next."

Pen's stomach dropped. She shook her head slowly. "I don't know."

For the first time, she saw that answer unsettle him. But not in the way she expected. His expression shifted-not closing down, but opening. Like a door he'd kept locked, suddenly revealing light beyond it.

She could almost see the thought forming behind his eyes—if the future wasn't fixed, then maybe his grief wasn't either. Maybe his loneliness wasn't permanent. Maybe they weren't impossible.

Connor stared at her for a long moment, and something in his expression softened in a way that made Penelope's chest ache.

Then his face tightened again, control snapping back like a door slammed shut, not out of cruelty, but survival.

"We should... return downstairs," he said, voice quiet and strained. "You should sleep."

Penelope nodded because she didn't trust herself to speak.

They left the nursery behind them.

But the air felt changed.

Like the house had listened.

Like it had approved.

They separated at the top of the stairs.

Connor paused near the railing, his hand on the banister, posture rigid again, yet not quite as distant as before. He looked like a man trying to decide whether to run or stay. "Goodnight, Miss Ward," he said.

"Goodnight," Pen whispered. And then, because the truth had cracked something open in her, she added, "Connor."

He froze at the sound of his name on her lips.

For a heartbeat, she thought he might say something, anything. Instead, he nodded once, stiffly, and disappeared down the hall.

Penelope stood there for a moment, Mina brushing against her calf as if to anchor her.

The house was too quiet now.

Too full of what they had done.

Pen entered her room, undressed with clumsy fingers, and crawled into bed like she could hide under blankets from the weight of time itself.

Mina curled against her hip, warm and steady.

Pen pressed her palm to the pendant at her throat. It felt heavier tonight. Not with metal. With meaning. "Please," Pen whispered into the dark. "If this is real... if any of this is real... help us."

Sleep pulled her under like a tide.

~

CONNOR ~

Connor waited until Penelope's footsteps faded down the hall before he released the breath caged in his lungs. The nursery fell silent again. Not the gentle silence of a room at rest. But the hollow silence of a room abandoned by its joy. Moonlight lay in pale ribbons across the cradle, the tipped wooden horse, the faded wallpaper, everything preserved as if time itself had been ordered to stop here. Connor stared at the items in his hands as though they were poisonous.

The letter, in his own handwriting, that familiar slant, the pressure of the strokes betraying the despair he'd tried to bury.

And beside it...

A slip of paper that did not belong to any world he knew.

Hazelnut Latte – $6.25
DATE: 2-12-2026
Thank you for your purchase

Connor sat down heavily on the floor, his back against the cradle's curved wooden leg. The movement was not graceful. It was surrender. His knees drew up, boots scuffing the boards, as if he could make himself smaller, less visible to the truth now crowding in around him.

He stared at the receipt first.

The paper was too smooth. Too thin. Too perfect. It was not rag paper. Not pulp the way his own mills could press it. There was no visible grain, no stubborn texture. The ink did not bleed. It sat on the surface in uniform, mechanical precision.

Numbers identical as soldiers.

Letters printed without the tremble of a hand.

He turned it over.

Nothing.

No watermark. No maker's mark. No explanation.

Simply the same impossible cleanliness.

His throat tightened violently. "Impossible," he whispered.

But the word did not change what was in his hands.

He dragged a hand through his hair, gripping the back of his skull as if he could keep his mind from splitting open with the force of it. He read the date again.

Twenty. Twenty-six.

A year so far beyond his own it might as well have been myth.

And yet, this paper existed.

It was worn at the folds, softened at the edges from being carried. It smelled faintly, not of ink and cedar, but of something sharp and sweet and unfamiliar, as if the world it came from had its own scent. It had lived in her pocket. It had *been with her.*

And grief. Grief had become his only companion. Guilt his shadow. A constant penance. A constant proof that love, in the end, was simply another word for loss.

He closed his eyes, clutching the envelope until the edges bit into his skin.

A liar could invent a story. But a liar could not create a relic from another century. Not in his hands. Not in this room. Not with the cold certainty of texture and ink and impossibility pressing against his fingers. The realization trembled through him, cold and electrifying.

She is telling the truth.

His gaze drifted to the letter. To the pain he'd once poured into paper because there had been nowhere else to put it. No one to hear it. No one who could carry it with him without breaking.

He had written it on a night when grief hollowed him so completely he'd thought he might simply... stop.

Stop waking. Stop breathing. Stop remembering how it felt to be happy.

Connor swallowed, the motion rough.

He hadn't touched that letter since the day he hid it. He remembered the exact moment. The exact weight of the envelope in his hand. The way his stomach had twisted with shame as he shoved it deep inside the wardrobe drawer, like the wood might swallow his suffering whole. Like burying it might convince his heart to follow.

He had closed the drawer. Closed the door. Closed himself. And he had never opened it again.

Yet here it was. In the moonlight. In her hands. Knowing him. Before she ever stood in this room.

Connor's chest constricted. He pressed the heel of his hand hard against his sternum as though he could hold himself together by force. The pain was not sharp. It was crushing. Slow. The weight of four years of guilt settling into a new shape.

"How could you know?" he whispered into the room.

The cradle offered no answer. The toys remained tipped and silent. The blanket stayed folded, untouched by the child it had been meant to warm.

He looked down at the letter again. His own words stared back at him in memory, too raw, too unguarded, too intimate for any man to bear being witnessed in. Connor had written what no one was supposed to see: that he had failed Clara. That he had failed their child. That he had failed to save the only light he'd ever been allowed to hold.

Then, against his will, Penelope's voice replayed in his mind.

Not the bold words. Not the jokes. Not the chaos.

The softness.

The way she had said his name when she thought he might break. The way she had looked at Clara's photograph with sorrow instead of envy. The way she had stood in this nursery and offered him truth like a trembling candle—fragile, but deliberate. As if she understood it might burn him, and offering it anyway.

Compassion.

Connor was not used to compassion. He did not trust it. Not anymore. Compassion had always been followed by pity. By distance. By people speaking in lowered voices as if he were already half-buried beside his wife.

But Penelope's compassion had not contained fear. It had contained *understanding.* And that was far more dangerous.

Connor opened his eyes and stared at the cradle again. A room frozen in time. A man frozen with it.

Until she arrived.

He swallowed hard. "Penelope Ward," he whispered into the quiet, testing the name as though it held magic of its own.

She was impossible. Illogical. Chaotic. Vexing. And yet her presence had begun to thaw parts of him he'd sworn to keep buried.

He pressed the receipt against his chest. The paper was cold.

But the realization burned.

"I believe you," he said quietly.

Saying it aloud cost him something, like stepping off a cliff and trusting the air to hold him.

But it gave him something too.

Truth.

Connor's breath shuddered as his gaze fell to the wardrobe drawer, still open from where Penelope had pulled it free. The blankets sat disturbed. The space where the letter had slept for years now exposed.

He should have felt violated. Instead, he felt seen. And that was the strangest, most terrifying thing of all. He had not been seen, truly seen, since Clara's death.

He'd been observed, certainly. Assessed. Pitied. Spoken about in hushed tones.

But not seen.

Not like Penelope saw him.

As though his brokenness was not something to fear... but something to hold with care.

Connor's throat tightened again, this time around something that almost resembled hope.

And hope was a cruelty he had denied himself for years.

Because hope led to wanting.

And wanting led to losing.

He bowed his head, forehead nearly touching his knees. "Clara," he whispered, because the name was carved into him deeper than bone.

At first, there was only silence.

Then—

A shift.

So subtle he might have imagined it.

The air in the nursery seemed warm, not with heat, but with presence. The moonlight seemed to soften. The shadows in the corners seemed less sharp, less threatening. Connor lifted his head slowly, his breath shallow. And for a heartbeat, he smelled something that did not belong to dust and cedar and old grief.

Lavender. Fresh bread. Clara's perfume, faint, like memory, like sunlight caught in cloth.

Connor went perfectly still. His pulse pounded in his ears. "No," he breathed. "I—"

The pendant. Penelope's pendant.

He could not explain *how* he knew, but the knowledge arrived whole: whatever tethered Penelope to this century did not merely move bodies.

It moved doors. It moved souls.

The air near the cradle shimmered—not in any way he could quite name, not like a ghost story meant to frighten children, but as though the world had taken a quiet breath.

And then the warmth became unmistakable. A presence at his back. Not heavy. Not haunting. Just... familiar.

Connor's eyes burned. He didn't dare turn around, as if seeing her would shatter him completely. He whispered her name anyway. "Clara."

A voice, soft as an exhale, answered. "Connor."

His entire body jolted, not in fear, but in the way a starving man reacts to bread placed in his hands.

He turned.

She stood there.

Not pale. Not sick. Not the Clara from his worst memories.

Clara, as she had been before the end. Hair pinned neatly, eyes bright and kind, her smile trembling with love that had never learned how to stop.

Connor could not breathe. "Clara," he rasped, and the word tore out of him like a confession.

Her gaze moved over him, over the lines time and grief had carved into his face, over the hardness he wore like armor. And she did not flinch. Her expression softened with something achingly tender. "My love," she whispered.

Connor's knees threatened to give out. He gripped the cradle's leg, knuckles whitening. This was not a dream. This was real. He knew this with every fiber of his being. "I failed you," he choked. "I—"

"Stop," Clara said gently. The word was not sharp. It was not scolding. It was *mercy.*

Connor's throat worked helplessly. "I should have— I should have—"

"You did everything you could," she said, stepping closer. The room seemed to brighten around her, as if the moonlight itself leaned toward her warmth. "And you have punished yourself long enough."

Connor's eyes spilled over. He hadn't cried like this, openly, helplessly, since they lowered her into the ground. Even then, he'd tried to swallow it back. To be strong. To be composed. Now it broke out of him anyway, shaking his shoulders.

Clara's hand lifted.

He expected it to pass through him.

Instead, her fingers brushed his cheek like a whisper made solid.

Connor sobbed once, the sound torn from the deepest place inside him. "I love you," he gasped, as if saying it might anchor her here.

Clara smiled, eyes shining. "And I will always love you," she whispered. "And you will always love me."

The words should have been comforting. Instead, they were agony. Because they were true. Because they were goodbye.

Connor's breath shuddered. "Then why are you here?"

Clara's gaze flicked, briefly, toward the wardrobe, the letter, the proof clutched in his hand. Toward the door Penelope had walked through. "That girl," Clara said softly. "She is not here to replace me."

"I know," Connor whispered. But even as he said it, guilt twisted in him. Because knowing did not stop the fear. Fear that wanting Penelope, wanting warmth, laughter, life again, would be betrayal. Dishonor. A stain on the love he had sworn would never fade.

Clara's voice gentled into something almost fierce. "Do you think I would want you entombed with my memory?"

Connor flinched.

Clara stepped closer, and he felt her presence fill the room with a light no oil lamp could cast. "I know you," she whispered. "You would rather suffer than risk feeling joy that might be taken."

His jaw tightened. "Yes." That was exactly true.

Clara's hand rose again, pressing lightly over his chest, over the place he'd been holding himself together by force. "You have carried me like a punishment," she said softly. "But I was never meant to be your punishment."

Connor's tears blurred her face. "What am I without you?" he whispered.

Clara smiled. "Alive," she said simply. "Still alive."

Connor's throat closed around a sound that was half grief, half surrender.

Clara's gaze flicked toward the door again. "She has her own sorrow," Clara whispered. "You can feel it, can you not?"

Connor swallowed.

Yes.

He had seen it in the flinch behind her bravado. In the way her hand found the pendant when she thought no one was watching. In the grief she tried to laugh around, like laughter might keep it from swallowing her.

Clara's eyes softened. "Let her share it," she whispered. "And let yourself be human enough to share yours."

Connor shook his head faintly. "I don't know how."

Clara's smile trembled. "Then learn," she said. "And if you find yourself standing in sunlight again... do not step back into the dark out of guilt."

Connor's breath hitched. "Are you telling me to—"

"To live," Clara whispered.

The word was a blessing and a command.

Connor stared at her, breaking apart and rebuilding all at once. "I don't want to let you go," he whispered.

Clara's eyes shone. "You don't have to," she said. "Not in the way you fear." She leaned in, pressing her forehead to his.

For one heartbeat, Connor felt warmth. Not memory. Not imagination.

Warmth.

Clara's voice came soft and sure. "Love is not smaller because it grows," she whispered. "It is larger."

Connor's sob broke free again, quieter now, like surrender. When he opened his eyes, the warmth began to fade.

Clara's form softened, light thinning at the edges like mist touched by wind.

"Clara—" Connor reached for her instinctively.

Her hand caught his fingers for a breath. Then another. Then slipped away like a sigh. Her voice lingered, tender as dawn. "Be kind to yourself, Connor." And then she was gone.

He felt the silence return to the nursery.

But it was not the same silence as before.

Connor sat trembling on the floor, the receipt crushed lightly against his palm, the letter pressed to his leg. His chest rose and fell in ragged breaths. His face was wet. His throat raw.

And the strangest part... He did not feel empty. He felt... cracked open.

He looked down at the receipt again. Then at the letter. Then at the cradle.

Would letting go of guilt mean letting go of love?

Clara's words answered before he could ask again: *Love is not smaller because it grows.*

Connor dragged in a shaky breath and forced himself to stand. His legs protested. His hands trembled. He returned the letter to the drawer carefully, as if the paper contained a holy thing. He hesitated, then placed the receipt beside it.

Future and past, sharing the same cedar-scented space.

He slid the drawer back in.

Closed it gently.

Then he stood at the nursery door with his hand on the knob, still warm, impossibly, as if Penelope's presence lingered there.

He did not feel defeat. He did not feel despair. He felt an acknowledgment.

Truth, settling into him like a new foundation.

And for the first time in years... he felt the unbearable ache of hope.

Connor swallowed, staring into the dark hallway beyond the nursery. "Penelope Ward," he whispered, voice hoarse.

Not a prayer. Not a warning.

A name that meant *possibility*.

Then, with a breath that shook, Connor stepped out of the nursery and closed the door behind him, not like locking something away...

...but like laying a hand on a grave and deciding, finally, to keep living.

CHAPTER 11

Sunday Best

Penelope woke with the uneasy certainty that the house knew something she didn't.

It wasn't the creak of the floorboards or the distant rattle of the pump outside. It wasn't even the fact that she had slept through the night without once clutching the pendant in panic.

It was *quiet*.

Not the lonely quiet she'd grown used to since arriving, but a quieter quiet. Settled. Expectant. Like a held breath.

She lay still, listening.

Below her, the day was already unfolding. Footsteps moved with purpose. The stove clanked. Water poured. And beneath it all, Connor's voice, low, even, but no longer edged with the brittle restraint she'd learned to recognize.

Something had shifted.

Pen sat up slowly, heart thudding. Mina stretched beside her, yawned wide enough to show teeth, her pink tongue curling, then immediately pounced on the hem of Pen's folded skirt like it had personally offended her.

"No," Pen whispered, disentangling claws. "Today you behave. No crimes."

Mina chirped and bit the fabric harder.

Pen dressed with care, fingers fumbling slightly. When she descended the stairs, the scent of fresh bread and coffee, *real* coffee, not a hazelnut latte with foam art, wrapped around her like a memory she hadn't earned yet. She hesitated at the threshold, suddenly unsure of herself in a way she hadn't been yesterday. As if she were stepping into a room where the rules had quietly changed overnight.

Connor stood at the table, sleeves rolled, tying off a sack of flour with methodical care. He looked up as she entered.

The moment stretched. Not with suspicion or distance. But something akin to recognition. And there it was, written on his face. Not with a smile, or even the softness that snuck its way in. But awareness. His gaze lingered a fraction longer than usual.

"Good morning, Miss Ward," he said.

Her name, spoken gently. Not as armor. Not a formality.

"Good morning," she replied, unsure what to do with the flutter in her chest.

Mrs. Porter emerged from the pantry, wiping her hands on her apron. She took one look at Connor... then at Penelope... then paused. The look in her eyes was brief. Barely a blink.

But Pen saw it.

"Well," Mrs. Porter said mildly, "someone slept."

Connor cleared his throat. "The day requires it."

Mrs. Porter's lips twitched. "So does the house, sir. It's been restless for years."

Pen blinked. "The house?"

Mrs. Porter set a loaf on the table. "Walls remember. Floors too. You'd be surprised what settles when grief finally loosens its grip."

Connor didn't argue.

That alone was shocking.

Mina chose that moment to leap onto the table, skid across the polished surface, and knock over the butter dish. Connor let out an exasperated sigh. "It is Sunday," he spoke matter-of-factly, as if that explained everything.

Penelope sat down after rearranging the butter dish and sending Mina off with a delicate pat on her rump. "Okay," she said, extending the O.

"Church," he said.

"What?" Penelope almost choked on the coffee she was sipping. "Um. No, thank you. I don't do religion."

"I wasn't asking." His crisp tone was back—then softened almost immediately. "It will do us good to get out of the house today."

Breakfast unfolded with an odd, fragile politeness. Connor passed dishes instead of retreating behind his paper. He asked Penelope if she preferred honey or jam. Mina stole a biscuit and fled under the table, crumbs flying.

At one point, Connor reached down and rescued Penelope's napkin from Mina's claws.

Their fingers brushed.

He froze.

So did she.

Mrs. Porter pretended very loudly not to notice.

The house settled around her once breakfast ended.

Not loudly. Not insistently. Only the quiet, lived-in sounds of a place that knew its own rhythms, Mrs. Porter moving dishes in the kitchen, the faint creak of floorboards adjusting to the morning, Mina thumping down the hallway before leaping onto the back of the settee like she'd claimed it weeks ago.

Pen lingered in the parlor, smoothing nonexistent wrinkles from her sleeves, watching dust motes drift lazily through the sunlight slanting in from the tall windows. The air smelled faintly of coffee and soap, and wood polish.

It felt... whole.

That tiny crack she'd glimpsed in Connor, just for a moment, just enough, had widened into something she couldn't stop seeing.

Not weakness but humanity. A man who carried grief like a second skeleton, invisible but heavy, and who still found space to be careful with her.

Careful. Protective. Present.

She leaned against the window, pressing her fingertips to the glass. It was cool beneath her skin. Solid. Real.

In 2026, she had money. A bank balance she rarely checked because it didn't change how empty her evenings felt. A Victorian house she'd bought on hope and impulse, its rot hidden beneath cosmetic fixes. She had freedom in the abstract sense, no one waiting for her, no one depending on her, but she'd never felt less anchored.

Here, she had structure. Meals at set hours. Work that mattered. People who noticed when she entered a room. A place at a table.

She mattered here.

The realization slipped into her chest with alarming ease.

I want to stay.

The thought didn't come with panic. It came with relief.

She imagined mornings like this—sunlight, routine, quiet conversation. Learning the land, the house, and the town. Becoming something more than a curiosity. Becoming... known.

Her gaze drifted to the doorway where Connor had stood moments earlier. The memory of his presence lingered like warmth after a fire had gone out.

She touched the pendant without thinking.

It lay warm against her skin. Steady. Not pulsing. Not reacting. Just there.

Listening.

Pen swallowed, heart pounding with something dangerously close to hope.

For the first time since she'd arrived in this impossible place, she wasn't thinking about how to leave.

She was thinking about how to stay.

By the time they were ready to leave, Pen's nerves were wound tight.

The moment Connor offered his arm, Penelope understood: Church wasn't about God here. It was about *being seen*. Judgment. A town gathering disguised as reverence.

Connor offered his arm.

She took it.

The walk into town felt heavier than before. People were already watching. Windows cracked open. Conversations stalled mid-sentence.

Mina rode proudly on Pen's shoulder, tail flicking like she owned the road.

"She's going to cause an incident," Connor muttered.

"She *is* the incident," Pen replied.

The church bells rang as they approached, deep and resonant.

The building itself was modest: white clapboard, narrow windows, but the moment Penelope stepped inside on Connor's arm, she felt the collective attention land like a weight.

Everything stopped.

Every pew was filled. Every head turned. Murmurs rippled like wind through dry grass.

Penelope felt it then. Not curiosity.

Expectation.

Connor guided her down the aisle with a hand firm at her elbow. Not gripping. Not possessive. Protective.

Mina, riding proudly on Pen's shoulder, flicked her tail at a passing hat.

Penelope hissed under her breath, "If you knock someone's bonnet off, I will *die* of embarrassment."

Mina purred.

They slid into a pew halfway down. Penelope tried to sit properly, spine straight, hands folded, heart racing. She could feel eyes crawling over her dress, her posture, the cat.

She was starting to breathe normally again, when a familiar, warm voice whispered from behind.

"Well now. If it isn't the most discussed cousin in three counties."

Penelope turned to see Daniel Brookes sliding into the pew behind them, grin firmly in place.

"Good morning," he murmured. "You look radiant today, Miss Ward."

Connor stiffened beside her.

Pen smiled politely. "Good morning, Mr. Brookes."

Daniel leaned closer. "I was hoping you'd come. Church is dreadfully dull without proper company."

Connor's jaw tightened. "I'm surprised you attend at all," Connor said coolly, not turning around.

Daniel chuckled. "I find it improves my reputation. And occasionally introduces me to charming ladies."

Penelope shot Connor a look. *Let me handle this.* She turned back to Daniel. "You're very bold for a Sunday."

"I consider it my finest quality."

Mina chose that exact moment to step off Penelope's shoulder, onto the pew, and *plop* herself directly onto Daniel Brookes's hymnbook.

Daniel blinked. "Is... is your cat judging me?"

"Yes," Pen said. "She finds you suspicious."

Connor exhaled sharply through his nose.

Daniel laughed, unoffended. "I like a woman with... spirit. And pets that match." He leaned closer. "Perhaps I might walk you home sometime. Give your cousin a rest."

The air shifted.

Connor turned.

Slowly.

"No," her companion said.

It wasn't loud. It wasn't sharp.

It was final.

Daniel raised a brow. "I was asking her."

Connor's hand moved, enough to rest against the back of the pew behind Penelope, a clear, unmistakable line drawn. "She is under my protection," Connor said. "And that is not an offer."

Silence bloomed around them, curious and prickling.

Penelope's heart pounded.

Daniel studied Connor for a moment, then smiled again, thinner this time. "Very well. I wouldn't want to cause discomfort." His gaze flicked back to Pen, lingering. "Still. If you ever wish for conversation without... supervision."

Pen swallowed.

Before she could answer, Mina hissed. Not playfully, then she climbed back over the pew, settling on Pen's lap.

People glanced over.

Daniel chuckled awkwardly. "I'll take that as a no." He leaned back, chastened but far from defeated.

Connor didn't move his hand.

Penelope felt warmth bloom where his presence bracketed her. Comfort. Safety. Belonging.

The feeling that she *was* right where she belonged.

Her thoughts were brought up sharp when Mrs. Abernathy sat two rows ahead.

Of course she did.

She twisted around, smile sharp as a blade. "Miss Ward," she whispered loudly enough for God and half the congregation to hear, "how *lovely* to see you again."

Pen smiled thinly. "Good morning."

Mrs. Abernathy's gaze flicked to Connor. "Such a blessing, family. Clara would have been pleased to know her kin are cared for."

Penelope's breath caught.

Connor stiffened beside her.

"Clara's… kin?" someone murmured behind them.

Mrs. Abernathy nodded eagerly. "Distant, of course. But blood is blood. I always said Clara had such *fine* relations."

Pen's pulse roared in her ears.

Connor didn't correct her. Didn't deny it. Didn't move.

The lie slid into place like it had always been waiting.

The service passed in a blur. Pen barely heard the words, only the whispers.

"Did you know Clara had a cousin?"

"I didn't."

"Well, she does now."

"Explains why he's opened the house again…"

"Poor man."

"Or lucky."

When the final hymn ended and the congregation began to rise, Pen braced herself.

They didn't make it three steps down the aisle.

"Miss Ward!"

"How long will you be staying?"

"Are you settling in?"

"Back East, you say?"

"What was Clara like as a girl?"

The questions came fast and sharp and smiling.

Connor answered where he could. Deflected where he must. His hand never left her elbow.

Daniel Brookes appeared from the crowd like he'd been waiting for a second chance. "Well," he said cheerfully, "if church doesn't inspire scandal, what does?"

Connor's jaw tightened.

Daniel's smile softened, just for Penelope. "You handled yourself beautifully. Not easy being dropped into the center of things."

Pen swallowed. "I didn't realize *how* centered."

"Oh," he said lightly. "You are very centered."

Mina hissed.

Daniel laughed. "Your cat still dislikes me."

"She has good instincts," Connor said flatly.

Daniel raised a brow. "I see the family resemblance runs deep. Miss Ward," he tipped his hat. "I *will* be seeing you again."

The crowd pressed closer. Questions overlapped. Assumptions hardened into fact. By the time they finally escaped into the sunlight, Pen's head was spinning.

As THEY WALKED BACK through the fields afterward, the bells still echoing faintly behind them, Pen finally spoke.

"You didn't have to do that."

Connor glanced at her. "Do what?"

"Shut Brookes down. Publicly."

"I wanted to."

Her breath caught. "That's not the same thing."

"No," he agreed quietly. "It isn't."

"He doesn't give up, does he?" Penelope whispered to Connor.

"You have no idea. This isn't the first time he has made advances to a woman in my charge," Connor replied.

"Clara?" Pen whispered.

Connor simply nodded, leaving Penelope with more questions than answers.

They walked on.

Penelope's chest felt tight with something dangerously close to joy.

The people knew her name; they wanted her story. They saw her, wanted her.

Connor slowed.

"Miss Ward," he said quietly. "What they believe now... it will not fade easily."

Pen nodded. "Neither will what I'm feeling."

He looked at her then, really looked, and for a moment, neither past nor future mattered.

And beneath Penelope's blouse, the pendant warmed, just enough to remind her:

Time was still watching, too.

Mina bounded ahead, chasing something invisible through the grass.

Pen's chest felt too full. Hope pressed against panic, both sharp enough to hurt.

"Connor," she said, unable to stop herself. "I really am... from another time. If there's a way back... do you want me to..." she trailed off.

He didn't answer immediately. When he did, his voice was steady. "That is not a decision for today."

She nodded, even as something inside her twisted.

As the house came into view, sunlight spilling across its windows, Penelope felt it clearly for the first time.

She wasn't only surviving this place anymore.

She was choosing it.

And that was the most dangerous thing of all.

WHEN LATER THAT DAY, Daniel Brookes appeared in town at the same time as they did, Penelope stopped believing in coincidence.

She felt him before she saw him: that subtle tightening at the base of her spine, the instinctive awareness that came from a lifetime of being overlooked and suddenly, inexplicably, noticed. Mina shifted on her shoulder, claws kneading the fabric of Pen's sleeve, tail flicking once in agitation, then twice. A warning.

"Connor," Pen murmured, keeping her gaze on the window display they were passing. "We're about to be intercepted."

Connor's stride shortened by a fraction. His jaw tightened. "I see him."

They were halfway down the main street, arms full of parcels Mrs. Porter had requested: flour wrapped in brown paper, a bottle of lamp oil, a small bundle of ribbon Pen had lingered over longer than necessary. The afternoon sun cast long shadows across the packed dirt road, and the town buzzed with its usual rhythm: shop doors creaking open and shut, horses snorting and stamping, women lingering on stoops with the unmistakable patience of people who enjoyed watching lives unfold.

Daniel Brookes stepped directly into their path. "Miss Ward," he said brightly, removing his hat with practiced charm. "What a pleasure."

Connor stopped walking.

Not abruptly. Not aggressively. He simply halted, and by doing so, claimed the space beside Penelope with unmistakable intent. He didn't touch her, but his presence pressed in, solid and unyielding. Penelope felt it immediately: the way Connor's presence sharpened, like a blade sliding free of its sheath.

"Brookes," Connor said flatly.

Daniel's grin widened. "Halden. I was simply remarking to Mrs. Abernathy how fortunate you are."

Connor's gaze flicked briefly past him, to where the woman in question hovered near the bakery door, pretending to rearrange nothing at all. Her eyes gleamed with interest.

"Fortunate?" Connor echoed coolly.

Daniel's gaze lingered on Penelope, far too long to be polite. "To have such delightful company."

Heat crept up Pen's neck. "That's... kind of you," she said, unsure whether courtesy or deflection was safer.

Connor's fingers tightened around the parcel in his hand, causing the paper-wrapped parcels to creak with alarm.

Daniel chuckled. "I was hoping I might steal Miss Ward for a moment. Show her a few places around town. Properly welcome her."

Connor answered before Pen could. "That won't be necessary."

Daniel arched a brow. "She can speak for herself, can't she?"

Pen opened her mouth, then hesitated.

The street had gone quieter. Not silent. But attentive. Conversations slowed. Glances sharpened. She felt suddenly like she were standing on a stage she hadn't agreed to step onto.

"I don't mind seeing more of the town," she said carefully. "But I'm not alone."

Connor turned his head toward her. Slowly. His expression remained composed, but his eyes were dark, turbulent. Searching.

Daniel smiled. "Of course you're not. But even family doesn't need to hover."

Connor's voice dropped, dangerously low. "Choose your words carefully."

The temperature between them shifted. Penelope felt it like pressure in her chest.

Daniel lifted his hands, feigning innocence. "No offense meant. Only concern. A woman such as Miss Ward should enjoy her freedom."

Pen stiffened. "My freedom?"

"Yes," Daniel said easily. "You're new. Unencumbered. Untethered. Surely you don't intend to remain hidden away in that house forever."

Connor inhaled sharply through his nose.

"I am not hidden," Pen said, sharper than she intended. "And I'm not untethered."

Daniel's gaze flicked between them. Something calculating passed through his eyes. "Then perhaps you are more... bound than you appear."

Connor stepped forward. Only one step, but it was enough to silence the space between them.

"You will stop," Connor said quietly, "implying anything about Miss Ward's character. Or her situation."

A murmur rippled through the gathered onlookers. Mrs. Abernathy leaned forward, delighted.

Daniel's smile thinned. "I was only offering kindness."

"I am offering restraint," Connor replied. "Do not mistake it."

Penelope's pulse pounded. She hadn't meant for this. Hadn't wanted to be a spectacle. But suddenly, she understood this was the cost of being seen.

Daniel tipped his hat again, slower this time. "Very well. I'll take my kindness elsewhere... for now." His gaze lingered on Pen once more. "If you change your mind, Miss Ward... you know where to find me. I'll be seeing you again *soon.*"

He disappeared into the crowd.

Connor didn't move until he was gone. Then, abruptly, he turned. "We're leaving."

Penelope had to jog to keep up.

They walked in silence until the buildings thinned and the road stretched open again. The fields beyond shimmered green and gold.

"You didn't have to do that," Pen said at last.

Connor didn't slow. "Yes. I did."

She frowned. "You didn't even let me answer."

His jaw worked. "Because I know his type."

"And what type is that?"

Connor stopped walking.

Pen nearly collided with him.

"He sees a woman who doesn't quite belong," Connor said tightly, "and he thinks that makes her available. Make her *his.*"

"That's not fair."

"No," Connor agreed. "It is not."

Something in his voice, not anger but fear, made her chest ache.

She took a breath. "Were you angry because he was rude... or because he was right?"

"Right?" he questioned.

"About me being more bound than I appear."

Connor looked at her then. Really looked. "Which would trouble you more?" he asked quietly.

Pen swallowed.

He turned away again. "We should return home."

But as they walked, Pen couldn't shake the feeling that something fragile had cracked, not broken, but no longer whole.

Connor's silence wasn't distance.

It was restraint.

And restraint, she was learning, could be far more dangerous.

THE RUMORS REACHED the house before sunset.

Mrs. Porter heard them first.

Penelope knew because the woman paused mid-stir at the stove, spoon hovering, brows knitting together in a way that meant *news*. Not good news.

"They're talking," Mrs. Porter said finally.

Pen's stomach dropped. "About... me?"

Mrs. Porter glanced toward the doorway. Lowered her voice. "About you and Mr. Halden."

Connor, seated at the table repairing a leather strap, went utterly still.

"Miss Pope stopped by with some of her apple preserves and a loaf of that sourdough she's always making. Anyway. She was told by Mrs. Watkins that they're saying," Mrs. Porter continued delicately, "that perhaps you are not his cousin after all."

Penelope felt the room tilt. "They can't—"

"They always do," Connor said. "They have nothing better to do than speak ill of others, to hide their own family shame."

Mrs. Porter sighed. "Well, she said Daniel Brookes has been... conversational. Seems he thinks if he can not have you, no one should. He is aiming to ruin you. So no decent fellow would court you when and if the time comes."

Connor's hand clenched, creaking the leather in his hand.

"He wouldn't!" Pen exclaimed.

"He would, and he has. He is telling folks that there is something different about you. But he is not saying what he thinks it is. Letting them use their own thoughts to create mischief. I worry he is trying to ruin Mr. Halden, as well," Mrs. Porter continued.

"He has to let that go," Connor gruffed.

"Let what go?" Pen inquired.

"Mr. Brookes has not forgiven Mr. Halden for-"

"That is enough!" Connor roared.

Penelope took a step back in shock.

He had never once raised his voice in anger. And yet, now he bellowed at his dear, sweet housekeeper.

Penelope let out a deep breath. "I'll go."

Both of them turned to her.

"I'll leave," she said again, heart hammering. "I won't stay if I'm causing trouble—"

Connor was on his feet in an instant. "No."

The word was sharp. Final.

She stared at him. "Connor—"

"I will not have you driven out by gossip," he said, voice tight. "Not after—" He stopped himself.

After what?

After defending her?

After wanting her?

After failing to stop it?

Mrs. Porter cleared her throat. "Perhaps a walk on the grounds would do you both some good. I'll have dinner waiting when you return. But take your time."

Connor didn't argue. He retrieved their overcoats and guided Penelope out the side door, leaving Mrs. Porter and Mina in the kitchen.

They walked toward the edge of the property, the sky bleeding pink and gold above them. Crickets sang. The air cooled. The small distance between them said more than any words could.

Penelope hugged her arms around herself. "I never meant for this."

"I know," Connor said.

"I don't want to be a problem."

"You are not," he said instantly, then faltered. "You are... complicated."

She laughed weakly. "That might be the nicest insult I've ever received."

He almost smiled.

They stopped near the old fence line. The land stretched wide, quiet, theirs alone.

"I don't understand what I'm feeling," Penelope admitted softly. "One moment I want to disappear. The next..." She gestured helplessly. "I don't."

Connor swallowed.

"You don't belong here," he said.

Her heart sank, but she knew he was right. In all truth, she didn't belong anywhere. She was unwanted and unnoticed in her own time. The only thing worth going back to was already here, with her. Mina. There was the money her parents left for her, but what good was it when she'd still be alone in a house full of ghosts.

"And yet," he continued, voice rough, bringing her back to him, "I cannot imagine this place without you now."

She looked at him.

The honesty in his deep blue eyes stole her breath.

"I wake expecting to hear your voice," he said quietly. "I watch the door without meaning to. And when Brookes looked at you —" His jaw clenched. "I felt something I have no right to feel."

"You have every right," she whispered.

"No," he said. "I don't."

She stepped closer; the pull to reach out to him was so strong. Yet she moved slowly. Gave him time to pull away.

He didn't.

The space between them narrowed until she could feel his breath. Smell the faint scent of pine and smoke and something undeniably *him*.

"Connor," she murmured.

His hand lifted. Hovered near her cheek, so close she could feel the heat of it.

He stopped.

"This cannot happen," he said hoarsely.

"Why?"

"Because I have already buried one woman I loved."

Her heart broke.

"I'm not Clara," she whispered.

"I know," he whispered. "That is what terrifies me."

The pendant at her throat felt warm, pulsing, insistent.

She reached for him.

He let her.

Just for a second.

Slipping her arms around his torso, feeling the pounding of his heart against her breast, the heat of him. She sighed when he returned the embrace, holding her as tightly as she held him. As if they were putting the broken pieces of each other back together again.

Penelope loosened her hold enough to lean back and glance at his face.

The deeply carved lines in his forehead said everything his lips did not. Then, he leaned down.

Pen's breath caught in her throat. Hoping he would continue closer, just a little closer.

Their foreheads touched. Breath mingled. The world narrowed to that fragile, unbearable closeness.

Penelope closed her eyes. Waiting for that one moment. Her heart slammed into her ribcage like a professional boxer.

And then he stepped back.

"I won't do this," he said, voice shaking. "I won't take something I cannot keep."

Pen's eyes burned.

"I didn't ask you to," she said.

"I want to," he admitted. "And that is precisely the problem."

He turned and walked away.

She stayed where she was, heart aching, pendant warm against her skin.

CHAPTER 12

What Was Not Taken

Breakfast was agony.

Connor arrived precisely on time, as he always did. He greeted Mrs. Porter with polite efficiency. He nodded once at Penelope and took his usual seat.

He did not meet her eyes.

Penelope felt the absence like a bruise.

But she noticed Mrs. Porter, gaze moving between them—Connor buttering his toast without eating it, Penelope's own untouched tea, Mina glaring at Connor as though personally offended by his emotional withdrawal.

"Something wrong with the eggs?" Mrs. Porter asked mildly.

"No," Connor said.

"They're cold," Penelope said at the same time.

Mrs. Porter hummed. "Funny. They were hot when I served them."

Silence.

Connor set his fork down carefully. "I'll be in the study." He stood, nodded once more, and left.

The door closed softly behind him.

Penelope exhaled shakily.

Mrs. Porter turned to her then, eyes kind but sharp. "He hasn't slept. He was in his study half the night."

Pen swallowed. "I didn't mean to cause trouble."

Mrs. Porter snorted. "Child, you didn't cause anything. You revealed it."

Pen blinked.

"This house has been holding its breath for four years," Mrs. Porter continued, gathering plates. "Men like Mr. Halden don't break loudly. They fracture quietly. And when something finally shifts, it's never gentle."

Pen looked down at her hands. "People are talking."

"Yes," Mrs. Porter said calmly. "And people always will."

"That's not comforting," Penelope whispered.

"It's realistic."

Pen managed a weak smile.

Mrs. Porter paused at the doorway. "If I may be so bold, whatever is between you and that man... decide what you want before others decide for you."

The words lingered long after she left.

THE FIRST SIGN that the gossip had teeth came right after midday.

Penelope was outside. Alone. Mrs. Porter had wrangled her to help with the household chores by hanging laundry in the yard, an exercise in patience, humiliation, and wind. She was fighting with a bedsheet when Mina froze on the fence post, ears flat.

Pen felt something was off, too.

The sense of being watched.

She continued to work against the wind, using the battle with the linens to get a better view of her surroundings without being obvious. When she couldn't get a view of what was behind her, she turned, reaching into the backet for another piece of laundry. That's when she saw him.

Daniel Brookes stood at the edge of the property, hat tipped back, smile gone.

"Miss Ward," he called. "I see you are alone. The timing is perfect. We need to talk."

Penelope straightened, the linen held tight in her hand. "About what?"

"About the stories," he called back, stepping closer.

Her stomach dropped. "I'm not interested in silly gossip. Thank you, but please leave."

He continued closer anyway. "They're saying you appeared out of nowhere."

Pen's pulse thundered, her grip and the fabric tightening to the point her knuckles hurt.

"They're saying you're not his family at all," he continued.

"I don't owe you explanations." She started running through her options—how she could use the sheet in her hands to stop him if he continued to get closer.

"No," Daniel agreed. "But the townfolk think you do." He was so close now; Penelope could see the blue of his eyes.

Mina hissed.

Daniel glanced at the cat, his expression dismissive. "Someone claims they saw you... before you arrived at the Halden house. Wearing strange clothes. Appearing as though from thin air."

Cold spread down Pen's spine. She knew he told the truth, but who would believe it?

"A boy," Daniel continued. "A farmhand. Swears you weren't there one moment... and then you were."

"That's ridiculous," she said.

"Is it?" he pressed. "Because people are asking questions they don't like the answers to."

Penelope's voice shook. "Why are you telling me this?"

Daniel studied her, his flirtation replaced by something colder. Calculation. "Because I don't think you're dangerous. I think you're trapped."

"That's not your concern."

"It could be," he said quietly. "If you'd let it. I can protect you in ways Halden cannot."

"No, thank you. I am fine right where I am. At my cousin's house," she said, hoping her voice didn't give away the terror she was feeling deep in her gut.

"You and I both know you are no cousin to Halden. Or Clara. I knew her well. Very well. She had no cousins. I can take you away, where you won't have to lie about who you are and where you come from."

"I said, No, thank you," Pen pressed again.

He stepped closer, right on the other side of the clothesline. "Let me be clear, Miss Ward. I am not asking. I am telling. You *will* come with me."

Her chest tightened with indignation and fear. "You're threatening me?"

"I am warning you," Daniel corrected. "This town forgives widowers. It does not forgive scandals. I will clear everything up with the townsfolk when you are mine." He lunged forward, ducking underneath the line, clearly on a mission to get to her.

In her panic, she shifted to her left, tripping over the basket of laundry. Brookes lunged where she had been—and fell to his knees, just missing her.

Pen's heart pounded in her ears. It took a long moment for her to realize it was the sound of boots on hard earth. It was footsteps that thundered behind her.

Connor.

He came down the porch steps fast, face carved from stone.

"Get off my land," he said, rolling up his sleeves, exposing arms of steel that had spent a lifetime working timber.

Daniel turned. "You should be careful, Halden. Harboring a woman the town doesn't trust—"

His words were cut off with a right hook to his cheek.

Penelope saw the spray of blood came from somewhere in the region of his mouth or nose; she wasn't sure.

"Leave," Connor said again. "Now. Or the next shot will be with my pistol."

Daniel hesitated, then smiled thinly, wiping the blood from his mouth with a white handkerchief. "You can't protect her from everything."

Connor stepped forward. "Try me."

Daniel tipped his hat and backed away. "I hope she's worth it, Halden. This time, I'll take not only your woman, but your land as well."

When he was gone, the silence roared.

Penelope turned to Connor. "Someone saw me."

Connor shocked Pen when he pulled her into his arms and held her close, like the shield he was becoming.

"That's what he came to tell me. Someone saw me arrive," she whispered. "I didn't know anyone could."

He swore under his breath—harsh and vicious. She'd never heard him sound like that before.

"They'll go to the sheriff," Penelope said. "Or the church elders. Or—"

"They won't touch you," Connor snapped. "I won't allow it."

"You can't control a town." She wanted to weep.

"No," he said fiercely. "But I can stand between you and it."

"Connor... if this gets worse—"

"I will not lose you," he said. The words tore out of him raw and unguarded, and coming deep from within him. She felt the vibrations as he spoke the words aloud.

Her breath caught. "You don't know what you're asking."

"I don't care," he growled.

The pendant pulsed hard against her skin, once, twice, like a warning.

Or a countdown.

. . .

THAT NIGHT, Pen lay awake listening to the house settle. The sounds were small at first: timbers contracting with the cold, a soft knock somewhere in the walls, the distant sigh of wind through the eaves. Ordinary sounds, Connor had told her once. The language of an old house finding its balance.

But tonight, the sounds felt deliberate.

Measured.

As if the house itself were awake, listening too. She was sure it was only her internal fears projecting outward. But after all that had happened the past week, she was ready to believe that houses could be haunted. Not in the sense of dead people walking around, but more of the energy, the memories, the essence of those that had lived within the walls of the house. It gave her an odd sense of peace, thinking that the house had feelings, too.

Penelope lay on her back, hands folded over her stomach, the unfamiliar weight of the stays pressing against her ribs. The bed beneath her was firm and narrow; the mattress filled with horsehair that smelled faintly of lavender and dust. Moonlight slid across the floor in pale ribbons, catching on the edge of the wardrobe, the chair, the washstand.

And at her throat—

The pendant pulsed. Not hot. Not cold. Just... warm. Alive.

Pen swallowed and shifted onto her side. The movement did nothing to calm the sensation. The metal loops rested against her skin like a second heartbeat, slow and irregular, as if responding to something she couldn't hear.

"Stop," she whispered, pressing her fingers lightly against it. "Please."

The warmth intensified.

Mina stirred against her hip, tail flicking once in irritation. The cat let out a low, questioning chirr and lifted her head, ears swiveling toward the door.

"What is it?" Pen murmured.

Mina didn't answer; she never did, but she slid off the bed with uncharacteristic caution, landing silently on the floor. Her body went low, muscles coiled, tail puffing enough to signal unease.

Penelope sat up.

"Mina?"

The cat padded toward the door, nose twitching, eyes wide. She stopped short of the threshold and hissed, soft, warning, nothing like her earlier displays of chaotic bravado.

Pen's heart kicked.

She swung her legs over the side of the bed and stood, bare feet sinking into the rug. The floorboards were cold. Too cold.

"Mina," she whispered again, reaching down to scoop her up.

The moment her fingers brushed the cat's fur, the pendant flared.

Heat bloomed across Pen's chest, sharp and sudden enough to steal her breath. She gasped, clutching at the chain as the warmth surged, then receded, leaving her trembling.

"Okay," she breathed. "Okay, that's new."

Mina squirmed in her arms, clearly unhappy. Pen held her tighter, pressing her cheek briefly against the familiar softness of her fur. The cat smelled faintly of flour and wood smoke and the clean soap Mrs. Porter favored; comforting, grounding.

Pen crossed the room and eased the door open.

The hallway beyond lay empty, lit only by moonlight and the faint glow of a single oil lamp farther down. Shadows stretched long across the runner rug, pooling near doorways like something alive.

She listened.

Nothing.

Still, the feeling wouldn't leave her. That prickling awareness along her spine. That sense of being watched, not maliciously, but with intent. Pen stepped into the hall.

Mina growled low in her throat.

"I know," Pen murmured. "I don't like it either." She closed the door quietly behind her and padded toward the stairs. One hand on the banister, she paused and looked down the long hall-way. The one where the nursery and other bedrooms were.

Connor's door stood ajar.

A sliver of lamplight spilled across the floor.

Penelope hesitated. She had no reason to intrude. No invitation. And yet, after the way he'd looked at her tonight, after the way his voice had gone tight when he'd said her name, after the way the town had circled them like vultures wearing polite smiles—

He exhaled slowly, then looked away. "Brookes came back to the house tonight."

Penelope's stomach dropped. "What? When?"

"After supper. While you were upstairs."

"And?"

"And I told him to leave."

Pen waited.

"He did not," Connor continued. "Not immediately."

"What did he say?"

Connor's hands curled into fists. "Enough."

The answer chilled her.

"Connor..."

"He suggested," he said carefully, "that you would be safer elsewhere."

Pen felt something cold slide into her chest. "Elsewhere, how?"

Connor met her gaze fully now. "With him."

Mina hissed violently.

Pen's pulse roared in her ears. "He said the same to me. But worded it as if I didn't have a choice. I told him he doesn't get to decide that."

"No," Connor said, voice darkening. "He does not."

"And what did you say?"

"I said," Connor replied, each word precise, "that he would never speak your name in my presence again."

Pen's breath caught. "And when he ignored that?" she pressed.

Connor looked at the floor. "Then I stopped being polite. Again."

The room seemed to tilt.

Pen stepped closer without realizing it. "Are you in trouble?"

Connor's mouth curved humorlessly. "Not yet."

Yet.

The word echoed.

"Connor," she whispered, "this is because of me."

He shook his head sharply. "No. This is because men like Brookes believe kindness is permission and grief is weakness."

"That doesn't make it less dangerous."

"No," he agreed. "It makes it inevitable."

The pendant pulsed again, stronger this time.

Pen gasped, grabbing the chain. Heat flared, spreading across her collarbone, down her spine, into her limbs. The air around them seemed to thicken, humming with something unseen.

Connor noticed immediately. "What is happening?"

"I don't know," she breathed. "But it's getting worse. Your books? Did they say anymore about how this thing works?"

"The texts were unclear. But this charm—your pendant—may not simply move its wearer through time. It may bind them emotionally to the person or place meant to change them."

"To change me? Or the place I ended up?" she whispered.

"I do not know. Again, it is all speculation."

Mina leapt from Pen's arms and darted down the hall, skidding to a stop near the stairs. She hissed again, fur fully puffed now.

Connor moved instantly, stepping between Pen and the hallway.

"Stay here," he ordered.

"I'm not leaving you," she shot back.

"I was not asking."

Before she could argue, a sound drifted up from below.

Footsteps.

Not inside the house.

Outside.

Pen's blood went cold.

Connor held up a hand, silencing her. He crossed to the window and peered out, muscles taut.

After a moment, he straightened.

"Someone closed the gate," he said.

Pen's heart hammered. "At this hour?"

"Yes."

The pendant burned.

Penelope swayed.

Connor was at her side in an instant, steadying her by the elbows. The contact sent a jolt through her, electric, undeniable. From the way his fingers tightened, he felt it too.

"Penelope," he said, her name rough. "Look at me."

She did, her heart pounding. Whether from fear, or the fact he said her given name rather than being formal, she wasn't sure.

His face was inches from hers. She could see flecks of gold in his blue eyes, a faint scar along his jaw, the tension coiled in every line of him.

"I will keep you safe," he said. "Do you understand me?"

Her throat closed. "I know."

"No," he said fiercely. "You don't. I mean it. Whatever comes. Whatever they think they know. You are not alone."

Something inside her cracked.

"Connor," she whispered, "it's not what's outside that scares me."

His head cocked to the side in confusion.

She continued, bile tickling at the back of her throat. "What if we get... separated?"

The question hung between them, fragile and terrifying.

His grip tightened, not painfully, but with desperate clarity. "Then I will find you."

The words were a vow.

Before she could respond, a sharp crash sounded from below.

Mina yowled.

Pen and Connor moved at the same time, racing toward the stairs.

They reached the landing right as Mina exploded into view, fur bristling, dragging something behind her with her teeth.

"A mouse?" Pen shrieked.

"No," Connor said grimly. "A message."

The cat dropped her prize at their feet.

A scrap of paper, wrapped around a rock and tied with a string. It had been the string Mina had grabbed onto.

Connor picked it up slowly, removing the paper.

His face hardened as he read.

"What does it say?" Penelope asked, heart pounding.

Connor looked at her, eyes blazing.

"They know something is amiss," he said. "And they are done waiting."

The pendant flared white-hot.

The house groaned around them.

And Penelope feared that somewhere in town, plans were already being made.

CHAPTER 13

The Town Decides

By morning, the house felt different.

Not quieter. Not louder. Watchful.

Penelope noticed it the moment she opened her eyes: the way the air felt thicker, like it was holding its breath. The pendant lay warm against her skin, no longer pulsing, but not still either. As if it were listening. Waiting.

Mina was already awake, perched on the windowsill, tail flicking in sharp, irritated snaps. Her ears tracked something outside: movement, sound, intent.

Pen swung her legs over the side of the bed. "I know," she murmured. "I feel it too."

Downstairs, voices carried. Connor's low and controlled. Mrs. Porter's, clipped and unusually stern.

Pen dressed quickly, fingers clumsy with nerves. She tucked the pendant beneath her blouse without thinking, an instinctive act, like hiding a wound.

When she stepped into the hallway, the house creaked underfoot, familiar and suddenly fragile. She paused at the top of the stairs, listening.

"I will not have her spoken of like that," Connor was saying.

"And I will not have men coming to the door before breakfast," Mrs. Porter snapped. "This is a respectable household."

Pen's stomach dropped. She descended slowly.

Connor stood near the dining table, already dressed for the day, coat buttoned, jaw set like stone. Mrs. Porter stood opposite him, hands planted on her hips, cheeks flushed.

They both looked up when Pen entered.

Connor's expression shifted instantly: relief, tension, something dangerously close to guilt.

"Good morning," Penelope said softly.

Mrs. Porter's gaze softened. "Good morning, dear."

Connor crossed the room in three strides. "Did you sleep?"

"Some," she lied.

His eyes flicked briefly to the pendant's hiding place, then back to her face. "We will be going into town."

That wasn't a question.

Pen swallowed. "Why?"

"Because," Mrs. Porter said sharply, "if they are going to talk, they will do it to our faces."

Pen's pulse quickened. "Who came here this morning?"

Connor hesitated just long enough to tell her everything. "Mr. Brookes. And Mr. Hale."

"And?" Pen pressed.

"And Mrs. Abernathy was watching from across the street."

Of course she was.

Pen let out a slow breath. "What did they want?"

Connor's mouth thinned. "Answers."

Mrs. Porter sniffed. "As if they're owed any."

Penelope looked between them. "And you're taking me into town because...?"

"Because," Connor said quietly, "I will not have them thinking you are hiding."

The words landed heavily. Hiding meant guilt. Hiding meant shame. Hiding meant danger.

Pen nodded. "All right."

Mrs. Porter's eyes sharpened. "You will keep your chin up."

Pen managed a small smile. "I've been practicing."

Connor almost smiled. Almost.

THE TOWN SQUARE buzzed like a disturbed hive. And Mrs. Abernathy was the queen bee, Mr. Brookes right beside her.

Penelope felt the tension the moment they stepped into view; the way conversations stalled, the way bodies subtly shifted to face them, the way eyes lingered too long and too openly.

This wasn't curiosity anymore. This was an assessment.

For once, Pen was glad she made Mina stay at home with Mrs. Porter and the bowl of cream she'd offered the calico.

Connor's hand hovered near Pen's elbow, not touching, but close enough that she could feel the heat of him.

They reached the general store.

Mrs. Abernathy stood front and center, flanked by two other women whose names Pen didn't know but whose expressions she recognized: righteous concern disguised as politeness.

"Well," Mrs. Abernathy said brightly. "If it isn't the Halden household."

Connor inclined his head. "Mrs. Abernathy."

Her eyes slid to Pen. "Miss Ward."

Penelope nodded. "Good morning."

"Oh, it is," Mrs. Abernathy said. "Though I fear it may not stay so."

Connor's spine stiffened. "If you have something to say—"

"I do," she replied smoothly. "Several things, in fact. And I believe the town would appreciate hearing them."

A small crowd had gathered now, trying not to be obvious, but close enough to hear the drama unfolding.

Pen's heart hammered. She could feel the pendant warming again, a warning hum beneath her skin.

Mrs. Abernathy clasped her hands. "We have been very patient."

"Patient? With what?" Pen asked before Connor could stop her.

Mrs. Abernathy smiled thinly. "With your... circumstances."

Connor's voice cut in, sharp as a blade. "My cousin's circumstances are none of your concern."

A murmur rippled through the crowd.

"Cousin," someone whispered.

"Is she?"

"I heard she was Clara's kin."

Penelope froze.

Connor turned slowly. "Who said that?"

Mrs. Abernathy tilted her head. "It makes sense, doesn't it? She looks a bit like her. Same eyes."

Pen felt the ground tilt beneath her.

"She does not," Connor said flatly.

"Oh, I don't mean closely," Mrs. Abernathy went on. "Distantly. A cousin from Clara's side. Explains her presence. Explains why she's here now. You lost one wife, and now you are looking to replace her with another."

Pen's breath came shallow. She glanced at Connor.

His face had gone dangerously still.

"That is a lie," he said.

Mrs. Abernathy's smile sharpened. "Is it? Because Mr. Brookes says otherwise."

The crowd parted.

Daniel Brookes stepped forward, the black and blue reminder of his encounter with Connor visible to everyone. He looked infuriatingly calm. Confident. Pleased.

"Good morning, Penelope," he said warmly.

Connor moved instantly, placing himself half a step in front of her. "You will not address her."

Brookes chuckled. "You don't own her, Halden."

Pen's pulse roared. "I can speak for myself."

Connor shot her a glance, warning, protective, pleading all at once.

Brookes's gaze softened. "Of course you can. That's rather the point, isn't it?"

He turned to the crowd. "We've all been polite. We've all been accommodating. But people are starting to wonder."

"Wonder what?" Penelope demanded.

"Whether you're safe," Brookes said. "Whether you're being kept here against your will."

A gasp went through the onlookers, murmurs of agreement.

Connor's voice dropped. "Careful, Brookes. You are on dangerous ground."

Brookes ignored him. "A young woman appears out of nowhere. No family claims her openly. She lives alone with a widower known for keeping to himself. We want answers. We deserve the truth!"

"That's enough," Connor bellowed.

"And now," Brookes continued smoothly, "we hear she may be Clara Halden's cousin. Which would make her—"

"Stop," Penelope said sharply. She knew this was the time to come clean, as much as she could, without having the crowd cry witch. If she were to stay here and things progressed with Connor, she couldn't be living as his 'cousin' and not expect the drama to continue.

All eyes turned to her.

She stepped around Connor, heart pounding, Mina's claws digging into her shoulder. "You want the truth?"

The crowd responded in scattered voices: yes... please... it is about time...

"I am not Clara's cousin."

The crowd gasped.

"And I am not Connor's kin, either. Not by blood. His father and mine go way back. And when my parents died, Mr. Halden was the closest thing to family I had. He took me in when no one else would. He is my protector. My guardian. I am not being *kept*," Pen said clearly. "I am here because I choose to be."

Brookes smiled. "Do you?"

"Yes." She turned to him, hoping the anger she felt toward him reflected in her eyes.

"Then you won't mind coming with me," Brookes pointed out.

The words hit like a slap.

Connor went rigid.

"Excuse me?" Penelope said. "Go with you?"

Brookes gestured vaguely. "A walk. A meal. Somewhere public. Somewhere you won't be... supervised."

Connor grabbed his arm. Hard. "That will not happen." His voice was a deep rumble.

Brookes yanked his arm free. "Let go of me, Halden."

The crowd buzzed, tension spiking.

Penelope felt the pendant flare; she reached for it without thinking.

"Connor," she whispered. "Don't."

Brookes leaned in, voice low. "You're damaged, Halden. Everyone knows it. Don't drag her down with you."

Connor's expression shifted—something dangerous. In the blink of an eye, he punched Brookes. It happened fast, too fast for anyone to intervene. A sharp, brutal movement. Fist to jaw. The crack echoed across the square.

Chaos erupted. Shouts. Gasps. Someone screamed.

Penelope stood frozen, horror and awe crashing through her.

Connor stood over Brookes, chest heaving, eyes blazing with something wild and unrestrained.

"You will not touch her," he said, voice shaking with fury. "You will not speak her name. You will not threaten my household again."

Brookes spat blood and laughed. "You've just proved my point.

The second time he has assaulted me in just as many days," he said loud enough for the entire gathered crowd to hear. "Someone get the sheriff."

Hands grabbed Connor's arms, pulling him away—from Brookes and Penelope.

Voices shouted.

"Enough!" an unknown man shouted.

"This has gone too far!" Another bellowed.

Penelope surged forward. "Stop it!"

Mina leapt from her shoulder with a shriek, launching herself at Brookes's face, seeking revenge.

Absolute pandemonium.

Brookes screamed as claws met skin. Men scrambled. Someone tripped. Someone else swore.

Penelope scooped Mina up, heart racing, fighting to hold the angry cat in check.

Connor tore free of the hands restraining him and turned to Penelope.

Their eyes met.

Everything unsaid burned between them.

"We're leaving," he said.

No one stopped them.

No one dared.

As they walked away, whispers followed like smoke.

"She is dangerous."

"He's lost control."

Pen didn't look back.

But she knew.

The town had made its judgment.

And it would not be kind.

THEY DIDN'T SPEAK on the walk home.

Connor's stride ate the road like he meant to grind it into dust.

Penelope had to lift her skirt higher than was dignified to keep pace, boots slipping in the packed dirt, lungs burning in the cold air.

Pen couldn't stop seeing it.

Connor's fist.

Brookes's face snapping to the side.

The sound, God, the sound, like a branch cracking in winter.

The town's collective inhale.

And the way Connor had looked at her afterward, like he'd been yanked into some terrible truth he couldn't take back.

The pendant, hidden beneath Pen's blouse, was warm enough to make her skin itch.

When the house finally came into view, Pen's relief was immediate and fleeting, because the sight of it also meant the confrontation was no longer behind them.

It was coming home with them.

Connor didn't slow until they were up the path. He didn't pause for the porch step. He didn't offer his hand. He simply opened the front door and motioned her inside with a clipped, rigid sweep of his arm.

Mrs. Porter and Mina met them in the entryway. She took one look at Connor's face and stopped breathing.

Then her gaze snapped to Pen, hair loosened, cheeks flushed, and finally to Connor's knuckles.

They were scraped.

Slightly red.

Not bloody, but angry enough to tell a story without words.

"Oh," Mrs. Porter said quietly. "Who?"

Connor shut the door behind them with too much control. It clicked into place like a lock. "Brookes."

Penelope's stomach twisted. "Mrs. Porter—"

"Go sit down," Mrs. Porter said, not unkindly, but with an authority that brooked no argument. "Both of you."

Connor looked like he intended to ignore her.

Mrs. Porter's eyes narrowed. "Mr. Halden."

Connor's jaw flexed. His shoulders rose and fell once.

Then he moved.

Not to the parlor.

Not to his study.

To the kitchen, as if the warmth and the order of it were the only things keeping him upright.

Penelope followed, Mina right behind, the pendant pressing hot against her chest.

Mrs. Porter shut the kitchen door behind them. The sound was small. Final. She crossed to the table, planted her hands on the worn wood, and stared at Connor like she was trying to decide whether to scold him or pray for him. "What happened," she said, voice flat as a line, "in town."

Connor didn't sit. He remained standing near the counter, one hand gripping the edge hard enough to whiten his knuckles. "He purposely provoked me."

Mrs. Porter's eyes flicked to Pen. "Did he provoke you into bleeding as well?"

Connor's nostrils flared. "It is nothing."

Pen's throat tightened. "It wasn't nothing."

Connor's gaze snapped to her. Sharp. Warning.

Penelope held it anyway.

"It was... a lot," she finished, softer.

Mrs. Porter exhaled, slow and weary, like a woman who had survived too many winters to be surprised by the cruelty of people. "Did anyone see?"

Pen let out a humorless laugh. "Brookes planned it. The townfolk there, Mrs. Abernathy knee-deep in Brookes' lies. It was clear this was exactly what he hoped for. An audience, and a spectacle."

Connor's jaw tightened further, as if her words had claws.

Mrs. Porter pressed her lips together. "God help us."

Connor's voice dropped. "I will handle it."

Mrs. Porter's eyes flashed. "Will you? Like you handled it in town? With your fist?"

He stiffened.

Penelope flinched at the sudden edge in the room, Connor's quiet fury meeting Mrs. Porter's fierce worry, sparks catching in the air between them.

Mrs. Porter's voice softened a fraction. "You cannot strike a man in public, Mr. Halden."

"He threatened—"

"He baited you," she cut in. "And you gave him what he wanted. Brookes won't stop at rumors and baiting. He'll bring the law with him. You and I both know he has always wanted what you have. And he will do anything to take it."

Connor's throat worked, as if he was swallowing words he couldn't say without revealing too much.

Penelope felt the pull of it; how his restraint had been a dam, and Brookes had taken a hammer to the cracks.

She sat at the table because her knees finally gave up pretending they weren't shaking.

Mina immediately jumped onto the chair beside her and began grooming herself like she hadn't just committed assault.

Pen stared at the cat in disbelief. "You're... fine?"

Mina blinked slowly, then licked a paw with utter satisfaction.

Connor's eyes closed briefly as if he, too, had no idea how they were living with this creature.

Mrs. Porter turned her gaze to Pen. Her expression changed then, not judging, not suspicious. Protective. "They spoke ill of you," she whispered. Not a question. A clear statement.

Pen swallowed. "Yes."

Mrs. Porter's mouth thinned. "Did they call you—"

"A lying harlot?" Penelope offered, because she'd heard it in the whispers. In the way Mrs. Abernathy had smiled. In the way the crowd's eyes had sharpened.

Mrs. Porter's face hardened. "Vultures."

Pen's chest ached. "They... they said I *might* be Clara's cousin. That I had her eyes. And that I was here to replace her."

Connor's hand tightened on the counter so hard the wood creaked.

Mrs. Porter's eyes widened, then narrowed. "Who said that?"

"Mrs. Abernathy," Pen said, voice tight. "And Brookes."

Mrs. Porter's jaw clenched. "That woman should be banned from polite society."

Connor finally spoke, low and dangerous. "She has no shame."

"No," Mrs. Porter agreed. "And now she has a story."

Silence settled, heavy and sick.

Penelope looked down at her hands in her lap. They trembled. Her fingers drifted unconsciously toward the pendant beneath her blouse, pressing it like a bruise.

Connor noticed.

His gaze dropped briefly, then jerked away as if he'd been burned.

Mrs. Porter noticed, too—not the pendant itself, hidden beneath fabric, but the gesture. The way Pen's body sought comfort in something hidden.

"Did he... truly threaten you?" Mrs. Porter asked gently.

Penelope hesitated. Because the word *threaten* felt too dramatic and not dramatic enough at the same time. "He said I should come with him," Pen admitted. "In front of everyone. Like... like it was decided. Like he could offer and I would simply —" She swallowed. Her eyes stung. "And when Connor told him no, he said Connor was damaged. Cold. That he'd drag me down."

Connor's breath came out sharp.

Pen looked up at him. "And then it was like... something snapped."

Connor's face appeared carved from stone. But his eyes weren't. They were too bright. Too haunted.

Mrs. Porter stared at Connor for a long moment. "You cannot

unmake a punch," she said quietly. "But you can choose what you do next."

Connor's voice was rough. "What I do next is keep her safe."

Penelope's heart stuttered.

Mrs. Porter's gaze flicked to Pen again, and something in her softened with a strange, aching pity. "Safety is not just bolts and distance," she murmured. "It is reputation. It is perception. It is knowing what people are capable of once they decide someone is a problem."

Pen's stomach sank.

"What are they capable of?" she whispered.

Mrs. Porter's lips pressed into a thin line. "Cruelty dressed up as righteousness."

Connor straightened. "They will not come here."

Mrs. Porter's eyes sharpened. "You don't know that."

Connor's jaw tightened. "I do."

Mrs. Porter pointed toward the window. "They already came once this morning. They will come again. And now they have a reason. Now they have a story that makes them feel justified."

Pen's fingers tightened around the edge of her skirt. She could still see Mrs. Abernathy's smile. That woman didn't want the truth. She wanted entertainment. A scandal was the closest thing this town had to theater.

And Penelope was the leading lady.

THEY TRIED to return to normal.

Which was, in itself, a kind of madness.

Mrs. Porter put the kettle on as if tea could fix a public brawl. Penelope washed her hands, scrubbing too hard as if she could scrub the town's eyes off her skin. Connor disappeared into his study for a stretch of time that felt like punishment.

Penelope sat in the parlor with Mina, who had become restless again, prowling along the windowsill, tail flicking, ears tracking every distant sound.

The rocking chair sat in the corner, perfectly still.

Pen looked at it and wanted to laugh hysterically.

Yesterday, Mina had tried to murder it.

Today, Penelope felt like she was the one being hunted. She heard Connor's boots in the hallway before she saw him.

He entered the parlor like a man carrying his own storm.

Penelope rose automatically. "Connor—"

"Sit," he said, not harshly, but with a tension that made it feel like a command to keep her from falling apart.

She sat.

He didn't.

He paced once near the fireplace, then stopped, fists flexing and unclenching like his body didn't know what to do with itself. "I should not have struck him," he said finally, voice like gravel.

Pen blinked. The admission hit her harder than the punch had.

Connor Halden did not apologize.

Connor Halden did not admit fault.

"I'm not..." Penelope searched for the right words. "I'm not angry."

His gaze snapped to her. "You should be."

"I'm not," she repeated, stubborn. "He wasn't... he wasn't being respectful. He was trying to corner me and disrespect us both, in front of everyone."

Connor's jaw worked. "That is what they do. They circle and circle until the prey is tired enough to make a mistake."

Penelope's throat tightened. "And you think I'm prey."

Connor went still. Something in his expression shifted, the armor cracking for a split second. "No," he said quietly. "I think *they* have decided you are."

Pen's stomach dropped. "What happens now?"

Connor's gaze held hers, and for the first time since she'd arrived, she saw him afraid. Not of her—his eyes weren't wary. Not of losing control again—his fear was too focused. But of losing her —the way he looked at her made that clear.

"They will come," he said simply.

A chill skated down Pen's spine. "Here? To the house?"

"Yes."

Mrs. Porter appeared in the doorway like she'd been summoned by the word. "They will," she confirmed. "They will come for you both."

Pen looked between them. "Why?"

Mrs. Porter's mouth tightened. "They won't come to shout," she said quietly. "They'll come to *correct*."

Penelope's voice was low. "Correct? Correct, what?"

Mrs. Porter let out a sigh, as if her words were causing her pain. "Mr. Halden assaulted a gentleman on Main Street. And there were witnesses. No respectable man would cause a ruckus out in public like that. He could be arrested for that alone. But more importantly, as a widow with a young woman living under his roof, who may or may not be family, they have the right to feel as though his guardianship is false. That he is seducing her. You."

The pendant warmed as Mrs. Porter uttered her last word. *You.*

Pen's hand flew instinctively to her chest.

Connor's eyes narrowed. "It's doing it again."

Pen swallowed. "It's... been warm since last night."

Mrs. Porter looked sharply between them. "What are you two talking about?"

Pen hesitated.

Connor's expression hardened. "Nothing you need concern yourself with."

Mrs. Porter's eyes flashed. "If a mob comes to the doorstep, Mr. Halden, I will concern myself with whatever I please."

Pen almost smiled until the fear tightened again.

Connor exhaled through his nose. He looked like a man being pulled in too many directions at once.

Then he said quietly, "We must be prepared."

. . .

PREPARED TURNED out to mean Connor doing things with a methodical calm that terrified Pen more than the town's gossip ever could.

He checked the back door.

Twice.

He tested the latch on the front door.

He went to the gun cabinet in his study—

Pen's heart lurched, and then returned empty-handed, as if he'd made a decision she didn't get to know about.

He pulled the curtains slightly, not enough to look like hiding, but enough to obscure the view.

He spoke to Mrs. Porter in a low voice, and she nodded grimly, then vanished into the pantry and returned with something wrapped in cloth.

Penelope's mouth went dry. "What is that?"

Mrs. Porter didn't look at her as she carried it toward the kitchen. "A rolling pin," she said briskly. "And if a sanctimonious woman thinks she's coming into our house to accuse a guest of sin, she can test its holiness with her skull."

Pen stared.

Connor's shoulders relaxed for the first time all day.

Just slightly.

Pen exhaled a laugh that turned into something close to a sob.

Mina chose that moment to leap onto the side table and begin pawing at a porcelain figurine.

"No," Penelope said quickly, grabbing her. "Not now. Not today. Please do not start a domestic war while we're preparing for a social one."

Mina meowed in protest, then wriggled free, launching herself straight toward Connor.

Pen's breath caught, expecting claws.

Instead, Mina landed on Connor's boot, climbed his trouser

leg like a furry mountain goat, and perched on his thigh with arrogant determination.

Connor froze like someone had slapped him with a live fish.

Pen stared. "She... she never does that."

Connor looked down at the cat, horrified.

Mina head-butted his knee.

Connor's face went blank—that particular blankness she'd come to recognize when something caught him completely off guard.

Mrs. Porter walked in, took one look, and made a sound suspiciously like amusement.

"Well," she said. "Even the cat knows where safety lives."

Connor's throat bobbed. "Get her off me."

Mina purred.

Pen's eyes stung.

Because even Mina, chaotic, feral Mina, was choosing him. As if she understood. As if she sensed what Pen was trying not to admit to herself: Connor was becoming her anchor.

And anchors were dangerous when you were meant to leave.

CHAPTER 14

The Fallout

By mid-afternoon, the first sign came.

A wagon rolling past the house slower than necessary with two men inside, their casual glances anything but casual.

Pen stood at the parlor window, curtain pinched between her fingers, heart pounding.

Connor appeared behind her silently. "Don't stand there."

Penelope turned. "They're already—"

"I know."

She lowered her voice. "What are they going to do?"

Connor's gaze was hard. "They will ask questions."

"And if they don't like the answers?"

Connor's jaw clenched. "Then they will pretend their cruelty is mercy."

A shiver ran through her.

She glanced down at the pendant again.

Warm.

Restless.

As if it agreed.

Then came the second sign.

Voices.

Not close at first. Then a distant sound carried on the wind: muffled words, the roll of a crowd.

Penelope's mouth went dry. "Connor…"

He moved to the front window and glanced out through the small gap in the curtain.

His face went completely still.

Mrs. Porter entered the room, wiping her hands on her apron. "They're coming."

Pen's pulse roared in her ears. "How many?"

Connor didn't answer.

Mrs. Porter did grim. "Enough."

The pendant flared so hot Pen gasped and clutched her chest.

Connor's head snapped toward her. "Penelope."

The way he said her name, no Miss Ward, no distance, made her breath catch.

"What?" she whispered.

Connor stepped close, close enough that she could smell him: wood smoke, soap, something steady beneath it. He looked down at the spot where the pendant hid. "It wants something," he murmured, almost to himself.

Pen's throat tightened. "Or it's warning me."

Connor's gaze lifted to hers. "Same thing."

A knock hit the front door. Hard. Not polite. Not patient.

A second knock followed immediately.

Then a voice—loud, sharp, certain of its right. "Mr. Halden!"

Mrs. Abernathy.

Of course.

Pen's stomach dropped.

Connor's hand flexed once at his side, like he was remembering his fist.

Mrs. Porter squared her shoulders. "Stay behind me."

Pen stood frozen. "Mrs. Porter—"

"I said stay behind me," she snapped, then softened a hair. "Dear."

Connor moved past them both.

Penelope grabbed his sleeve. "Connor, don't—"

He paused, turning his head enough that she could see his profile. His expression controlled. But his eyes... His eyes looked like a man about to step into a fire—willing to burn rather than let her. "I will not let them take you," he said, so low only she could hear.

Pen's throat closed. "I'm not something they can take."

Connor's gaze flicked to her mouth.

Then away.

The moment was gone.

He opened the door.

The porch was crowded. Men in work shirts, hats in hand. Women in pressed dresses, eyes bright with outrage. A few children clinging to skirts, peeking around bodies. And at the front, like a queen of rot, stood Mrs. Abernathy.

Her gaze swept over Connor, then slid past him, searching.

Finding.

Pen's blood turned to ice.

"There she is," Mrs. Abernathy said sweetly. "Miss Ward."

Pen stepped forward despite Mrs. Porter's grip on her arm.

Mina chose that moment to launch from Pen's shoulder straight toward the nearest bonnet ribbon, clawing it like it had personally offended her.

A woman squealed.

Someone shouted, "That cat is possessed!"

Penelope grabbed Mina mid-air, mortified. "She's not possessed... she's just... she's Mina."

Mrs. Abernathy's smile widened. "And isn't that just like her? Unusual. Wild. Unfeminine."

Connor's voice cut like steel. "State your business."

Mrs. Abernathy clasped her hands, eyes glittering. "We are concerned, Mr. Halden. Concerned for the welfare of a young lady living under... unusual circumstances."

Connor's body went rigid beside her.

Behind Mrs. Abernathy, Daniel Brookes stood with a bruised jaw and a satisfied gleam in his black eye.

Pen's stomach turned.

He had wanted this.

Connor saw him—she watched his gaze land and harden.

A muscle jumped in Connor's cheek.

Mrs. Abernathy continued, louder now, for the crowd. "We have heard troubling things."

Connor's voice was low. "From whom?"

"From people who care," she said. "From people who saw what happened in town."

Brookes's mouth curled. "From people who saw you lose control."

Connor didn't look at him.

But Pen felt the heat of Connor's fury like a storm at her back.

Mrs. Abernathy's gaze flicked to Penelope. "And from people who say you are not who you claim."

Pen's heart hammered.

"We want to know," Mrs. Abernathy said, "why you are here."

Pen opened her mouth.

Connor spoke first. "She is family."

A murmur surged.

Mrs. Abernathy's eyes gleamed. "Ah. Yes. But which kind?"

Penelope's stomach dropped. "What—"

Mrs. Abernathy took a step forward. "We have heard you are Clara Halden's cousin."

Silence hit like a slap.

Connor's face went white.

Pen's lungs locked.

Mrs. Porter made a strangled sound behind them.

Brookes smiled like the cat with the canary.

Pen's mind flashed: Clara's portrait on the store wall. Clara's music book.

And now this.

This lie was not only a scandal.

It was cruelty.

Mrs. Abernathy lifted her chin. "If you are Clara's kin, then you have no business in Mr. Halden's home without a proper chaperone."

Pen's throat closed. "I've already told you, I'm not—"

"And if you are not," Mrs. Abernathy went on, voice rising, "then you are a stranger, and a strange one at that. And it is the duty of a town to protect itself from strangers who appear out of nowhere."

The heat from the pendant spread outward, sharp and breath-stealing, like it had pressed a warning directly against her heart.

Pen forced her hand away from her chest and lifted her chin.

"I am here because I choose to be," she said clearly, her voice shaking only slightly. "And Connor Halden has done nothing but protect me."

Mrs. Abernathy's smile thinned. "Protection can look an awful lot like possession, Miss Ward."

Connor took one step forward. "That is enough." His voice was calm. Too calm. The kind of calm that came right before a storm broke loose.

Mrs. Abernathy's eyes flicked past him again, hunting. Always hunting. "Then perhaps you will not object to the sheriff sorting it out."

As if summoned by the word, hooves sounded on the packed dirt road.

A wagon rolled into view at the end of the drive. The crowd shifted, making space as Sheriff Hollis climbed down, his expression already set in lines of weary authority. He took in the scene with one sweeping glance: the gathered townsfolk, Brookes's bruised face, Mrs. Abernathy's expectant posture, Connor standing squarely in the doorway like a man bracing against a siege.

"Afternoon," the sheriff said, voice steady. "Mr. Halden."

Connor inclined his head. "Sheriff."

Penelope's pulse roared in her ears.

Mrs. Abernathy stepped forward eagerly. "Sheriff, we've been most concerned. There's been an incident in town."

"I heard," Hollis replied. His gaze flicked to Brookes. "You were struck."

Brookes nodded solemnly. "Unprovoked."

Connor didn't look at him.

Penelope's fists clenched. "That's not—"

Connor lifted a hand, stopping her without touching her.

Hollis held up his palm. "Miss, I'll need you to stay back."

Pen swallowed hard and did as she was told.

The sheriff turned back to Connor. "There were witnesses. Several. Public assault is no small thing, Mr. Halden."

Connor's jaw tightened. "I will answer for my actions."

That—that was worse than denial.

Mrs. Porter made a sharp sound. "Sheriff, you know this man. You know his character."

"I do," Hollis said quietly. "Which is why I'm asking him to come peaceably."

Penelope's heart cracked.

Connor didn't hesitate. He reached for his coat from the hall hook and shrugged it on with deliberate care, like he was preparing for weather instead of loss.

Pen stepped forward, voice breaking. "Connor, please—"

He turned then, fully, and the look he gave her stole the air from her lungs. There was no fear, no regret. Resolve. "I will not have you dragged into this further," he said. "You have already been made spectacle enough."

Her eyes burned. "This is because of me."

"No," he said, so firmly it hurt. "This is because of them."

The sheriff cleared his throat. "Mr. Halden."

Connor nodded once. Then, before Pen could stop herself, she caught his sleeve.

"Connor," she whispered. "I don't want you to think—"

His hand closed over hers briefly. Just enough. "I know," he said.

That was all.

He stepped away.

The sound of the shackles felt impossibly loud in the sudden hush.

Mrs. Abernathy exhaled in something that sounded dangerously like satisfaction.

And then Brookes spoke.

"Well," he said smoothly, stepping forward. "Since Mr. Halden will be indisposed, it seems only right that Miss Ward be taken into proper care."

Pen recoiled instinctively.

Mrs. Porter moved faster than Pen thought possible, placing herself squarely between Penelope and Brookes. "Absolutely not."

Brookes smiled thinly. "I only mean—"

"You mean to take advantage," Mrs. Porter snapped. "And you will not do it under this roof."

Hollis raised a brow. "Mrs. Porter—"

"She stays," Mrs. Porter said, voice iron. "With me. In this house. Where she has been treated with respect."

Penelope felt tears spill over.

Brookes scoffed. "She's not family."

Penelope drew a shaky breath. "I never said I was," she said. "But Connor Halden is my guardian. And I will not be passed like property because he bruised your pride."

A murmur rippled through the crowd.

Hollis studied her for a long moment, then nodded once. "Miss Ward may remain here under Mrs. Porter's supervision."

Brookes's smile vanished.

Connor closed his eyes briefly, relief flickering across his face before he masked it again.

The sheriff placed a hand on Connor's shoulder. "Let's go."

Connor walked down the steps without looking back.

Pen watched him go, every step tearing something loose inside her chest.

The crowd followed, buzzing, satisfied, already spinning the story.

When the last wagon disappeared down the road, the house fell silent.

Utterly.

Pen stood frozen, staring at the empty drive.

In the kitchen, Mina let out a thin, broken cry and bolted for the door, claws skidding uselessly against the wood.

"No," Pen whispered, sinking to her knees. "No, no, no..."

Mrs. Porter scooped the cat up, pressing her to her chest as Mina wailed, the sound raw and unrestrained. "Hush, love," she murmured, tears streaking her own cheeks. "Hush now."

Penelope collapsed onto the parlor floor, the strength draining out of her all at once.

The house felt hollow.

Connor was gone.

And suddenly, with terrifying clarity, Pen understood the truth she'd been avoiding all day.

She *had* wanted to stay.

And because she had wanted it, because she had let herself believe it, everything had fallen apart.

Her fingers curled around the pendant as sobs tore free.

"This is my fault," she whispered into the quiet. "If I hadn't come... if I hadn't stayed... he would be safe."

The pendant burned against her palm.

Not warning.

Not anger.

Calling.

And somewhere, deep in the walls of the house that had begun to feel like home, something ancient and patient shifted... and waited.

~

CONNOR ~

The cell smelled of iron, damp stone, and old regret.

Connor Halden sat on the narrow bench bolted to the wall, his elbows braced on his knees, his hands clasped loosely between them. The shackles were gone, but the imprint of the iron still seemed to bite into his wrists, phantom pressure where freedom had been removed and then reluctantly returned.

He had not resisted.

That fact troubled him more than the arrest itself.

He had walked beside Sheriff Hollis through the town he had helped build, past faces he had known since boyhood—men who had once clasped his shoulder in sympathy after Clara's funeral, women who had brought bread and casseroles and solemn prayers. Now they watched him with something else in their eyes.

Judgment.

Suspicion.

Relief that it was not them.

Connor had met none of their gazes.

Because the only face he could see was hers.

Penelope. Standing in the doorway of his house, pale and shaking, trying so desperately not to break that it had nearly undone him. The way her fingers had tightened in his sleeve. The way she had looked at him as if he were the last solid thing in a world gone unmoored.

And the way he had let go.

His jaw clenched.

The door at the end of the narrow corridor opened with a heavy scrape. Boots sounded against stone. Connor lifted his head, expression already locked into place, spine straightening by instinct rather than choice.

Sheriff Hollis stopped outside the bars.

"You holding up?" Hollis asked.

Connor inclined his head. "As well as can be expected."

Hollis studied him for a moment, then sighed. "You know I didn't want this."

Connor's mouth twitched humorlessly. "Intentions do not alter outcomes."

"No," Hollis agreed. "They rarely do."

He gestured to the bench opposite the bars. "Mind if I ask a few questions? Officially."

Connor nodded. "Of course."

Hollis leaned back, folding his arms. "You struck Daniel Brookes. In full view of witnesses."

"Yes."

"No attempt to deny it?"

Connor shook his head. "None."

"Why?"

The question hung there, deceptively simple.

Connor looked down at his hands. Hands that had built houses, split timber, held Clara gently when she was afraid. Hands that had clenched into fists when Brookes had leaned too close to Penelope, when his voice had turned suggestive, when entitlement had dripped from every word.

"She was being cornered," Connor said.

Hollis raised an eyebrow. "She?"

"Miss Ward."

"Your cousin."

Connor's jaw tightened. "No."

Hollis's gaze sharpened. "No?"

"She is not my cousin by blood," Connor said evenly. "Nor is she my ward by law. But she is under my protection."

Hollis let out a slow breath. "You understand how that sounds."

Connor lifted his eyes. "I understand exactly how it sounds."

"And yet you still struck him."

"Yes."

Hollis rubbed a hand over his mouth. "He claims you warned him off once already."

"I did."

"And when he persisted?"

Connor's voice dropped. "He implied she would be better off without me. That she was... confined."

Hollis studied him. "And that warranted violence."

Connor met his gaze steadily. "It warranted correction."

Silence stretched between them.

Finally, Hollis sighed. "You know how this goes. Public disorder. Assault. You'll be held overnight. Possibly fined. Depending on how hard Brookes presses it."

Connor nodded once. "I understand."

Hollis hesitated. "There's more."

Connor's shoulders tightened.

"The town's... concerned," Hollis continued carefully. "A young woman appears out of nowhere. Lives under your roof. Wears odd clothing. Speaks oddly. Has no family to vouch for her."

Connor's stomach tightened.

"They think you're compromised," Hollis finished. "Or worse. She is."

Connor leaned back against the stone wall, the chill seeping through his coat. "And what do you think?"

Hollis was quiet for a long moment. Then he said, "I think you've been lonely for a very long time."

The words struck deeper than any accusation.

Connor closed his eyes briefly. "Loneliness is not a crime."

"No," Hollis agreed. "But it makes men careless."

Connor thought of Penelope's laugh in the kitchen. Of the way she had looked at Clara's piano with reverence rather than fear. Of the way she had stood on his porch and declared—clearly, bravely—that she chose to be there.

Careless.

If that was carelessness, he would bear the charge.

"I will not harm her," Connor said.

"I know," Hollis replied. "But the town doesn't know her. And they don't understand what they can't categorize."

Connor opened his eyes. "Neither do I."

Hollis straightened. "Get some rest. I'll return in the morning."

The sheriff left.

The door closed.

The silence rushed back in.

Connor leaned forward, elbows on knees, hands clenched now despite his efforts. The cell felt smaller with every passing moment, the stone walls pressing in like the weight of years he had spent holding himself rigid and alone.

"I should never have let you stay," he murmured into the quiet.

But the lie tasted bitter.

Because the truth was this—

He had never let her stay.

She had walked into his life like something inevitable. Like fate, or punishment, or grace. And now, sitting alone in a cell, stripped of control and certainty, Connor Halden faced the thing he had avoided since Clara's death.

He was afraid.

Not of judgment.

Not of punishment.

Not even of losing his carefully ordered life.

He was afraid of losing *her*.

Because somewhere between etiquette lessons and shared silences, between laughter and grief and the impossible truth of her existence, Penelope Ward had become something he had not allowed himself to want.

Hope.

Connor pressed his forearm against his eyes, breathing through the ache burning behind them.

"Clara," he whispered, the name a prayer, and a wound all at once. "What have I done?"

The stone offered no answer.

But deep in his chest, beneath the guilt and fear and longing, something else stirred.

A quiet certainty.

If Penelope was taken from him—by the town, by fear, by time itself—he would not survive it unchanged.

And for the first time since the cell door had closed behind him, Connor Halden allowed himself to feel it fully.

The unbearable weight of loving someone he could not protect.

~

MRS. PORTER DID NOT ASK Penelope's permission.

She simply stepped forward, scooped Mina into her arms with firm, practiced efficiency, and turned toward the kitchen as if this were any other evening, as if the world had not just cracked open on the front porch. "Come along, you dreadful creature," she murmured, voice brisk but not unkind. "We'll have some fish. And cream. And you'll stop that noise before you frighten yourself half to death."

Mina protested immediately. Not with her usual offended yowl, but with something sharp and raw, a sound that sliced straight through Penelope's chest. The cat twisted in Mrs. Porter's arms, paws scrabbling desperately, eyes locked on Pen as if she were being dragged away across water.

"Mina—" Penelope croaked.

Mrs. Porter did not turn. "She needs feeding," she said, practical to the last. "And warmth. And quiet. And you—" Her voice softened slightly. "You need a moment where she is not looking at you like that."

The words landed like a mercy Penelope did not feel strong enough to accept.

The kitchen door closed. The sound was ordinary. Mundane. Final. It echoed through the house like a verdict.

Penelope stood frozen in the parlor, arms hanging uselessly at her sides, heart pounding so hard she was certain it must be visible beneath the fabric of her dress. The house felt suddenly enormous, every corner too sharp, too loud with memory.

Connor's absence pressed in on her from every direction. The fireplace where he had stood, braced like a man holding himself upright. The doorway he had passed through, back straight, jaw set, knowing what waited for him. The space beside her where his presence had begun to feel... expected.

Safe.

She swayed slightly and sank down onto the sofa, skirts pooling around her like spilled wine. Her hands shook as she pressed them to her face, breath stuttering in and out of her lungs as if she'd forgotten how to do it properly. Her corset felt too tight. Her skin too thin. The house, *Connor's* house, seemed to loom around her, every wall heavy with memory and judgment and things she did not belong to.

This is my fault.

The thought arrived fully formed, heavy and absolute.

If I hadn't come...

Connor would still be free.

Mrs. Porter wouldn't be bracing herself against the town's whispers and accusations.

Mina wouldn't be crying in confusion and fear.

This house wouldn't be under siege by whispers and judgment.

Connor Halden had survived grief before her.

He had survived loss.

He had survived loneliness.

He had survived four years of silence and restraint and aching control.

She was the variable.

She was the disturbance.

Penelope folded forward, elbows braced on her knees, forehead pressed into trembling hands. A sob tore free before she could stop it, rough and humiliating and real.

"I ruin everything," she whispered.

Tears slid down her cheeks, dripping onto her skirt, her hands, and the polished floor beneath her feet. She barely noticed. Her mind was spiraling too fast, chasing the terrible logic her grief offered so convincingly.

The pendant warmed. Not sharply. Not violently. Just... attentively.

She gasped, fingers curling instinctively around the chain at her throat. The metal felt warmer than before, like it had been resting against skin already heated by fever. "No," she whispered, panic threading through the grief. "No, not now." Her breath came faster as memories flooded her in merciless succession.

Connor adjusting her gloves in town, careful not to touch bare skin longer than necessary.

Connor standing in front of her on the porch, voice steady as iron as the crowd pressed closer.

Connor's eyes when he'd said, 'I will not let them take you'.

And she had let him be taken instead.

Because of her.

"I never should have come," she said hoarsely, the words scraping her throat raw. "You'd be better off," she sobbed, the words tearing free at last. "All of you. If I'd never existed here at all."

The pendant pulsed. Once. Slow. Steady. Like a heartbeat answering another.

Penelope shook her head violently. "That's not what I mean. I don't want to leave him. I don't—" Her voice broke. "I don't want to leave."

But the truth sat heavier beneath the protest.

She believed, deep down, in the marrow of her bones, that Connor would be better off without her. That belief wrapped itself around her grief like a blade.

The room tilted.

Not dramatically. Not yet. Just enough that she had to reach for the back of the sofa to steady herself. A low vibration thrummed beneath her skin, spreading outward from the pendant, down her spine, into the floorboards beneath her feet.

The house felt like it was listening.

"No," she whispered again, louder now. "Please. I didn't mean—"

But she had. That was the cruelest part.

The pendant did not care that she was wrong. It did not care that love had just begun to bloom. It cared only that she believed she was the wound.

Her chest tightened painfully as the air thickened around her, the edges of the room blurring as if the world itself were being smudged away. Her ears rang, a high, distant sound like wind through glass.

"Mina!" Penelope cried suddenly, stumbling toward the kitchen. "Mina, no! Don't send me back, not without—" Her foot caught on the edge of the rug. She fell hard to her knees, pain flaring briefly before being swallowed by something much larger. The pendant burned now, not searing, but insistent, a pull that wrapped around her heart and tugged. "Stop," she sobbed. "Please stop. I'll stay. I'll fix it. I'll—"

The parlor dimmed, lamplight stretching and warping like reflections in water. The piano across the room shimmered, its polished surface catching light that no longer behaved properly.

She reached out blindly. "Connor," she whispered, the name torn from her like a prayer.

And she felt herself pulled away into nothing.

***

Mrs Porter and Mina

The kitchen was warm with lamplight and the familiar, comforting scent of fish.

Mrs. Porter knelt by the hearth, setting a small saucer on the floor with practiced care. "There you are," she murmured. "Eat. You'll feel better."

Mina leapt down immediately, devouring the offering with frantic intensity, tail lashing, ears twitching toward the parlor with every sound, or lack of one.

Mrs. Porter straightened slowly, wiping her hands on her apron. "Miss Ward?" she called. "Penelope?"

No answer.

A chill crept up her spine.

She walked back toward the parlor, steps measured, deliberate, the way a woman walks when she is already afraid of what she might find.

The room was empty.

The sofa cushions were askew.

A single tear-darkened mark stained the rug.

The air felt thinner. Wrong. Like a door left open in winter.

Mrs. Porter stopped short. "Oh," she whispered.

Behind her, Mina padded into the doorway, sniffed the air once... and froze.

Then she screamed.

Not a meow. Not a cry. A raw, broken sound that tore through the house, clawing at the walls, echoing into every empty corner Penelope had left behind.

Mrs. Porter sank slowly into the nearest chair, one hand pressed to her mouth, eyes burning.

"Oh, my dear," she whispered. "What have you done?"

Outside, the house settled.

Penelope was gone.

THE HOUSE DID NOT SLEEP that night.

Mrs. Porter knew this because she did not sleep, and the Halden house had always mirrored the state of its keeper. When Connor was gone, truly gone, the house held its breath. When grief ruled it, the walls remembered.

Tonight, the house mourned.

Mina prowled.

Not with her usual imperious confidence, tail high, nose twitching in arrogant inspection of her domain—but low to the ground, shoulders hunched, steps uneven. She moved from room to room like she was searching for something that had fallen through the cracks of the world.

Mrs. Porter followed her at a distance. She did not try to stop the cat. She had learned, long ago, that some kinds of grief must be walked through, not managed.

Mina padded into the parlor first.

She leapt onto the sofa, sniffed hard at the cushions, kneaded once, sharply, as if trying to pull something back into existence. Her ears flicked toward the doorway. She hopped down again, restless, and let out a thin, questioning sound.

Mrs. Porter's chest tightened. "She's not there, love," she whispered, though her voice shook despite her effort. "I know."

Mina did not believe her.

The cat trotted to the fireplace, sniffed the hearthstone where Connor had stood so often, then pivoted toward the hall. Her movements grew frantic, her small body vibrating with unease. She ran upstairs.

Mrs. Porter followed more slowly, one hand gripping the banister, the other pressed flat against her sternum as if to hold her heart in place. Each step felt heavier than the last. The upstairs corridor was dim, the oil lamp casting long shadows across the familiar doors.

Mina stopped outside Penelope's room. She pawed at the door. Once. Twice. Harder.

"Mina..." Mrs. Porter whispered.

The cat meowed sharply, an urgent sound, then pressed her face to the crack beneath the door as if scent alone could summon her person back.

Mrs. Porter opened the door.

The room was exactly as Penelope had left it. The bed neatly made. The lavender dress folded on the chair. The faint scent of soap and something indefinably *her* lingering in the air.

The absence was suffocating.

Mina leapt onto the bed and spun in tight circles, then froze, ears flat. She sniffed the pillow once and let out a broken, keening sound that ripped straight through Mrs. Porter's composure.

"Oh, my dear," she whispered, crossing the room and sinking onto the edge of the bed. "Oh, my poor, foolish girl..."

Mina collapsed against the pillow, body curled tight, eyes wide and shining. She cried then, not loudly, but continuously, a soft, wounded sound that refused to stop. Each noise scraped against Mrs. Porter's heart like a blade.

She reached out, hands trembling, and gathered the cat into her arms.

Mina fought her. Not violently. Not with claws. She simply struggled, twisting and stretching toward the door, toward the hall, toward anywhere Penelope might still be.

"She didn't leave you," Mrs. Porter said fiercely, as much to herself as to the cat. "Do you hear me? She didn't choose this."

Mina did not care about words.

She cried harder.

Mrs. Porter pressed her cheek against the cat's fur, tears slipping free despite her years of practiced restraint. She had buried a husband. She had buried a sister. She had buried children she'd helped bring into the world.

But this... This was different. This was the wrong kind of empty.

"She loved you," Mrs. Porter whispered, rocking slightly now, unable to stop herself.

Mina's cries softened into shuddering breaths, her small body trembling against Mrs. Porter's chest.

The house creaked. A sound like settling wood. Or a sigh.

Mrs. Porter stayed there a long time. Long enough for the lamp oil to burn low. Long enough for the moon to crawl across the floor. Long enough for the night to press in around the house like a held breath.

Eventually, Mina's exhaustion overtook her grief. She curled tighter, paws clutching at Mrs. Porter's sleeve as if afraid she too might disappear.

Mrs. Porter did not move. She sat there in the quiet, holding what remained. "Connor will come back," she said into the dark. "And when he does... this house will need to remember how to hope again."

Mina did not answer. But her grip tightened.

And somewhere, across time and stone and impossible distance, something listened.

CHAPTER 15

The House That Forgot Her

Penelope woke on the floor.

That was the first wrong thing.

The second was the silence.

Not the soft, breathing silence of the Halden house at night. Not the familiar creak of old wood settling around a hearth that had known grief for more than a century.

This silence was hollow. Empty in a way that felt careless.

Pen's eyes flew open.

She was lying on her side in the parlor of the Victorian. *Her* Victorian. The one she'd bought with a phone call and a stack of paperwork and the naïve belief that a house could be a beginning. The wallpaper on the walls was peeling again. The floorboards beneath her cheek were uneven, one edge digging into her jaw.

No oil lamp. No fire. No warm breath of another life sharing the room.

The pendant lay against her chest, cool and inert.

"No," she whispered.

She sat up too fast, dizziness slamming into her. Even in the quickly spreading darkness of nighttime, her gaze swept the room in a frantic arc.

The sagging couch. The cracked windowpane. The half-filled garbage bag she hadn't finished piling the trash into because she'd been pulled *away*.

Away.

"Mina?" Her voice cracked immediately. "Mina, come here."

Nothing.

Her heart knew before her mind would allow it.

She scrambled to her feet, vintage shoes skidding on the uneven floor, and ran the best she could, laced tight in stays and petticoats.

"Mina!" she called again, louder now, panic rising. "Mina, baby, come on, this isn't funny!"

She checked the kitchen first.

The semi-modern appliances sat where she'd left them, cold and indifferent. No Mrs. Porter humming at the stove. No smell of biscuits or coffee strong enough to make your eyes water. Only week old mail on the counter and a smear of dust she hadn't yet wiped away.

"Mina?" she tried again, weaker now.

She dropped to her knees and looked under the table.

Nothing.

The pantry, the powder room. The closet where Mina liked to hide when she wanted to ambush unsuspecting ankles.

Empty.

She ran upstairs.

Her breath came sharp and shallow as she pushed open each door, dread blooming with every room that offered no flash of calico fur, no indignant meow, no accusing stare.

"Mina, please," she whispered, voice breaking now. "Please be here."

She checked the nursery last.

The room was unfinished in this time, bare studs where walls had been removed, insulation exposed, the faint smell of rot and mouse droppings lingering in the corners. No cradle. No warmth.

Her knees buckled.

She slid down the wall and pressed her forehead to the cool drywall, breath hitching. "She's still there," she whispered, like a prayer and a curse. "She's with Mrs. Porter. She's safe. She's…"

The word *safe* shattered her.

Because safe wasn't the same as *with me*.

She pressed her palm to the pendant.

Cold.

Unresponsive.

"You weren't supposed to do this," she said hoarsely. "You weren't supposed to take me without her."

No answer.

The house creaked, a sound she used to find comforting, now hollow and wrong.

She stayed there until the shaking slowed. Until her throat burned from crying, and no more tears came. Then she stood on unsteady legs and made her way to her bedroom.

She peeled the Victorian dress from her shoulders, fingers fumbling with buttons that had been second nature hours ago. Each layer she removed felt like stripping away proof that it had been real. That he had been real.

She was exhausted—not only from the physical strain, but from losing Mina, losing Connor, losing everything. But removing her garments from *his* time felt like she was accepting it—she'd returned.

Final.

She slipped into her pajamas, which were right where she had left them a week before.

Was it really only a week?

And climbed into bed. The brass headboard was the only constant in her sleeping arrangements. She was now sleeping in what had been his room—same place, different time. A room she had never fully stepped into in its prime. The paint was chipping in places, exposing bare plaster underneath.

"Please let this all be a bad dream," Pen whispered to the room, as the darkness draped over her and she finally drifted to sleep.

THE SUNLIGHT SPREAD across Penelope's face, waking her from fitful dreams. She couldn't remember details, only the overwhelming sense of grief. She hadn't felt it this heavy since her parents had died when she was seven. It took everything in her power to climb out of bed and face the fact that she was utterly alone. No Mina, no Mrs. Porter, no... Connor.

Out of a newfound habit, she went to her pile of Victorian clothing and began to dress. She knew if she stayed in the house, she would fall apart. She caught a glimpse of herself reflected in the broken mirror and let out a devastated sigh. She couldn't walk through town dressed as she was. She'd had enough of this town's criticism. Even if it had been the current town folks' ancestors. Pen painstakingly removed her dress and underthings, replacing them with a t-shirt and jeans. The fabric felt ... wrong. Uncomfortable.

Penelope let out a deep sigh as she grabbed her key and wallet, which still lay on the wobbly broken end table by the door, and stepped out in the world she no longer felt a part of.

WALKING DOWN MAIN STREET, Pen realized how much had changed in one hundred and thirty years. And how little. But the realization that hit harder than she expected was the fact that the town had not noticed her absence. Even though they had very much noticed her arrival.

The coffee shop on Main, *The Tipping Bean*, newly renovated and aggressively modern, buzzed with the same low hum of conversation and espresso machines it previously did. The barista glanced up and smiled, practiced and pleasant.

"What can I get for you?" she asked. "Are you new in town?"

Pen replied automatically. "Hazelnut latte. And yes. I'm new."

"Large?"

"Yes."

"And your name?"

Penelope felt that old sense of—*I'm invisible*—when the woman asked. It had only been a week since she was here last, and the woman hadn't remembered Pen, that she was, in fact, new in town.

She paid without thinking, her card tapping against the reader with a chirp that felt obscenely loud. The barista called her name, Penelope, and it echoed wrong in the space.

She took the cup with shaking hands.

The smell hit her first.

Sweet. Warm. Familiar.

She stared down at the foam, at the little leaf the barista had etched into the top, and her chest caved in.

Connor would have hated this place.

Too loud. Too chaotic. Too careless with time. He would have stood stiffly near the door, hat in hand, eyes narrowed in polite discomfort, clearly wondering how anyone could tolerate such noise before noon.

Pen carried the coffee outside and sat on the bench beneath the awning. She took a sip. It tasted wrong. Too sweet. Too thin. No bite. No substance. She swallowed it anyway.

Across the street, people passed her without a glance. A woman laughed into her phone. A man jogged past with earbuds in. A child dragged a scooter along the sidewalk.

A week had passed for her.

Here, it had been nothing.

No missing person report. No concern. No one wondering where she'd gone.

Invisible.

The word settled into her bones.

She finished the coffee she didn't want and stood, suddenly

unsure what to do with herself. She knew she couldn't go back into the house, not yet.

Her feet carried her toward the library without conscious thought.

THE LIBRARY SMELLED THE SAME. Dust and paper and the faint, comforting tang of old glue. It was quiet in the way only libraries were allowed to be, reverent, patient, untouched by urgency.

Pen walked straight to the local history section. She didn't hesitate. Her fingers brushed spines she now knew too well. Halden. Timber. Early settlement records. Census rolls. Land deeds. She pulled one book after another, stacking them on a table near the back where she'd first sat days ago—*centuries* ago, it felt like.

Connor Halden.

His name appeared exactly as it had before. Prominent landowner. Timber advocate. One hundred acres planted and managed. Community contributor. Widower. No mention of an arrest. No mention of scandal. No mention of a woman who fell into his life like a comet and tore it apart. She went back to the deeds she'd researched before.

Was that only a week ago?

It seemed lifetimes.

Her chest tightened.

Land purchased by Mr. Halden in 1857. House complete in 1860.

"That must have been his father," Pen said to no one.

Property sold in 1897 to Mr. Wallace P.

No—Mrs. Wallace P.

The S was barely there, as if it was intentionally microscopic.

"Mrs. Porter!" Pen practically shouted.

A shush came from somewhere behind her.

"Sorry," she whispered before turning back to the pages. "Why did he sell it to Mrs. Porter?" Pen spent the next hour trying to find an answer, only to be left with more questions. She found that Mrs. Wallace Porter was a widow with a son, Wallace Jr., who married a Miss Callowell in 1894. They had a son, but he unfortunately died in 1955 from a railway accident. Penelope couldn't find an obituary for Mrs. Porter.

"I ruined him," she whispered. "Why else would he sell his family property?"

After hitting more dead ends, she called it a day. She didn't want to go home; it wasn't home anymore. It was simply a shell she had dreamed would someday be home. And for a very short time, it had felt that way.

But the pendant had brought her back.

And seeing that Connor sold his family home and property to his housekeeper, told her exactly what she thought. She had ruined him. She could only speculate why he sold it.

"Maybe to keep it safe," she whispered as she continued walking back. "Maybe Brookes kept pushing for retribution. Since he couldn't get me, he tried to take Connor's land. Mrs. Porter would keep it safe."

But women rarely owned land back then.

Penelope shook her head, trying to stop the intrusive thoughts.

"He's gone. They are all gone," Pen cried as she tried to open the front door. The key couldn't turn. She tried again. Like a lock in desperate need of oil, it would not budge.

Ready to scream at the world for all its cruelties, Pen slipped over to the stairs of the front porch, sat on the top step, and put her face in her hands, resting elbows on knees.

She couldn't stop the flow; the tears she thought she'd already shed came back with a vengeance. Crying is not pretty. It's filled with snot and red cheeks. But she didn't care. There was no one to see her.

Wiping her eyes and her nose with the napkin she'd grabbed at the coffee shop and stuffed in her pocket, she tried the lock again.

Nothing.

Not wanting to go in, and yet needing to get inside, Pen walked around the house to the east side, where the storm doors that let to the cellar were. She'd recalled when the librarian had mentioned that kids used to break in through there. And she hadn't bought a lock yet. Sure enough, with a little elbow grease and strength she hadn't used since chopping wood with Connor, Pen lifted up the wooden door and slipped in.

She'd only been down there once, the day she'd moved in. She'd walked through the entire house, envisioning her new home. This would be where the laundry room was going to be. Penelope made her way to the stairwell, which led up to the kitchen. She stopped mid-step.

Listening.

Silence.

Pen let out a sigh. "Quit spooking yourself out," she said to herself, the sound almost echoing in the empty stairwell. She took another step and stopped again. This time, she was *sure* she heard something that sounded like footsteps above her. In the kitchen.

Running up the last few steps, she burst into the kitchen, fully expecting to find those teenage boys lurking in her house. But there was nothing, no one. Pen checked the house, room by room, looking for any disturbance. Everything was how she'd left it.

She started to say, "This house isn't haunted," but caught herself mid-word. That wasn't true. The house *was* haunted. But not in the traditional way. It was haunted by the loss that not only was she carrying, but that had lived within the wall for over a century.

Dinner that night was a cold can of Spaghetti O's and a Sprite.

Mrs. Porter would be appalled.

That night, she lay in bed, the pendant resting against her skin under her pajama shirt.

Penelope had thought of taking it off and putting it back where it came from. But she couldn't. It was truly the only thing still connecting her to Connor... and Mina. The metal was cold. Even the warmth of Pen's skin did nothing to add heat to the metal.

Morning came with new thoughts and the smallest glimmer of hope.

Penelope dressed quickly, still putting her coat on as she rushed out the front door.

She couldn't believe she hadn't checked when she was at the library the day before. Pen had only been focused on the past. On Connor. But there was something else nagging at her. The future. In the past.

Pen shook her head, trying to knock the time-travel garble out of her head.

Once in the library, she pulled a slip of paper from a stack labeled "scrap paper" where she'd scribbled half-mad notes about the pendant the last time she and Connor had spoken of it.

Heartbound charm. Folklore. Second chances. Binding to what is needed, not wanted.

Her fingers tightened around the pen.

"What did you need me for?" she asked the empty room. "What was I supposed to fix?"

She moved to the reference desk and requested older folklore volumes, obscure ones. The librarian eyed her curiously but complied.

Penelope spent hours there.

She read until the words blurred.

Mentions of talismans tied to grief. To unfinished bonds. To love left unresolved. Objects that did not obey linear time, but emotional truth.

One passage made her breath stop.

The heartbound charm does not choose permanence. It chooses reckoning.

Pen closed the book slowly.

Reckoning.

Connor arrested. The town turning. Mina left behind. Being ripped from the only place she had ever truly belonged.

The pendant hadn't brought her home because she *wanted* to leave.

It had brought her home because something had broken beyond repair.

Or because it was trying to save what it could.

Pen pressed her fingers to her mouth and stared at the words on the page. There was no clear answer to how it worked. This made the dark hole in Pen's soul ache even deeper.

"I'm coming back," she whispered fiercely. "I don't know how, but I am. I will not leave them like this."

The pendant lay quiet against her skin.

Waiting.

As if to say: *Then you must understand me first.*

Outside, the sun dipped lower over a town that didn't know she'd ever been gone.

She imagined somewhere, across time and grief and locked doors, a cat cried herself to sleep in a house that still remembered her.

PENELOPE DIDN'T REMEMBER the walk home.

She remembered unlocking the door.

The sound echoed too loudly in the empty house; the click of the lock ringing like a finality she wasn't ready for. She stepped inside and closed it behind her, leaning her forehead briefly against the wood as if the door itself might hold her upright.

Nothing had changed.

And everything had.

The half-painted trim. The faint smell of dust and old wood. The quiet hum of a refrigerator instead of a hearth.

She shrugged off her coat and let it fall where it may. No Mrs. Porter to scold her for leaving garments on the floor. No Mina to immediately claim it as a bed.

That thought cracked something in her chest.

"Okay," she whispered to the empty room. "Okay. I'm here."

The house did not answer.

Her feet carried her toward her bedroom—without conscious thought—toward the place where it had all begun. The wardrobe door was open.

And sitting on the shelf was the envelope.

The paper was thicker than anything made now, ivory-toned and time-stained, the edges softened by decades.

Her hands closed around it.

Connor's letter.

She pulled it free and sat back on her heels, clutching it to her chest for one long, shuddering breath before forcing herself to look.

The envelope was intact. His handwriting still slanted across the front in ink that had soaked lovingly into the paper fibers. The sight of it nearly undid her.

"I didn't imagine you," she whispered. "You're here. You're real."

Her fingers slipped inside.

The letter unfolded with familiar resistance, the paper whispering softly as if resentful of being disturbed again. She didn't read it this time. She couldn't. The words were too heavy, too intimate.

But something else slid free with it.

A second piece of paper.

Smaller. Thinner. Modern.

Her breath hitched.

The receipt.

She stared at it, disbelief and relief crashing together so hard she swayed. It was folded, creased along familiar lines, worn soft at the corners like something carried often.

Proof.

Her hands shook as she unfolded it.

And then—

Nothing.

The ink had faded almost completely; the glossy thermal paper bleached pale by time and exposure. Where bold black letters had once been, there was now only a ghost of shapes. She could *almost* see the outline of words, the impression of numbers, but they were unreadable. Gone.

Of course they were.

That kind of paper wasn't meant to last. It wasn't pressed. It wasn't made to endure decades, let alone centuries. It was designed for moments, not memory.

Pen let out a broken laugh that dissolved into a sob.

"It was there," she said fiercely to the room. "It was real. I know it was."

She pressed the faded receipt against the letter, against the thick, enduring paper that had survived grief and time and neglect. One fragile. One eternal.

Just like them.

She folded both carefully and slid them back into the envelope, her hands gentle, reverent. Then she tucked it back into its long-time home, in the back of the wardrobe drawer... not hidden, not buried.

Kept.

The house creaked softly around her.

For a wild, irrational moment, she expected to hear boots in the hallway.

She didn't.

Night fell quietly.

No oil lamps to light. No shared supper. No voice calling her name, no *Penelope*, spoken low and careful like something precious.

She went upstairs alone.

The bedroom felt cavernous now. Too large. Too bare. She stripped off her clothes mechanically and pulled on an old T-shirt, one of Mina's favorite shirts to knead against when she slept.

The bed was cold.

She curled on her side, facing the empty space where Mina should have been, where warm fur and a steady purr should have anchored her to sleep. Her chest hurt. Not sharply. Not dramatically. Just constantly. "I left her," Pen whispered into the pillow. "I left her with strangers." Her throat closed.

Mrs. Porter was not a stranger. She knew that. She was kind. She was capable. Mina would be fed and spoken to, and loved.

But she wasn't with *her*.

And Connor—

The thought of him behind bars, of his rigid control finally broken by her presence, made something deep inside her twist violently.

"If I hadn't come," she whispered. "If I had just stayed invisible... you'd be safe."

The pendant lay cool against her skin.

Silent.

Unmoved by her tears.

Pen cried herself empty that night.

The kind of crying that left her ribs aching and her throat raw, and her eyes burning long after the tears stopped coming. The kind that didn't resolve anything, didn't cleanse or heal. Only marked.

When sleep finally claimed her, it was thin and restless.

The house creaked around her, settling into a shape that did not include her grief.

And for the first time since she'd bought the Victorian, Penelope Ward felt truly, devastatingly alone.

~

CONNOR ~

Connor Halden was released right before dusk.

The sheriff did not make a show of it. There were no speeches, no dramatic pronouncements, only the heavy scrape of the key in the lock and the solid click of iron surrendering to inevitability.

"Mr. Halden," Sheriff Hollis said, opening the cell door. "You're free to go."

Connor rose without a word, joints stiff from a night spent sitting upright against stone. He rolled his shoulders once, testing himself, then stepped into the narrow corridor. His coat was returned to him. His hat. The small, quiet dignity of a man reclaiming his things.

Daniel Brookes stood near the door, jaw still shadowed with bruising, arms crossed as though he meant to block the exit by sheer arrogance.

"This isn't finished," Brookes said.

Connor didn't look at him.

Sheriff Hollis did.

"It is," Hollis replied calmly. "You were warned."

Brookes scoffed. "I was assaulted."

"You were told to leave a woman alone," Hollis corrected. "Multiple times. Witnesses confirmed it. Including three women who don't particularly like Mr. Halden and still said you wouldn't stop."

Brookes' lips curled. "So that excuses violence?"

"It explains restraint," Hollis said evenly. "You pushed until a line was crossed. And you did it in public because you thought the crowd would protect you."

Connor finally turned then, his gaze flat, unreadable.

"It won't," Connor said quietly.

Brookes bristled. "This town—"

"This town," Hollis interrupted, "does not belong to you."

Silence settled thick and uncomfortable.

Hollis cleared his throat. "Go home, Mr. Brookes. And consider this matter concluded unless you wish to explain to your mother why her name was nearly dragged through the mud."

Brookes' face flushed. His gaze flicked once toward Connor, then away.

He left.

Sheriff Hollis sighed and turned back to Connor. "You should go straight home. Keep a low profile for a few days. Town'll settle."

Connor nodded. "Thank you."

Hollis hesitated. "You were protecting her."

"Yes."

Hollis studied him. "That matters."

Connor did not trust himself to speak again.

THE WALK home felt longer than it should have.

The road was familiar, every bend, every fence post etched into him by years of repetition, but something was wrong. The air felt... thinner. The house appeared exactly as he'd left it, standing solid against the fading light, but it did not *reach for him* the way it usually did.

The windows were dark.

No movement at the parlor glass.

No cat perched on the sill like a sentry.

Connor's steps slowed.

She's frightened, he thought. *Mrs. Porter kept her in.*

He mounted the porch and opened the door.

The house was quiet.

Not peaceful. Empty.

"Penelope?" His voice echoed too loudly.

No answer.

"Mina?" he tried.

Nothing.

Mrs. Porter appeared from the kitchen, wiping her hands on her apron. Her face was drawn. Her eyes were tired in a way that made something cold twist low in his chest.

"You're home," she said.

"Yes," Connor replied. "Where is she?"

Mrs. Porter hesitated.

Connor knew then.

The knowledge did not strike him like a blow. It settled instead, slow, heavy, absolute.

"She's gone," Mrs. Porter said. "I think the pendant took her."

The room tilted.

Connor braced one hand on the back of a chair. "You knew about that?"

"I know everything that goes on in this house. I may be a widow, and my boy may be grown with a wife of his own, but I will always be a mother, with a mother's ears and intuition. She didn't leave by choice. That I know for a fact."

"When?" he barely whispered, taking a seat.

"Last night. After they took you." Her voice wavered. "She was crying. Alone. Mina was with me in the kitchen."

That was when Mina appeared.

She padded into the room slowly, tail low, ears flattened. When she saw Connor, she stopped, then crossed the distance and climbed into his lap with deliberate care, curling tightly against his chest.

Connor froze.

Then his arms came around her.

Mina pressed her face into the fabric of his vest and purred, a broken, uneven sound that hurt to hear.

"She's been like this since," Mrs. Porter said quietly. "Won't settle. Keeps checking doors."

Connor stroked the cat's back mechanically. "She'll come back," he said. He did not know how he knew. He only knew that he did.

. . .

DINNER WAS NEARLY SILENT.

Connor ate because Mrs. Porter placed the plate in front of him and watched until he did. Mina refused her own bowl, choosing instead to sit in Connor's lap, paw pressed against his chest as though anchoring him.

Afterward, Mrs. Porter retired early.

Connor sat alone by the fire.

The chair across from him remained empty.

The night pressed in.

When sleep finally came, it was restless.

And then—

"Connor."

He turned in the dream, heart leaping.

Clara stood before him, whole and warm and smiling the way she had when she wanted him to listen.

"You're not losing me," she said.

"I'm afraid," he admitted.

"I know."

"You gave me permission," he whispered.

She reached for him. "I gave you *life*."

Her hand pressed briefly to his chest.

"When she comes back," Clara said, fading softly, "do not be afraid to choose joy."

Connor woke with tears on his face.

WITH THE MORNING sun came new hope.

Mrs. Porter had yet to rise. Mina lay curled on the hearth rug, one paw twitching in her sleep as if chasing something she could no longer see. The silence was different now, no longer simply empty, but *expectant*, like the house itself was holding its breath.

Connor sat at the small desk in his study, lamp turned low, quill resting idle between his fingers.

He had not written a letter like this in years.

Not since Clara.

He stared at the blank page for a long time before beginning, his handwriting careful, deliberate—each word chosen as if it might one day matter more than he could yet understand.

Penelope,

I do not know if you will ever read this. But I have learned, in these last days, that certainty is a luxury I no longer possess.

I once believed I was living. I see now that I was only surviving. After Clara died, the world narrowed. I told myself it was strength to keep the house orderly, the days predictable, the grief contained. I believed endurance was the same as purpose.

You proved me wrong.

In less than a week, you and your impossible cat overturned a life I had been carefully preserving like a relic. You brought noise and laughter and chaos into rooms that had learned only silence. Mrs. Porter started smiling again. There was light in a house that had only known darkness for so long. You asked questions I had avoided answering. You stood in my grief without trying to fix it, and that, I think, is when the walls first began to fail.

I did not realize how lonely I had been until you were gone.

Mina searches for you. Mrs. Porter pretends she does not. And I find myself listening for footsteps that will not come.

If Clara had lived, she would have loved you. Not merely liked you, loved you. She had a gift for recognizing good souls, and she would have seen in you what I see now: courage, kindness, and a heart that refuses to harden even when the world gives it reason to.

If Clara could have chosen someone for me, someone to remind me how to live again, it would have been you.

I do not believe loving you dishonors her. I believe refusing to live would.

I will always love her. But love does not vanish simply because it made room. She would not want the house to remain a mausoleum. But to be what we built it to be. Let it hold laughter again. Let it shelter more than sorrow.

If the magic that brought you here took you away, then it misunderstood you. Because nothing was broken by your arrival. Everything was mended.

I do not know how to bring you back. But I swear to you that I will try.

Until then, know this: you were not a passing disruption. You were a beginning.

—Connor

He set the quill down with hands that did not quite steady.

When the ink had dried, he folded the letter carefully and sealed it, not with wax, but with pressure, firm, intentional, like a promise.

Then he rose.

The parlor felt different without her. Larger. Colder.

Connor knelt beside the place she had shown him, the floorboard she'd said had felt *wrong* beneath her fingers. He ran his hand over the wood, lingering where the grain shifted slightly, where age and pressure had weakened it.

"This is where you came through," he murmured.

He fetched a small pry bar from the tool rack, hesitated only once, then wedged it carefully into the seam.

The wood resisted.

Then gave.

Not enough to splinter. Just enough to crack, subtle, intentional, leaving a narrow crevice that caught the lamplight at the wrong angle. A flaw. A future catch-point.

Connor slid the letter into the cavity, pressing it deep, then replaced the board, tapping it back into place with the heel of his hand.

When he stood, the room looked unchanged.

But it wasn't.

The house had been altered.

Time, he suspected, had been given something to hold on to.

Connor rested his palm briefly over the spot, then straightened.

"Find her," he said quietly to the house, to the pendant, to whatever strange mercy governed this impossible thread between them.

Behind him, Mina stirred and let out a small, questioning sound.

Connor turned, crouched, and lifted her gently. She pressed her face beneath his chin, purring as if she understood.

"I will," he told her. "I promise."

CHAPTER 16

What Remains

O ver the course of the week since Penelope had returned, she told herself she had to try.

That was the lie she clung to as she stood in the middle of her kitchen, sleeves rolled up, hair twisted into a knot that wouldn't stay, hands wrapped around a sponge she'd already forgotten to rinse.

Try to return to life. Try to be normal. Try to pretend she hadn't been ripped out of a century that had begun to feel more like home than this one ever had.

The kitchen smelled faintly of dust and lemon cleaner. The counters were bare except for a single mug, cold coffee she'd poured and forgotten hours ago. Sunlight filtered in through the grimy window, catching on the cracked tile floor and the peeling paint along the cabinets.

She scrubbed anyway.

The motion was automatic. Back and forth. Press. Wipe. Press harder, as if she could scour the ache out of her chest the same way she scoured the counter.

For a moment, only a moment, she could almost see her.

Mrs. Porter, standing at the counter beside her.

Sleeves rolled neatly, flour dusting her apron and her cheek, hands strong and practiced as she kneaded bread with a steady, comforting rhythm. There would have been warmth in the room then. Heat from the stove. The quiet confidence of a woman who knew exactly where everything belonged.

Pen's throat tightened.

"I burned the biscuits," she whispered into the empty room, her voice sounding too loud, too modern, too alone. "You would've scolded me for that."

No answer came. Of course, it didn't.

Her sponge slipped from her fingers and hit the sink with a wet slap. She stared at it, breath catching, and then turned away before the tears could gather enough strength to spill.

This wasn't working.

None of it was.

She wandered out of the kitchen and into the hallway, the old house creaking softly beneath her feet. The Victorian was exactly as she'd left it, half-renovated, half-abandoned. Exposed beams. Buckets catching phantom leaks. The smell of old wood and long-settled dust.

This place had once felt like a promise.

Now it felt like a hollow thing. A shell she'd poured money into because she hadn't known where else to put herself.

Her steps carried her, without conscious decision, toward the conservatory.

The room was colder than the rest of the house; the glass panes were clouded with grime and age. Sunlight filtered in weakly, casting long, fractured shadows across the floor. And there, against the far wall, sat the piano.

The decrepit upright she'd found when she first bought the house. Too damaged to move. Too broken to fix. She'd meant to sell it. Or gut it. Or cover it with a tarp and forget it existed.

She hadn't done any of those things.

Pen approached it slowly, fingers brushing the chipped wood

along its edge. The surface was cool beneath her touch, the varnish long gone in places, leaving the grain exposed like bone beneath skin.

"I never asked you to play," she murmured. "I don't even know why you're still here."

The piano did not answer.

She sat on the bench, anyway.

It creaked under her weight, one leg wobbling slightly. The keys were yellowed, several cracked or sunken, some so stiff they barely moved.

She lifted one finger.

Pressed.

The note that emerged was wrong.

Not just off-key, *wounded*. A hollow, warbling sound that shuddered through the room and died like something ashamed of itself.

Pen flinched. "Oh," she whispered. "Oh, that's awful."

She pressed another. Then another. Each sound was worse than the last. The notes clashed and sagged, the melody she tried to form collapsing before it could exist. It wasn't music. It was grief, translated into sound.

Her hands dropped into her lap.

And suddenly, she wasn't in the dilapidated conservatory anymore. She was somewhere else. Somewhere she'd never been but could picture with devastating clarity.

1896.

The Halden House. She could *imagine* Clara's music book open on the stand. The careful handwriting. The pressed flowers tucked between pages. Connor standing in the doorway, silent, listening, not daring to step closer—as if sound itself might shatter him.

Clara filling the house with music.

Connor listening.

Before everything ended.

And now—

Pen's chest caved inward.

"Now he's lost you twice," she whispered, tears finally spilling free. "Once to death. Once to me."

Her shoulders shook.

She pressed her hands to her face, breath coming in broken pulls. "I didn't mean to," she said to no one. "I never meant to take anything from him."

But she had.

Hadn't she?

She had arrived like a storm, uninvited, impossible, and everything had shifted around her. The house had breathed again. Connor had softened. Mrs. Porter had smiled. Mina had chosen.

And then she'd vanished.

Left him standing in the wreckage.

Again.

Penelope rose unsteadily and backed away from the piano, as if it might accuse her if she stayed. Her feet carried her out of the conservatory, through the hallway, toward the parlor.

She hadn't meant to go there.

But her body remembered the way, even if her mind resisted.

The parlor was quiet. Sunlit. Still.

And the floor—

Her breath caught.

The floorboard near the center of the room was open.

Not pried up roughly. Not splintered.

Just... opened.

Pen froze in the doorway.

Her pulse roared in her ears as she stepped closer, heart pounding so hard it hurt. The pendant had ripped her and Mina away, the removed board still sitting where Pen had set it when she'd picked up the bundle. She glanced inside. The cavity beneath the floor was darker than she remembered, deeper.

Her knees weakened, and she sank to the floor beside it, fingers trembling as they hovered over the opening.

"No," she whispered. "You couldn't..."

But of course he could.

Connor Halden did not leave things unfinished.

She reached inside, and her fingers brushed paper. It was brittle, like the kind she remembered from the first letter. And just the same, this was folded with care. Pen drew it out slowly, reverently, as if afraid it might vanish if she moved too quickly.

The handwriting on the envelope stole her breath.

Connor's. Strong. Slanted. Familiar.

Her name was written across it.

Penelope.

Her vision blurred completely this time.

She clutched the letter to her chest and bowed over it, a sound tearing out of her that was half-sob, half-laugh, half-prayer.

He had written to her. He had believed she would find it.

And in that moment, before she even opened it, Penelope finally understood.

She hadn't been sent away because she was a mistake. She had been sent away because she still *believed* she was the mistake.

The house seemed to sigh around her. The floorboard creaked softly beneath her weight.

And somewhere deep in her chest, beneath the grief and guilt and fear, something long dormant stirred.

Hope.

PENELOPE DIDN'T OPEN the letter right away.

She couldn't.

She knelt there on the parlor floor, the wood cold beneath her knees, the envelope pressed to her chest like a second heart, terrified that once she read it, there would be no going back. That whatever was written inside would rearrange her beyond repair.

Connor Halden had never wasted words.

If he had written to her, *really* written, it would be honest. It would be careful. And it would hurt.

Her fingers traced the edge of the paper, feeling the faint indent of his handwriting through the envelope. The pendant rested against her sternum, unusually warm now, as if aware of what she was about to do.

"I'm afraid," she whispered, voice breaking in the empty room. "I don't think I can survive wanting something this much."

The house did not answer. But it didn't feel empty anymore.

With a shaking breath, she slid her finger beneath the flap and opened the letter.

The sound of paper unfolding felt thunderous in the quiet.

Her eyes moved over the page slowly at first, careful, reverent, then faster, then halting, as the words landed not only in her mind but in her bones.

She sank back onto her heels. Her chest ached. Her vision blurred.

Connor's voice filled her head, not the stern, controlled one he wore like armor, but the quieter version she'd only glimpsed in moments of vulnerability. The man who had written in the dark. The man who had learned how to survive without living.

By the time she reached the part where he spoke of Clara, of loving her, of *always* loving her, of how love did not vanish simply because it made room, Pen's breath was coming in sharp, broken pulls.

"Oh, Connor," she sobbed. "You beautiful, impossible man."

Her tears dropped onto the page, blurring the ink. She didn't wipe them away. She let them fall, baptizing the words, as if grief itself needed to acknowledge what he'd given her.

He had not accused her. He had not blamed her. He had not asked her to fix him. He had simply told her the truth.

That she had changed him. That she and Mina had disrupted

his house, his routines, his carefully constructed numbness, and that it had been *good*.

That Clara would have loved her. That Clara would have wanted him to live.

Pen pressed the letter to her lips, a broken sound escaping her as something deep inside her finally gave way.

All this time, she had believed love meant taking.

She had been so careful not to steal anything from him.

But Connor had *given*.

Freely. Bravely. Knowing the cost.

The pendant pulsed. Once.

Hard enough that she gasped.

Penelope's hand flew instinctively to her chest as heat spread beneath her palm, not painful, but insistent. Alive. The metal loops seemed to hum, the vibration she'd felt beneath the floorboards echoing now inside her ribcage.

"No," she whispered, panic flaring. "Not yet. I just found you again."

The pendant did not listen.

It grew warmer.

Brighter.

The air in the parlor thickened, the same way it had that first night, the world seeming to lean inward, reality holding its breath. Dust motes slowed. Sound dulled, like cotton pressed against her ears.

Pen staggered to her feet, clutching the letter in one hand, the pendant in the other.

"I know," she said desperately, voice shaking. "I know what I want now. I choose him. I choose *there*. Please—"

The house creaked. Not settling. Responding.

The pendant surged with heat, no longer subtle, no longer patient. The metal burned, not painful, but with purpose. With *direction*.

Pen's knees buckled.

The letter slipped from her fingers, fluttering to the floor.

"No—!" She lunged for it, but her hand passed through air that felt suddenly thick, resistant, like pushing against water.

The world tilted.

The parlor blurred.

The Victorian, her Victorian, stretched and shimmered around her, edges dissolving into light.

And through it all, one thought rang louder than the rest, clear and devastating:

It isn't sending me away.

It's bringing me home.

Pen reached for the letter one last time as the light swallowed the room.

"Connor," she whispered. "I'm coming."

The pendant flared.

The house exhaled.

And Penelope Ward vanished, not in grief this time, not in fear, but carrying something she hadn't had before.

Certainty.

THERE WAS NO FALLING.

No light.

No dark.

Just... suspension.

Penelope existed in a space without edges, without floor or ceiling, as though she had been caught in the pause between two heartbeats. The air was neither warm nor cold. It did not press against her skin. It *held* her.

She became aware of the pendant first.

It no longer burned. It pulsed, slow and steady, matching the rhythm of her heart. For the first time since she'd found it beneath the floorboards, it felt... satisfied.

"I'm not lost," Pen whispered, though she wasn't sure who she was reassuring.

No, came a presence, not a voice, not sound, but understanding. *You are choosing.*

Images drifted around her, weightless as breath.

Connor at the table, sleeves rolled, jaw tight as he tried not to watch her too closely.

Mina in the sunlight, belly up, utterly unbothered by the rules of any century.

Mrs. Porter's capable hands kneading dough, anchoring a house that had nearly forgotten how to be a home.

Then, soft as memory... Clara.

Not as Pen had seen her in photographs. Not frozen, or pale, or distant. But warm. Whole. Smiling with a gentleness that carried no jealousy, no sorrow.

Only love.

"You don't have to carry it alone," the presence said, and Pen knew, with a certainty that made her chest ache, that Clara was speaking *through* the space, not standing within it.

Pen's breath hitched. "He thinks loving me means losing you."

A pause. A kindness.

Love doesn't vanish when it grows, came the reply. *It widens.*

Tears slid down Pen's cheeks, drifting instead of falling.

"In the beginning, I didn't mean to change anything," Pen whispered. "I simply wanted somewhere to belong."

And you found it, Clara's presence answered. *So did he.*

The pendant warmed again, not urgently now, but with purpose.

Pen felt the pull, not a yank, not a demand, but an open door.

Go, the space seemed to say. *Not because you were taken. Because you chose.*

The world tilted gently.

Time inhaled.

And Penelope stepped forward.

~

CONNOR ~

Connor Halden told himself he was working.

The ledger lay open before him, columns neat and orderly, numbers marching down the page with the kind of obedience he had always relied upon. His quill moved; the ink flowed. His hand performed the motions it had learned over decades of necessity.

But his mind was nowhere near the page. The last week had been one of the hardest since Clara died. Connor had lost twice. He was finally opening his heart and soul, letting someone enter his personal tomb, and just when he felt it was safe to care again, to truly live again, it was ripped away from him. All that was left of her was currently lying sprawled across his desk.

Mina was directly atop a stack of correspondence that he had already read twice without retaining a single word. She had claimed the space with imperial confidence, belly half-up, paws tucked, tail flicking lazily whenever his quill scratched too close to her whiskers.

"Unacceptable," he murmured, though without heat.

The cat blinked at him, slow and unimpressed, then resettled herself more firmly against his forearm.

Connor sighed and leaned back in his chair, fingers tightening around the quill.

The letter pressed against his thoughts like a bruise.

He had written it the night before. Not carefully. Not with the restraint he usually applied to every word that left his hand. He had written it because if he did not, the feelings would have remained trapped inside him, pacing, clawing, demanding to be acknowledged.

He had written it to Penelope.

And then, because some part of him still believed in rituals, in places holding meaning, he had placed it beneath the floorboard.

In the exact spot she had described. The spot where the impossible had first entered his life.

He had told himself it was foolish. Sentimental. Hopeful in a way he had sworn never to be again.

Yet now, as his gaze drifted to the window and the afternoon light slanted across the shelves, he found himself wondering…

Has she found it yet?

Had she opened it with trembling fingers, reading his words in that quiet, intent way she had, like she was listening for something beneath the ink?

Had she cried?

The thought tightened something in his chest.

Connor closed his eyes briefly.

A future without her stretched before him, stark and colorless. The house returned to its careful silence. Meals eaten with polite efficiency. Mina prowled restlessly, searching corners, listening for footsteps that would never come.

He would survive it.

He always survived.

But survival was no longer enough.

The quill stilled in his fingers.

Something… shifted.

Not a sound. Not a movement. Just a sensation, subtle as the change in pressure before a storm. A ripple through the air, through the house itself, like a deep structure settling into a new alignment.

Connor's spine straightened.

He frowned, breath slowing.

No.

He had imagined too much lately. Allowed himself too much room for possibilities. He had been doing that since she left, measuring every silence against her voice, every empty space against the shape she had filled.

He looked down at the ledger again, forcing his hand to move.

Ink bled into the paper.

Mina's ears twitched.

Connor stilled.

The cat lifted her head, pupils blown wide, body suddenly coiled. She stared, not at him, but past him, toward the hallway.

"Mina?" he said quietly.

She exploded into motion.

The cat launched herself across the desk in a streak of fur and fury, scattering papers like startled birds. The ledger slid sideways. The inkwell tipped, spilling black across months of careful accounting.

"Damn it—" Connor surged to his feet. But the words died in his throat.

Mina did not flee the chaos she had created.

She ran.

Straight for the door.

Straight for the parlor.

Connor's heart slammed against his ribs.

Only one thing ever sent her into that kind of frenzy.

His breath caught. His hand gripped the edge of the desk, knuckles whitening as his mind rebelled even while his heart surged forward.

No, it was not possible. He had already endured one miracle. He would not...

A sound drifted down the hall.

A sharp inhale.

A gasp caught between disbelief and sobbing relief.

Connor moved.

He did not walk.

He did not hesitate.

His boots hit the floorboards hard as he crossed the hall, the house seeming to lean toward him as he went, as though it, too, recognized what was unfolding.

The parlor door stood open.

Sunlight poured in through the windows, catching dust motes in a golden hush.

And there...

Standing in the center of the room...

Was Penelope.

She looked exactly as she had when she first arrived and entirely unlike she had ever belonged.

Her dress was wrong... garishly modern, fabric unfamiliar, color too bold for the century. The pendant lay against her chest, glowing faintly, unmistakable.

Gripped tight in her hands... was his letter. Crushed slightly at the edges and held like something sacred.

Mina skidded across the rug and launched herself at Penelope's legs, climbing her like she had been gone for a lifetime.

Pen laughed, a broken, beautiful sound, and dropped to her knees, clutching the cat, her shoulders shaking.

Connor could not breathe.

The world narrowed to the sight of her. Alive. Here. Real.

She looked up.

Their eyes met.

The room tilted.

Connor crossed the space between them in three long strides and stopped. Stopped because every instinct screamed to touch her, and every fear begged him not to scare her away.

"Penelope," he said, her name a revelation.

She stood, unsteady, still holding the letter. Her eyes were bright with tears and something fierce beneath them. "I found it," she said softly. "I read it."

His chest ached. "I know."

Her lips trembled. "You meant it."

"Yes."

The word left him without armor.

She took one step closer.

Then another.

The pendant warmed, brightened, then stilled, as if satisfied.

Connor reached for her, not carefully this time, not cautiously, but with certainty. His hands came to rest at her waist, solid, grounding, as though anchoring her to this moment, this place, this life.

"You came back," he said, voice rough.

Pen nodded. "I chose you."

The house creaked softly around them, like it was exhaling at last.

CONNOR WAS aware of exactly three things.

The warmth of her where his hands still rested at her waist. The pendant, quiet now, like a heart that had finally found its rhythm. And the unbearable fact that if he did not kiss her *now*, he might never survive the restraint again.

Penelope swayed toward him, as though gravity had finally decided which way she belonged.

"I didn't know if I could," she whispered, voice unsteady. "I thought maybe... maybe wanting to stay meant I was selfish."

His thumbs tightened instinctively, grounding her. "Wanting to stay," he said lowly, "means you are alive."

Her breath shuddered. "Connor—"

That was all it took.

He kissed her.

Not carefully.

Not properly.

Not with the distant, measured restraint he had been clinging to since the moment she arrived.

He kissed her like a man who had buried his heart and had clawed it back out of the earth.

His mouth found hers with a desperation that startled him, that seemed to take her breath away. Warm, firm, unmistakably real. The kind of kiss that erased time, erased doubt, erased every careful rule he had built his life upon. His hands slid up her back, fingers spreading as if he needed to *feel* that she was solid, here, not a dream he would wake from aching.

Penelope gasped softly into his mouth, the sound breaking something open in him.

She kissed him back with equal urgency, one hand fisting in his shirtfront, the other coming up to his jaw as if she needed to anchor herself there. Her lips moved against his with hunger and relief tangled together, too open, too expressive, too modern for this century, and utterly perfect for this moment.

Connor felt it then.

The guilt.

A flicker of Clara's memory... not as accusation, but as presence.

And instead of pulling away, instead of breaking—

He deepened the kiss.

Because loving again did not erase the love that had come before. Because grief did not get to dictate the rest of his life. Because Clara had loved him *alive*, not entombed.

Penelope's knees nearly buckled. Connor caught her without thinking, drawing her closer until there was no space left between them. He kissed her slower now, reverently, as though learning her, as though promising something without words.

When they finally broke apart, breathless, foreheads resting together, the silence felt holy.

Improper.

Unforgivable by every rule he had ever lived by.

And yet...

Penelope laughed softly, a tear sliding free. "That was... definitely not appropriate for 1896."

Connor huffed a quiet sound that might have been a laugh himself. "No," he agreed, brushing his thumb gently along her cheek. "It was not."

She searched his face, vulnerable and hopeful all at once. "Do you regret it?"

He didn't hesitate. "Not for a single second."

Behind them, Mina jumped up onto the settee, flicked her tail, and let out a smug little chirp, clearly satisfied with the state of affairs.

Connor pressed his forehead to Penelope's once more, eyes closed.

The house creaked softly, like approval.

And for the first time in years, the future did not feel like something to fear.

It felt like something he was finally brave enough to choose.

Epilogue – Heartbound

Four days after Penelope's return, she found Connor in the morning room.

He sat in the wingback chair by the window, newspaper folded across his knee. Mina was draped across his lap like a fur stole, paws tucked beneath her, purring loud enough to hear from the doorway.

Penelope stopped, teacup halfway to her lips.

Connor glanced up, saw her watching, and his expression did something she'd never seen before. It softened. Not into a smile—not quite—but close. Something gentler than she knew he was capable of.

"She's claimed me, I'm afraid," he said, one hand resting lightly on the cat's back.

Mina cracked one eye open, flicked her tail once, and settled deeper into his lap with a smug little chirp.

"She has excellent taste," Penelope replied.

The corner of his mouth twitched. Almost a smile.

He looked back down at his paper. Mina purred. The morning sun slanted through the stained glass, painting rainbow patterns across the floor.

It was the first morning that didn't feel borrowed.

It felt like theirs.

And Penelope, well, she finally found home.

The night she'd returned, Penelope had slipped the pendant off and tucked it into a drawer. She was right where she belonged. The magic could rest.

She understood now—they were heartbound souls, pulled together to mend what grief broke. And that sometimes, things need to get a little messy before they can be set right.

Late one evening, after dinner had been cleared, Penelope brought up what she learned in the future about the past. They sat in Connor's study so he could take notes.

"I gathered information about the property," she began, "once when I first found your letter, then again, when I went back. I was looking to see if your life had gotten better, after I was gone."

"No, it did not," Connor pressed.

"I know. The property records showed something strange," Penelope said, spreading her notes on his desk. "The house was sold in 1897. To a Mr. Wallace P."

Connor's brow furrowed. "I haven't sold—"

"Hold on. That was the confusing part. But, if I had to guess, you sold it to Mrs. Porter to keep the property 'safe' from Brookes."

Connor chuckled. "I would say that once again, you are correct. Brookes and I go way back." HIs jaw tightened. "When I first started courting Clara, he tried to steal her away."

"Seriously?" Penelope leaned forward.

"Her heart was already spoken for." A ghost of a smile crossed Connor's face, then vanished. "He vowed he would have my life one day. At first, I thought he meant to kill me outright. But he does not have the backbone for something that vile.

"So he has been chipping away at your reputation," Penelope finished.

"For years. When you arrived... Connor's expression darkened. "It gave him the fuel he had been waiting for."

"What a jerk."

Mrs. Porter's voice drifted from the hallway. "Language, Miss Ward."

"You may come in and listen, Mrs. Porter, if you like," Connor invited.

The housekeeper took a seat.

"So what do we do now... about Brookes?" Penelope inquired.

"Nothing. Sheriff Hollis put Brookes in his place civilly. I do not think he will try anything again. But if he does, we will handle it together."

Mina picked that moment to run headlong into the room, with a mouth full of something... furry.

She jumped up onto Connor's desk, scattering the documents he had stacked there into a blizzard of paper. Before Connor got them straightened, Mina dropped the item she'd been carrying in his lap. She sat down; her face full of pride.

Connor reached down and picked it up. Holding it by the tail, he presented the item.

A mouse. Very dead.

"I guess she really likes you," Penelope laughed.

"She does this if she likes you?"

"Yeah. See, she brought you a meal. She sees you as family, and she wants to take care of you." Penelope reached across the desk and gave her best friend a gentle pat on the head."

Penelope looked back at the notes Connor had jotted down, then at the room around them—the mahogany desk, the built-in shelves, the stained glass casting colored light across the floor.

"I guess this means we've changed history," she said quietly. "You won't need to sell."

Connor followed her gaze around the room. "No. I suppose I won't."

"Good." She met his eyes. "This house should stay in the family."

Something shifted in his expression. Warmed. "Yes. It should."

ONE YEAR Later -

Morning arrived quietly.

Not with urgency or alarm or the sharp insistence of a world that needed something from her, but softly, like a breath released after being held too long.

Penelope woke to warmth.

Real warmth. Not the artificial hum of a radiator or the inconsistent chill of a house that hadn't yet learned her rhythms. This warmth was layered... sunlight filtered through lace curtains, the weight of a quilt stitched by hands that knew how to care, the solid, steady presence of another body beside hers.

Connor.

His arm was draped over her waist, possessive without being tight, protective without restraint. His breathing was slow and even, the rise and fall of his chest anchoring her in place. Penelope lay still, afraid to disturb the fragile perfection of the moment, afraid it might unravel if she moved too quickly.

But it didn't.

Because this wasn't magic holding her here.

It was *choice*.

She turned her head slightly, watching the early light paint his features. The lines at the corners of his eyes had softened in the months since... everything. Since her return. Since the storm. Since the long, painful reckoning that had nearly torn them apart before it bound them together for good.

The sharp furrow between his brows had smoothed. His jaw, no longer clenched even in sleep. The house had stopped haunting him.

Mina butted her head against Pen's hand, then Connor's arm, as if ensuring they were both real.

"You'd think she was the one who lost us," Connor muttered.

Penelope stroked the cat's fur. Mrs. Porter had told her later how the cat slept on Connor's chest every night, as if guarding his heart.

Some bonds didn't need explanation.

The house stirred beyond their room, soft footsteps, the creak of a rocking chair, the faint murmur of a woman humming under her breath.

Mrs. Porter.

Penelope closed her eyes briefly, letting the sound wash over her. It still amazed her how much the older woman had become, without effort, without declaration, the maternal presence Penelope hadn't realized she'd been searching for her entire life.

She rose slowly, careful not to jostle Mina, and dressed with the ease of someone who no longer felt like she was wearing borrowed skin.

Connor watched her, his expression softening. "You look..." he began, then stopped, searching for the right word.

"Here," Penelope supplied.

"Yes," he said. "That."

They made their way downstairs together, hand in hand, the house greeting them like an old friend. The parlor was bathed in morning light.

The pendant.

Penelope glanced instinctively toward the sideboard where it now lay, nestled in a velvet-lined box. Cold. Inert. Ordinary.

It had not warmed in months.

Its work here was done.

Mina hopped down and claimed her usual spot on the rug, tail curled neatly around her paws. Penelope and Connor took their places on the sofa, the familiarity of it all striking her anew.

Mrs. Porter stood near the window, rocking gently, her expression softened with a joy she didn't bother to hide.

In her arms slept a newborn.

Elizabeth Claire Halden.

Penelope's heart clenched. Every time. That fierce, impossible love that made breathing difficult.

Mrs. Porter looked up, smiling. "She's been changed but is ready to be fed. And she's got your stubbornness already, Mr. Halden. Refused to settle until I started humming."

Connor rose instantly, crossing the room as if the floor might shatter beneath him. He leaned over, brushing a finger along his daughter's tiny hand.

"She has her mother's timing," he said.

Penelope joined them, resting her head against Connor's shoulder as she gazed at the baby.

Elizabeth Claire.

Named for Penelope's mother, Elizabeth... and for Clara.

Not a replacement.

A continuation.

A bridge between love lost and love found.

"I used to think," Penelope said quietly, "that I needed to get back. To 2026. To my old life."

Mrs. Porter hummed softly, rocking. "And now?"

Penelope met Connor's eyes. "Now I know there is nothing to get back to. This is it."

Connor turned to her, cupping her face with both hands. The tenderness of the gesture still stole her breath after all this time.

"Mrs. Halden," he said, and her breath hitched the way it always did.

He kissed her then, not the restrained, careful kisses of propriety, not the desperate ones born of fear, but a kiss full of certainty. Of tomorrow. Of vows spoken and kept.

Penelope smiled into the kiss, the world aligning around her in a way she'd once thought impossible.

Mina flicked her tail in approval.

. . .

THE PENDANT NO LONGER WARMED.

Penelope noticed it one morning while standing at the parlor window, Elizabeth Claire warm and heavy against her chest, Mina draped across the back of the chair, sphinx-like and watchful. Outside, the fields stretched green and orderly, the timber rows growing strong beneath Connor's careful stewardship.

She pressed her fingers to the small velvet box on the sideboard.

Nothing.

No hum.

No pulse.

No whisper beneath her skin.

For a long moment, panic flickered—old instinct—hard to kill, but it faded almost as quickly as it came. She smiled instead.

Connor glanced up from the ledger at the dining table. "What is it?"

"I think," she said softly, "it's finished."

He stilled. Not with fear. With understanding.

He crossed the room, resting a hand at the small of her back, grounding her without thinking.

"For good?" he asked.

Penelope nodded. "For us."

Connor looked at the pendant, then at their daughter, then at Mina, who chose that moment to flick her tail and knock a quill onto the floor.

"If that thing ever wakes again," he said mildly, "it will answer to me."

Penelope laughed, leaning into him. "I think it is time we put it where it belongs."

Connor nodded, then momentarily left the room. When he returned, he carried a small bundle of fabric. He shook it out to reveal Penelope's Razor's Edge t-shirt. "I feel it most appropriate that this keeps it company, returning it to you, in the future, or the past as it may be."

She kissed his cheek, then took the shirt—faded band logo, soft from years of wear—and wrapped the pendant inside.

Together, they tucked it neatly away in the crevice Connor had created in the floorboard.

They spoke of planting seasons.

Of Elizabeth's future.

Of whether Mina could be trained not to steal biscuits (she could not).

The pendant remained where it was.

Silent.

Complete.

***

Years Later

The Victorian house stood restored, its windows bright, its floors solid, its walls warm with memory.

A key turned in the front door. Footsteps crossed the parlor. A hand brushed the mantle.

Then paused.

One floorboard sat slightly uneven.

Not broken.

Not rotten.

Simply... waiting.

The board lifted. Beneath it, wrapped in time and cloth, something faintly gleamed.

The pendant stirred. Not awake. Not yet. But ready.

THE HEARTBOUND CHARM does not choose lightly.

It waits.

For the broken path.
For the moment, love and loss intersect.
And when the time is right—
It binds again.

END OF BOOK ONE
- Order Book Two Here -

Amaryllis Madsen is the pen name of author Andrea Hurtt.

After her grandmother asked her to write something a 97-year-old woman could read (without having a heart attack from the shock), The Heartbound Chronicles were born.

Amaryllis Madsen is the sweet, clean side of Mrs. Hurtt's wild imagination.

Stay tuned for more to come from Ms. Madsen, and if you're looking for something a little more steamy, check out Andrea Hurtt's full collection of books.

https://www.instagram.com/andreahurttauthor/

https://www.facebook.com/AmaryllisMadsen/

https://www.tiktok.com/@poppublishing

Acknowledgments

Page Edge Design:
    Painted Wings Publishing

www.ingramcontent.com/pod-product-compliance
Lightning Source LLC
Chambersburg PA
CBHW071539030726
47598CB00001B/164